1

To Keith

My First Book

[signature]

*This book is dedicated to all the people in my life
who have been an inspiration to me.
May God Bless each of you.*

The characters and events portrayed in this book are fictitious. Any similarity to real persons living or dead is coincidental and not intended.

Knights Rising
Book 1 of
The Silver Knights Saga
By
Greg Carter

Chapters		Page

Chapter 1
Memories of the Past

Every muscle in his body tensed when he saw the flaming red eyes and glistening white fangs staring at him through the campfire's dying light. With one powerful lunge and the beast was on him, sending both of them crashing backward to the ground.

Hot steamy breath bellowed in his face reeking with the stench of death. Immense pain exploded though his left shoulder as the devil's fangs tore through his plate armor, boring deeply into his flesh.

Michael hoped he could get to his feet and unsheathe his sword. A sudden downward thrust of his arms, he pushed his legs forward, managing to dislodge the filthy beast long enough to get on his feet.

His sword was drawn he welcomed the fight; kill the beast or die trying. He didn't care now that he was in full battle rage and the fight was on.

Furious at being denied an easy kill, the foul creature lunged forward; arms outstretched in a wild attempt to tear him apart. In its brainless haste the incompetent bastard underestimated him. He turned and lowered himself the instant the beast reached him. He drove his sword straight through its ribs, pierced its heart and threw it to the ground. The filthy animal was dead before it touched the earth.

Temporarily exhausted after the surprise fight, he had to rest and tend to his wounds, which by now were burning intensely. He rekindled his campfire and surveyed the deep bloody wound on his left shoulder underneath the damaged plate armor.

He fumbled through his pack trying to find ointments prepared by the Priests of Honos in the last temple. He pulled out the glass vial containing the healing mixture; broke the wax seal and poured a small amount in his right hand.

White light and burning pain blinded him the second he applied it to the bleeding wound.

He closed his eyes to the glorious agony he felt as his skin slowly stitched itself back to together. He knew he was being healed, yet didn't know which was worse; the fight or the medicine. He finished tending to his shoulder, then knelt and prayed. Thankful to his holy god Honos for another victory and then stretched out on his worn bear hide blanket to rest.

Anymore all he did was stay in the forest; after all he had no reason to live anywhere else. His enemy wasn't in cities or villages; they were out here.

He had been running into more and more of the wretched devils in pairs which were odd. The foul creatures usually roamed in packs of at least twelve or more. He knew they must be scouting; either that or they splintered off of larger groups; why, he had no idea.

The world was quieter out here, yet the demons from his past still haunted him wherever he went. Nowhere would he safe from them; running to the ends of the earth wouldn't help.

How could he suppress the voices from his troubled past, that spoke to him from the darkest recesses of his mind? What had he ever done to deserve such a fate? Why was he chosen to live a tortured life? Did he have any chance for happiness? It wasn't his fault he was born. Questions of his life raced through his head, until his eyes grew heavy and finally he fell into a fitful sleep.

Unable to suppress them any longer, painful memories came into sharp focus. Torrents of grief spilled through his torn soul, like a rain swollen river overflowing its banks. He felt like he would drown by the strength of the raging currents; too weak to fight.

A small boy watching in horror as his mother fell to the floor sobbing uncontrollably. Tiberious, his father's longest serving knight brought news of his death. He was been with him when they were ambushed northeast of Cinnibar by the foul Scarious, or what later became known as black devils. They were a constant plague in those days, coming down from the northern regions and ransacking village after village.

The only item Tiberious returned was his father's sword. The very one he now carried. Michael was too young to fully understand what had taken place. All he saw was his mother crying and telling him daddy was gone and wouldn't be coming home.

Then the scene changed to a woman. The only true love he had ever known. Her smile could melt a heart of stone. Her long brown hair flowed past her shoulders soft as silk. Oh how the thoughts of her warmed his soul. However this was the worst demon of all: her death was his fault. Why did she have to die?

How he wished it was him instead. Damn Her! Why did she ever get in front of him? She was worth so much more than he was. Fate was cruel and never allowed second chances when it came to death. It was final and no one could change it, only her memories remained to haunt him.

He made it from one day to the next, living on hatred and rage of the murderous beasts who took the love of his life. The all-consuming desire for vengeance of the deaths of Kara and his father drove him on. Gnawing at him like an endless hunger; an unquenchable thirst for his enemies' blood.

Opening his eyes he scanned his surroundings as the soft morning sun beamed down through the trees on his face. He saw nothing more than typical forest life and an old buzzard pecking at the lifeless corpse of the wretched beast he'd slain the night before.

With no other signs of danger, he packed up camp and noticed he was running low on rations. Damn it, he hated going into towns.

It had been almost a year since Kara's death. He kept telling himself things would get better, but they never did. At times he felt like he was going insane. He spent too much time alone. The bloodlust for the black devils was overwhelming, clouding his judgment.

If he just get to their leader somehow and kill him. Over time he had been learning more information about him. An insane mage in the Northern Wastes named Soladar; most were rumors, but his name always came up.

On the plus side, with a trip into town he could get his armor fixed and do some much needed drinking. Michael looked into his coin pouch and counted twenty-two gold and fifteen silver pieces. Plenty to buy a decent horse and all the rations he needed. Cold weather came early in the Carrillion region and soon he would have to carry along a tent and extra provisions.

He set out on an old dirt road, passing farmers with horses pulling carts over filled with

grain. Beautiful hard maples lined both sides of
the road with their blazing red color. Fall was in
full swing in all its dazzling glory.

The closer he came to the city, the more
people he saw traveling the various roads
spanning the countryside. The main entrance was
easy to see, even at a distance because of its
massive size. It had to be at least twenty horses
wide with large granite pillars at each side over
three stories high topped by a single granite
capstone. Engraved deeply in the front was its
name, 'City of Lawrence.'

He had heard of the city during his travels,
but this would be his first time in it. It had a
reputation of a lawful city ran by the great
general, Sir Lawrence Meracius. Who had fought
in the Great War and as a reward for his service
the city was given and named after him by King
Galanar himself.

Lawrence was a thriving place, the largest
city northwest of Cinnibar. Townspeople
bartered their wares in large open street markets.
The air in the city was festive and jovial as he
entered; which was in direct contradiction to the
way he felt.

Michael looked around and realized it was the first day of October, The Hallowed Month. For the next thirty-one days celebrations would take place, beginning at midnight and continuing until the last day.

It was official; he had lost Kara one year to the day. Some anniversary he thought, this will certainly make his supply-run a pain in the ass.

A veteran of more than a few brawls in cities, he knew to mind his own business unless he wanted trouble. He walked down one of the busier streets looking for a blacksmith. King's Way was the main avenue running straight through Lawrence; which was overcrowded with vendors of all kinds who came out for the festival.

Fire-eaters and funny dressed men juggling all sorts of dangerous looking object. Tables spread as far as he could see filled with mounds of food and trinkets. Mages and wizards of all types had come out to show off their magical talents. What festival would be complete without mages? Michael thought sarcastically. Smug bastards think they can do everything with magic, afraid to get their pretty little hands dirty.

It's a miracle any left or even allowed around civilized people. The great mage war nearly destroyed the top half of the continent, leaving behind the infamous Northern Wastes. Only one mage Michael trusted, and that was Garian a priest.

He actually enjoyed musicians though, especially the harp players. While he was here he was going to try to make the best of it. At festival time they were always plenty of people selling food; a welcomed relief from having to cook it yourself. He ate mostly dry rations when he ate, which was little. Some days he had to force himself to eat, just to keep his strength up.

It was tough to make his way through the hordes of people with children darting back and forth in the broad cobblestone avenue. Crowds always made him nervous; unconsciously he tightened his hand around the hilt of his sword. Apparently people walking towards him could tell and were doing their best to give him a wide birth.

He stopped dead in his tracks, almost midstride. Was he seeing things? As she got closer to him; he swore it was. No; damn it he was going to have to stop thinking they were any

way she could still be alive. However she looked
so much like Kara striding by him gracefully. He
turned in her direction after she walked by and
wondered if he should go and tap her on the
shoulder. What then, idiot?

Could people come back from the dead?
God she did look like Kara; he thought for a brief
moment before walking after her. He heard a
monk say one time: 'The beauty of death is
rebirth.' Whatever the hell that meant, he had no
idea. Maybe the stories were true about the spirits
being set free to roam the land during All
Hallows Month.

Catching up to her he had the urge to turn
around, suddenly feeling like an idiot.

"Excuse me, miss?" Michael managed to
say sheepishly as he tapped her shoulder.
She turned around a little surprised.

"Yes?" The woman said in a soft light
tone.

She did indeed look like his Kara, but not
as much up close.

"Sorry ma'am. I thought you were
someone else." Michael said clearing his throat.

"That's okay handsome. For you I could be that, someone else." She said in a warm sultry voice.

"Perhaps another time," Michael replied, before turning and continuing on down the street. He hated to be rude, but he was in no mood for games.

A dark wooden cart filled with food came into view on his left and he stopped in front to inspect its offerings. It was over flowing with pork sausage links; ham hocks, all different colored breads, and some meats he didn't recognize. The smell was mouthwatering.

"What can I get for you?" A soft feminine voice called out from behind the cart.

Michael looked around the cart and saw its proprietor. A short well rounded woman with a funny bowl style haircut. He stifled a laugh because the voice didn't fit her image at all.

"What's your best meat sandwich?" Michael asked.

"Boy don't you have a deep voice," the woman said as she stood up.

"And not bad looking either I might add. Mm mm not bad at all," she finished half to herself.

He often got comments when he visited towns. With his six foot muscular frame; rugged good looks, black hair and hazel green eyes, women often made passes at him. It was something he was used to; even enjoyed in the past.

"Now, you were asking about my special, weren't you? Well, if you're up for a real treat. I got a fresh delivery of bugglewomp meat. I fix it in my own secret sauce and grill it till it's tender and juicy."

"No thanks." Michael replied.

"Have any pork sausage?"

"Well of course I do! After all, I have meats from all seven realms. Now how would you like it?" She asked.

"On black bread; with salt, pepper, poppy corn, and onions; oh yeah, and don't forget mustard. Now don't go light the dressings and they'll be a tip in it for you," Michael said finishing his order.

Before all the words were out of his mouth, she was already working on his sandwich with the speed of an expert. She finished; wrapped it in a square sheet of plain brown paper and handed it to him.

"Five coppers," she said.

He reached into his old leather money pouch, retrieved a silver coin, handed it to her, and took the sandwich. She started to make change.

"Keep the change. The sandwich is delicious," Michael said doing his best to contain the overly large bite from escaping his mouth.

He could see she was very pleased, not only with the tip, but his enjoyment of the sandwich as well.

"Thank you, pleasure doing business," she added as Michael turned to leave.

Boy he forgot how good food could be, or how hungry he was. Now he just needed to find a tavern, get something to wash the sandwich down with, and maybe a night or two of lodging. He rounded a corner turning off King's Way onto a smaller street named Crozet Street. It was lined with taverns; clubs, and possible houses of ill repute where no decent people go.

He passed by a few taverns with names such as *Mystic's Haven* and *Hezakara's Magical Emporium,* which obviously were ran by magical enchantments. Michael hated those kinds of places. Why anyone would want to go to a place and be served by phantom waiters and duck flying drinks was anyone's guess.

They were probably too cheap to pay for good help. It surprised him that Lawrence allowed magical ran businesses in the city, taking away honest jobs; no wonder people couldn't find work, mages were running everything. What was wrong with good old fashion work?

Then a comical thought came to him. How would a mage run a brothel? He snickered as he imagined what god-awful creation they would conjure up. It would probable maim or kill the first patron it tried to service.

He walked on a little farther and came to the Golden Paw Tavern and Inn. It looked like a decent place, ran by real people and well taken care of. However most importantly was the small sign in the window offering hot baths and rooms. Michael ate the rest of the sandwich by the time he reached the bar.

He sat down on the barstool and noticed two shadowy characters sitting at a table in the back whispering to each other. He always made it a habit to size up any place he went just in case of trouble.

A tall old wiry man with a stone grey beard hobbled over his way.

"No trouble, you hear," the wry old bartender said in a crisp crackling voice.

"Who me?" Michael replied, looking bewildered.

"I see yer glarin' at them two. Leave 'em be; you hear?" The gnarly old barkeeper said in his sternest sounding voice.

Michael didn't realize he was glaring at anyone.

"No worries, old timer. I'll leave well enough alone, just looking around that's all." Michael's voice sounded raspy, like it hadn't been used in a very long time.

"Still early, we'll be fillin' up soon. Now; what you'll have youngin'?"

"Pint of Rockbite," Michael replied.

With a huff the old barkeep set off with a half crooked grin filled a thick glass mug and handed it to Michael. He took the full stein of mead and downed half of it in one long drink.

"Ah, much better, but it will take more to quench my thirst." He mumbled after the rest of it went down.

Rockbite had always been his favorite mead. It got its name from people drinking too much and falling face first and 'biting rocks.' He always thought it was a made up story to enhance sales. Though he didn't care either way it was good mead.

"Another one and a room for a night or two and where's your baths located?" Michael belched out in a much clearer voice, though still with a baritone ring to it.

"Hold yer horses' youngin' one thing at a time; I ain't as fast as I used to be." The old bartender growled in his throaty dry voice hurrying off to refill the mug again.

"No rush, my good man." Michael said picking up the second round of mead off the well-worn counter, taking another large mouthful and swallowing.

"Ah, just what the doctor ordered." Michael said out loud.

"What's that youngin', my hearing ain't as good as it used to be?" The old bartender said in his dry rough tone, which seemed to belong to a man who had been wondering in a desert without water for three days.

"Nothing, just talkin' to myself." "Now what were you needin'?" The old barkeep asked as if asking the question to thin air.

"Oh yes a room; I have one left. They're upstairs across from the baths; although only one bath is workin' at the moment. Last door on the right, I'll send someone to get it ready. You can have my last room; down the hall, last one on your left." The old man sounded a little winded from all the speech.

Michael finished off the second Rockbite and ordered up another to take upstairs. They were at least one good thing left in life he thought, feeling the effects of the mead already. He should slow down a little after this one. Drinking too fast wasn't a good idea unless you wanted a hell-of-a-hangover. Besides, he had all the time in the world he thought spitefully.

First things first though, bath and then maybe some fun. The tavern was beginning to fill up with festival goers. Maybe staying here was a bad idea after all, he thought climbing the stairs.

Upstairs, last door on the right, ah there it is he told himself reaching the end of the hallway. He opened the door and found a large oval shaped tub made of blackened iron already half-filled with water. A long dark wooden bench stood along the right side wall providing a seat to take off boots. He sat his mead down on the bench and began undressing when someone knocked the door.

"Minute." Michael blurted out, and reached for the towel at the end of the bench.

"Come in," he said, after he had wrapped himself with the towel.

In staggered a shaggy blonde haired teenage boy carrying two pails of water larger than him.

"Here boy let me help you," Michael said and took the two large steaming buckets of water and poured them into the tub.

"Thank ya sir," the boy said sheepishly.

"No problem. Here ya go," Michael said as he handed him a copper for a tip, which certainly brightened him up. His blue eyes shined.

"Thank ya, sir. My name's Micknia, but you can call me Mick. Need anything else, sir?" Mick finished lightly in what Michael suspected was his best proper speech.

"No I'm good."

"Just ask for me if ya need anything else," Mick added as he turned to leave.

"Thanks, I will."

This will certainly be a treat, Michael thought as he got into the tub of hot water. "Ah yes." Michael said aloud to the empty room as he grabbed the bar of soap and washcloth.. He loved the smell of fresh soap, nothing like a hot bath to make you feel better. Another bad thing about living in the wilderness, it can be hard to get a decent bath or shave. His beard was getting unruly and worst of all it had streaks of grey through it. He was way too young to have any grey showing.

He got dressed and went downstairs to find the bartender. The bar was full by now and the poor old bartender looked as if he was going to have a stroke with sweat beading up across his wrinkled forehead.

"Just a minute sonny, I'll be right with ya," the old barkeeper said sounding surprisingly energetic.

"No problem." Michael replied.

The old bartender hobbled back over to Michael.

"Now what can I do ya for?" He asked.

"I was wondering where I could get a haircut and shave?" Michael asked.

"Well, ol' Barstova's Barber shop will do ya up just fine. Yup he's the best."

"I didn't get your name earlier?" Michael asked.

"Valkriss, and yours good sir?" Valkriss asked in an unmistakable courteous tone.

"Michael."

"Good to meet you Michael." Valkriss said extending his leathery hand out for a handshake.

"Same here," Michael said as he shook his hand.

"You have a strong handshake Valkriss."

"Things aren't what they always appear to be, now are they, judging by that sword you carry." Valkriss said with a half-cocked grin.

Yet Michael pulled his hand back, which went immediately to the hilt of his sword.

"Easy there young fellar, I'm just making an observation, that's all. Besides I'm in the tavern business, not the spying business," Valkriss added quickly.

"You have nothing to fear from me. Barstova's is down on Sorence Lane off King's way."

"Thanks; this is for my room and board." Michael said and flipped Valkriss a gold coin, which the old man caught in mid-air.

"Pleasures mine," Valkriss thanked him before turning to serve his other customers.

"Mick; Mick, dang it where are you boy?" Valkriss yelled, although his voice was hardly audible over the noise of the growing crowd.

"Over here sir, whatcha needin', Val?" Mick stammered as he came running from the other end of the bar.

"Dang blast it boy. I told you not to call me Val. Only my friends call me that, and I don't like you. Call me sir or Valkriss. Think you can manage the bar for a few minutes while I go to the cellar and get supplies?"

"Yes sir!" Mick said beaming.

"I'd better not catch you drinkin'. You're too young, got it mister?"

"Oh yes sir. No problem sir." Mick looked like he was standing at attention.

"And watch the Hellsbreath Ale, will ya? Last time someone drank that stuff, they nearly burnt the place down when they belched near a candle," Valkriss added, heading to the stairwell leading down to the cellar.

He could still hear Mick saying yes, sir as he made his way down the stairs. He worried Valkriss; hell anyone worried him when they actually acted excited about work.

"Damn it, Adrelia! You listen to me, you hear. He's not one to be messed around with!"

"I told you! Don't call me that Valkriss. It's Holly; remember that you old goat," she sneered through clenched teeth.

"Keep your voice down. They're ears everywhere in this damn town," Holly said, lowering hers as well.

"Fine, but there's something you need to know. Michael carries a sword I've seen before and if I'm right, it means trouble Holly; big trouble. Mark my words." Valkriss said as his old voice trailed off like he was recollecting old memories.

"What are you talking about old man?"

"The Silver Knights," Valkriss said half to himself.

"Have you lost your marbles? They only exists in stories Valkriss. Fairy tales told to little children at bedtime." Holly mocked in a motherly tone.

"Listen, girl, do not mock me. You know nothing of what once was. The sword Michael carries was once carried by Delwen Carlear. I know this because he used to stay here during the Great War. He spent time here with a lady by the name of Asuvalia Lyndhurst. Boy she was one gorgeous redhead of a woman, hell-of-a-temper though. If she hadn't been so crazy in love with that damn Delwen, I would have gone for her myself.

Anyway, she stopped hanging around here after he didn't come back. I suspect our dear boy Michael may not be an only child either. Ah sam's hell, I'm sorry Holly. I keep getting off track. Now where was I? Oh yeah. I may be getting old dear, but my memory is still as clear as ever. I was close to finding out the true lineage of the sword when Delwen was sent to battle by Sir Lawrence and never returned.

Decoros the sword of Glollas, the first Primericerus of the Silver Knights is well known and can only be used by a direct blood descendent of his," Valkriss said sounding a little winded from all the talk.

"What did you call Glollas? Primericerus."

"It means, true leader," Valkriss answered.

"So, how does this change anything?" Holly asked.

"Ah, my poor girl you still don't see, do you?" Valkriss smiled like an affectionate grandfather.

"It means Michael must be a direct relative of Glollas'; therefore, he may be Delwen's son. It's the only way he could have that sword. Somehow it must have found its way back to him over the twenty-two years since his father was killed."

"I still don't see how this changes things."

"I keep forgetting you've been locked away in that damn prison too long to know much." Valkriss said pointly.

"Trust me you will need to know this if you are going to be successful.

The Silver Knights formed after the chaos of the Mage War which had destroyed the foundations of law and order and laid waste the entire northern half of this continent. In its wake, entire civilizations descended into depravity, where the strong survived by plundering the remnants that were left behind. Glollas was the first leader of the Silver Knights, which at first consisted of merely a few dozen dedicated men.

Yet in time their ranks grew and grew until they were the most formidable fighting force on earth.

Once a knight was chosen, his first year he was trained in every weapon known to exist. Their second year was spent learning how to counteract all types of magic. Yet not one was trained to ever use offensive magic of any kind. They were forbidden to do so. The Code of the Silver Knights was quick to make an example of any who tried.

They were feared by even the greatest mages Holly. Some knights were immune to magic. A blessing bestowed upon them for their faithful and undying loyalty unto death by Honos, the holy god they served.

It was Glollas who killed the Vorlocks' high necromancer, Kavanaugh, breaking their power to this day. Be extremely careful about what you try on Michael. If he is who I think he is, anger him and Soladar will be the least of your worries." Valkriss said.

"How else am I going to kill Soladar?" Holly asked.

"Your mother, god rest her soul, was my only sister Holly and you're her only child. I don't want to see anything happen to you. Just drop it; please? You won't be able to pull it off, even with my help. However, you have whatever I can offer if I cannot persuade you otherwise," Valkriss finished with a sad ring to his aging voice.

Holly placed her hand on the side of Valkriss' face.

"Dear sweet uncle, thank you for everything you've done these last few months. Everything will work out, just wait and see. Don't worry, just stick to our plan. Okay? Besides I've already seen Michael once, and I think our plan will work wonderfully." Holly said matter-of-factly.

"What in sam's hell do you mean? You met him already? Haven't I told you to stay in the tavern and let me know if you're going out Adrelia? When did you meet Michael? And where? He just came in today." Valkriss said clearly upset at being left out of the loop.

"Don't call me Adrelia," Holly said as a reddish color flickered across her eyes in the old cellar's oil lamp lights.

"Ease up girl, your hokey pokey magic don't scare me, you're the one who needs to learn some fear Holly. You're just like your mom lass, stubborn as they come. Have it your way," Valkriss said, strained from the stress.

"I was in disguise uncle, quit worrying about me. I needed to know how effective it would be."

"Well, did he go for it?"

"Indeed."

"I have to get back up to tend the bar. That youngin' will have the place destroyed if I leave him alone too long.

One other thing, Michael's staying upstairs in the last room, you know the one."

"Indeed I do. Now off you go before Mick starts giving away shots of Hellsbreath and burns the place to the ground," Holly said smiling.

Chapter 2
Jealousy

It was four in the evening by the time he found Barstova's Barber shop. It was empty apparently everyone was out enjoying the festival. That suited Michael just fine, that way he wouldn't have to wait in line. He hated to get a haircut and shave when the barber was in a hurry. Something about a person using a straight razor around your neck; you didn't want them distracted, less they slip and you'd be the one paying the price.

The barber was a large burley man with a pot belly. He was middle aged by Michael's guess, with well-groomed dark brown hair and beard someone in his business should have.

"Gil's the name. How may I help?" The barber said in a booming jolly voice causing his oversized belly to shake.

"I need a haircut and shave." Michael answered in a light baritone tone doing his best to relax.

"Come on up and have a seat and I'll see what I can do for you," Gil told him.

His hair always got unruly and curly when it grew long; not to mention the grey showing in his beard. He always felt clean when he had a fresh shave. Kara used to joke, calling him 'Greybeard her curly haired warrior.' God, it seemed like a lifetime ago, yet he could still feel her soft hands running through his hair.

"All done, sir. How does it look?" Gil asked, bringing Michael back out of his daydream. The barber held up a mirror in so he could inspect his haircut and shave.

"Good job, thank you. How much do I owe you?" Michael asked clearing his throat.

"One silver sir," Gil answered. Michael dug into his money pouch, retrieved two and gave them to him.

"Many kind thanks, come back anytime," the barber said happily as Michael left his shop.

He had to get some fresh air, had to breath. It was too painful remembering how he felt after Kara's death. The rage welling up inside him and threatening to overtake his soul; should he it? Would they be any coming back if he did? Or would he be lost in a sea of hatred, forever adrift in endless despair. Never again to come ashore to the bountiful lands of, joy and love. A poem he wrote after losing her came to mind.

Shall my troubled soul wonder, eternally searching? Why? I have seen death; felt its icy grip close around me; pried it free, my life redeemed. Yet what shall become of my soul? A man driven onward to fight; for what I no longer know. My existence persists. I was grateful to be spared. However confusion darkens my mind and clouds my soul. My judgment is evil; I am condemned like a worthless thief caught unawares in the mists of night.

Am I worthy to be loved? Nay I say not. What then shall I be worthy of? Death and torment would not suffice for my fate. Yet, I am spared by His Most Gracious Host on High. Will I claim hope for salvation and redemption of my soul? Pain has been my companion and hatred my lover for so many years now, can I know any other? The future lies before me, shall I step forward? My strength has faded and burns only in memories of my youth. All that is left to me is smoldering coals of the fires of undying passion which once raged out of control. Yet left the warmth of reason comes with age tempered over time.

Damn it man get ahold of yourself, they're going to lock you up. Hell that might not be such a bad idea he thought, as he regained his composure and headed back to the tavern.

The evening wore on and the Hallows Eve festival got into full swing. The street lamps began to flicker to life with mulciber flies illuminating them. Many people called them lightening bugs; just a handful would light up an entire room.

They were a menagerie of people flowing through the street; all kinds with tattoos; large piercings. Still others with spiraling designs that glowed on their bald heads; even their women had them as well.

Michael had heard about them, Rune People they were called; said to have special powers depending on what type of runes they were born with. Their powers were not well understood or talked about. Most people feared them, maybe for good reason he thought.

He had never seen such a diverse assortment of individuals before, not even in Cinnibar and he found it to be extremely fascinating. He allowed his mind to wonder about what language they spoke and customs they had. There was even an occasional dwarf wondering through the crowd.

"Outta my way humie," one overly large dwarf kept shouting as he made his way through the crowd. Dwarves weren't the most subtle of people.

One thing that never died in Michael was his curious nature. If he could just get Kara out of his head he thought making his way back off Sorence to King's Way. He might be able to lead a normal life, but how could he do that when his life was all about killing the evil Scarious. The retched beast had invaded his life so early by killing his father.

His mother Myra made sure the warriors of Trayden trained him in all weapons of combat. His father's sword was still his favorite though. It felt light as a feather in his hand, like an extension of his arm. At times the sword knew what to do before he did, acting on its own accord.

He heard stories about how certain swords could become obsessed with blood and take on a life of their own. A sword which became possessed would exert its will over the wielder. He would become its slave and the sword his master. He always caulked it up to old wives tales and nothing more.

At five years old when he was presented his father's sword by Tiberious. He knew then where his destiny lay. It was a heavy burden to be placed on one so young, yet he took it willingly.

Kara was his fault; he had made an oath to his mother upon her deathbed when he was just eighteen years old: 'Upon my honor, upon my blood, upon my death, shall my father be avenged.' Michael remembered the words like he had spoken them yesterday.

He should have never strayed from his quest like he did, by falling for Kara. She was his first and his only love; why? Honos in heaven only knows why, he thought.

"Excuse me." A woman's voice said in front of him.

Then he realized he was about to walk right into a lady with a little boy standing in front of a street vendor selling all manners of sugary sweets.

"Oh, pardon me I'm sorry I didn't see you," Michael said apologetically.

The woman made her purchase, ignoring her little boy who was tugging on her dress in hopes he might get the big orange lollipop he was eyeing. Michael stepped up to the vendor and pointed to it.

"I'll take that one," he said, paid for it and handed it to the boy.

"Here you go little one."

The little fellow looked up with a broad smile and reached out for it the same time his mother turned around and saw.

"Are you supposed to take things from strangers?" The mother asked frowning. The little boy withdrew his hand. "I'm sorry, my name is Michael. How do you do, ma'am?"

"I'm Alana and this little beggar here is Branson," she said in a stern tone looking down at him.

"I guess it's okay. What are you supposed to say Branson?" Alana asked her son.

"Gee thanks mister," Branson said delighted to have his hands on the overly large orange lollipop.

"You're more than welcome Branson," Michael replied in a fatherly tone.

"Enjoy the fair and be safe," he added before setting off again.

"To you as well," Alana said softly with a slight twinkle in her eye.

It felt strange to act human again, Michael thought as he continued walking down the broad avenue.

"STOP!" screamed a woman from somewhere in the crowd behind him.

Michael's hands went for his sword instinctually as he spun around to see a man running toward him.

He simply stuck out his foot and tripped the buffoon, sending him crashing face-first on the hard cobblestone street. Michael was on top of him before he could move with his sword at his throat. The man tried to struggle in vain.

"Don't," Michael ordered harshly.

"Move and I'll slice your throat."

Within seconds a frantic woman appeared beside them.

"He took," she gasped trying to catch her breath.

"He took my handbag," she finally managed to get out.

"Really now, I just thought you were running for your health," Michael told the hoodlum sarcastically.

"I didn't do anything. You're crazy; both of you!" The hooligan spat out.

"Well, let's see if you're right shall we? Ma'am what color is your bag?" Michael asked politely.

"Purple with a black clasp," the lady answered indignantly.

Michael threw open the man's vest with his free hand.

"Why; what do we have here? Don't tell me, you're accessorizing aren't you?" Michael grabbed the handbag and handed it back to the lady.

"Is everything there?" He asked.

"I think so, let me check," she said going through her bag feverously.

"Yes, it looks like everything's here," she said satisfied.

"What are the value of your items and money in your bag ma'am?" Michael asked.

"What do you mean?" The woman asked.

"So the guards will know how to determine his punishment."

"Let me see, about ten silver. Yep that should be right," the lady answered.

"Oh, I'd hate to be you," Michael told the thief.

"Go to hell!" The man sneered.

"Oh maybe I will, but how about you first?" Michael said, glaring wild eyed at him. He could see the look of terror and shock run through the man's eyes, as he pressed his sword down on his neck.

"Please don't," the man gasped.

"I'm sorry, I didn't mean it," he whined, as a little trickle of blood ran down his neck from Michael's sword biting down on it, threatening to sever his head.

"That's enough, we'll take him now," a stern male voice called out from over Michael's shoulder.

"My apologies officer, my sword slipped and nicked the poor chap," Michael said as he got to his feet.

He knew the King's Law dictated that anyone caught stealing, had to work manual labor and repay seven times the amount stolen or attempted to. It always made for a very unhappy thief whenever they got caught.

He made his way through the thicket of bystanders who had been attracted by all the commotion.

"Well done!" A man's voice came from behind him with a pat on his back.

"Thanks, now if you'll excuse me." Michael said as he weaved his way through.

It was nothing to him; anyone would have done the same. He was just in the right place at the right time and it was definitely time to do some serious drinking and listen to music. Michael thought heading back to the tavern.

Soon he found himself back at a packed Golden Paw on the edge of dark. Luckily he found a table, but unfortunately it was at the dead center of the barroom.

At least he wouldn't be lonesome with all the noise in the place, he thought as a waitress walked up to his table.

"What'll you have?" She asked.

"Pint of Rockbite please," Michael answered.

"Anything else?" She asked with a smile.

"That's all, thanks," Michael replied.

He just wanted to enjoy his favorite mead and spend an actual night in a real bed. It wasn't long before the pretty young barmaid returned with his drink.

"Thank you, keep 'em coming and I'll make sure to tip you well. What's your name by the way?" Michael asked.

"Bree and your most welcome," she replied with a smile and turned to serve other customers.

The demons inside his mind wouldn't stop. They never did, always threatening to overtake him at any second. Over and over their shouts echoed in his head. It's all your fault; you're the reason she's dead. You killed her. End it Michael, put an end to your pain and suffering.

Maybe he should, yet he knew he could never dishonor Honos. However he could do something reckless. Maybe travel to the Northern Wastes and find a legion of black devils to attack. That single thought brought a wide smile to his face; at least it would be an honorable death.

"Hello handsome looks like you could use some company. You mind?" She asked, pointing to the empty chair at his table.

"Sure," Michael said clearing his throat and getting his mind back to reality. He looked up, and thought he'd seen her before. She was a very attractive woman a little younger than him, perhaps

"My name is Michael Carlear, and yours?" He asked politely and took another drink of Rockbite to clear his throat.

"Devona Thayer. Nice to meet you; do you come here often?" She asked.

Michael had to lean forward so he could hear her better through all the noise.

"Can't say I've been here before," Michael said coolly.

"Have I..."

"May I have your attention please?" A man's booming voice interrupted him before he could finish his question.

"We have a great band for your entertainment tonight. To start off All Hallows Month! Welcome to the Golden Paw Tavern... All the way from Sindara...The Merrimac's!"

"Oh they're good, I saw them play in Odessa just outside Cinnibar and they were wonderful," Devona told Michael.

Yet another demon from his past he had to deal with. At least the crowd got quieter when the band started playing. It was a four man band, three playing instruments and a singer; except they looked to be a man short. An enchantment was playing the drums.

Of course Michael had never heard of them. He'd only seen a couple of street musicians play before, not counting some of the folks in his village. They were a pleasant band to listen to, even if they did have help from magic he thought and turned back to Devona.

"Have I seen you before?" Michael asked causally.

"No, I would've remembered a handsome man like you," Devona said with a wink.

"You sure? I was out earlier, could have sworn I'd seen you some place." Michael asked again. He was always good at remembering faces.

"Sorry, I just got into town this evening," she replied.

"My apologies, where are my manners? What would you like to drink, my lady?"

"Now don't go getting all formal on me and besides who says I'm a lady?" Devona added laughing devilishly.

She had a beautiful smile and was far more striking than at first glance.

Maybe the smoke in the tavern blurring his eyesight, either that or the Rockbite had kicked in. Devona had beautiful wavy dark brown hair, long black eye lashes, warm rosy cheeks and with the low V-cut red velvet dress, not a bad figure to boot. Yep, the Rockbite was most assuredly kicking in, he thought with a smile.

"What are you smiling at?" Devona asked in a sweet melodious tone smiling.

Damn he was busted; oh hell he had to think of something fast.

"The song they're playing just reminded me of something funny that's all," Michael said trying to avoid her eyes.

He was never good at lying.

"Michael, they're playing a song about Glollas' last stand and him dying," Devona said crossly.

"Oh; it was a story I heard a long time ago about how one of the knights tried to flee in fear only to fall on his sword and die," he said putting on his best straight face.

"Boy your right that is funny," Devona said with a slight smile.

Thank goodness she bought it, or let him off the hook, either way he was happy.

"Now how about a drink; what would you like?" Michael asked.

"Double Cinnigin on the rocks, please."

"I'll be right back," he said and went to the bar himself since he didn't see a waitress anywhere.

The music wasn't half bad as he listened to it walking to the bar. The band was playing just off center of the far wall. They didn't have a proper stage. Some tables were pushed out of the way to make room. At least he could hear them and they were worth listening to. They had a great harp player, which he always loved to hear. Music was like food: when it was good you couldn't get enough; however if it was bad, you wouldn't eat another bite.

He finally managed to get to the bar and raised his hand to get somebody's attention.

Valkriss must have extra help tonight. There's no way he could handle all this, he'd stroke out Michael thought.

"What can I get you?" A husky male voice asked coming from under the counter.

"What?" Michael asked unsure if someone was talking to him and if so; where the hell they were?

"You heard me humie. What can I get ya?"

This time Michael looked over the bar and saw a dwarf who was as broad as he was tall. He looked kind of young, for all he knew about them. This one didn't have a beard, just coal black hair, big black bushy eyebrows, or maybe unibrow would be a better description.

"You starin' at me humie?" The dwarf bartender asked in a deep voice.

"Not at all good sir. I'll have a pint of Rockbite and a double Cinnigin on the rocks please," Michael said doing his best to lighten the dwarf up.

"Eight coppers."

Michael flipped him a silver coin. "Keep the change, my good man."

Michael headed back to Devona with the drinks, hoping the tip would make up for any ill feelings the dwarf may have toward him.

Bad enough to have an angry bartender, but a pissed off dwarf bartender, that could get a man killed. Michael almost spilled the drinks when he bumped into the table coming back, imagining the angry dwarf replacing his brand of drink with something like Hellsbreath. Good grief, the worst drinking experience of his life was in a little dive in Helcon. He nearly exploded after drinking that toxic brew.

He didn't see how anyone could enjoy something that can do that to you. It tastes great when you drink it, but oh boy you better watch out when you burp.

"Here you go," Michael said as he sat the drink down in front of her and moved around to sit in his seat.

"I'm sorry if I'm not good company tonight. I'm not much of a social person lately," Michael looked down at his mead.

"No worries here Michael. Like I said, I'm new in town and looking for some company, that's all," Devona said in a warm rich tone.

Damn everything about this woman is sexy, even her voice he thought. They talked for a long time and had more drinks, which was an extremely pleasant distraction from his demons.

Finally well after midnight they said their goodbyes and parted ways. He headed upstairs to his room after telling her he would be staying at least another day there at the tavern. And he found out she was going to be in town for a few days longer at the Fulcrum Hotel. If she didn't come by the Golden Paw tomorrow, he would venture out and see if he couldn't run into her by chance. Sleep came fast and dreamless that night for once.

He woke early the next morning, as he always did. He wished he could have slept a little longer, he had a splitting headache. Too much Rockbite, he thought getting out of bed making him feel even worse. How many drinks did he have last night? He wondered, searching for his pants. They were lying in the middle of the bedroom floor halfway to the bed. After locating all his clothes and washing his face in the wash bowl, he felt a little better. His first order of business would be to get some strong black coffee, another luxury he missed.

They were many things he missed, he thought sadly. Ok let's not start that again, he told himself heading out the door to go downstairs.

He was surprised to see the barroom in tip top shape after the size of the crowd in there last night. The smell of fresh brewed coffee drifted across urging him toward it at the bar. Planted squarely in the middle was a large white kettle with cups on both sides. Self-service, he thought with a smile.

This is good coffee, he thought sipping the piping hot beverage while he sat on the barstool.

"Be with you in a moment. Have some coffee while you wait." A young feminine voice called out from the back room, nearly causing Michael to spill coffee in his lap.

"Oh, thanks," Michael replied to the unseen voice.

If that was Valkriss, he must have gotten a mage to change him into a young woman. He was certainly going to have to work on his twisted sense of humor.

"Well good morning sir. I see my coffee has lifted your spirits. What's so funny?" She asked grinning, as she walked up behind the bar.

"Nothing, I was just thinking of something funny that's all," Michael said.

There's no way he would tell her the truth. She was far too beautiful to have ever been a man.

"My name's Holly; and yours?" She asked.

"Michael," he said rising off his seat as he answered

"No need for pleasantries. It's way too early for that," Holly said with a slight girlish quality in her voice, making her seem younger than she probably was.

"Now, Michael what can I get you to eat? My uncle Valkriss told me to take good care of you," she said smiling.

Sweet mercy, he loved the way she said his name. She was adorably cute as well he thought, trying to think of something to order. He really didn't want anything, he just wanted to talk to her more. "Do you have a menu?" Michael asked politely.

"Here you go," she said and reached him a small thick folded menu with a golden paw stamped on its front cover.

Michael pretended to read it, but he already knew he what he was going to order.

"I'll have toast and bacon."

"Ok I'll get right on it; be back in a few minutes," Holly said, turned and walked back into the room where Michael had heard the voice come from before.

He refilled his coffee. The first cup made him feel good enough to where he could eat a little. Within five minutes or so Holly returned with his order.

"Here you go. Hope you enjoy," she said, sitting his plate and silverware down in front of him.

"Smells delicious," Michael said with a smile.

"So did you say Valkriss was your uncle?" Michael asked trying to drum up a causal conversation.

"Yes; I came up from Cinnibar to help him out. He doesn't like to admit it, but he's getting too old to run the tavern and good help is hard to find now days. He doesn't have any children of his own. I kinda feel bad for the old goat," Holly said affectingly.

"That's kind of you," Michael said.

"So what brings you into town? Is this your first time in Lawrence?" Holly asked.

"Came in for the Hallowed Month festival; my first time here, I'm from Trayden," he said, not wanting to really tell her the true reason.

He knew it would not only turn her off, but make her think he was just another crazy warrior hell bent on self-destruction.

"How long have you been in Lawrence? I didn't see you around here yesterday," Michael hoped to change the subject.

"Not long, came up this summer," Holly replied.

"If you'll excuse me, I see some of our other guests have come down," she added before heading around the bar to see about the others who were sitting a couple tables behind him in the main bar area.

She hated these menial tasks and put on her best fake smile as she walked over to the table; where a slim balding man and short blonde haired woman sat waiting for service. She could care less about them or what they wanted. She couldn't wait to get out of Lawrence and back to her plans which were ten years in the making. She took their order and headed off to the kitchen.

"Duty calls," Holly told Michael as she passed by.

"I understand, maybe we can talk again," Michael said.

"Hope so," she said vanishing into the kitchen.

He finished breakfast with another cup of coffee and then went to see if he could find that blacksmith Valkriss had told him about. He found himself on King's Way trying to remember the directions.

He saw the street and turned and went down the old narrow brick lane filled with small local shops. He almost passed the blacksmith shop, but the clanging sound of metal made him stop.

It was a small place with an old weather-beaten sign that read: Lizemores Blacksmith Shop barely legible. The place certainly looked like it had seen better days. He peered into the large open front.

"Hello," Michael said loudly so he could be heard over the clanging noise coming from the back of the shop.

The sound stopped and an aged bearded man appeared from the back.

"Aye, what can I do for ya?" The old smith asked in a distinct accent Michael had never heard before.

"I was told you do good work on armor and might be able to know where I can buy a horse as well."

"Aye, may be able to do that; let me see what ya have that needs fixin'."

Michael handed him the piece of damaged shoulder plate.

"Owie, looks like you be havin' way too much fun, you have. What in de world did this? Must have been extremely hard whatever it was," said the blacksmith with a toothless grin, turning the piece over in his blackened callused hands.

"Well made, Trayden piece by de looks of it. Haven't seen anything from there in a while, good stuff it is," he said muttering to himself more than Michael.

"Well, Mr. Lizemore; you can fix it?"

"Call me Orndoff, laddie. I can fix it no problem, but it'll cost ya. This is good armor and good armor is hard fixed. Where'd you say you're from?" Orndoff asked.

"I didn't."

"No offense meant. Don't go gettin' your trousers in a bunch youngin'. Just asking that's all. I'll fix your armor; business is hard to come by since the Great War ended. Hell, all I do anymore is horseshoes; horseshoes, and more damn horseshoes. I swear if I never see another one, it'll be too soon, I tell you that."

Oh great Michael thought, a blacksmith on a rant.

"I'll have it ready for you first thing in de morning."

"That's fine."

"Wouldn't be interested in selling that sword there, would ya?" Orndoff asked offhand.

"My sword? No thanks. It's sentimental to me." Michael answered coolly, knowing he meant no harm.

"That's a nice one from the look of the hilt, it is."

"I'll be by in the morning to pick up my armor," Michael said curtly, having no desire to discuss any sale further and turned to leave; when he felt a vise-like grip grab his arm.

"Keep your head down youngin', times are dangerous and trust is seldom deserved," Orndoff said quietly letting go of his arm.

"What do you mean?" Michael asked, his right hand already gripped tightly around his sword's handle.

"Just what I said; you're no fool. You know full well what I mean," Orndoff said in a harsh tone.

"I can handle myself well enough. Don't worry about me, old timer," Michael said confidently and left.

He didn't bother to ask Orndoff where he could find a horse. Michael didn't like people nosing around in his business. And what the hell was the crazy old smith talking about? He had other things on his mind and getting killed was the least of them.

What he wanted to do now, was find Devona, or maybe find out more about Holly and see if she was single. Tough choice, he thought smiling.

His head spun as he walked down the old alleyway to the main street; first the comments from Valkriss at the tavern and now this Orndoff character. He knew his father's sword was special; no one had to tell him that, but why did everyone seem to know it somehow?

He only knew one man who held any answers and that was Tiberious. He had given up looking for him a long time ago. Though, if he were honest with himself, he stopped looking when he met Kara.

What was wrong with wanting to live a life of peace with someone you loved? Nothing unless you were him, he thought sarcastically. Heaven forbid he ever get anything he wanted. Still in many ways he was thankful for the time he had spent with Kara. They were the happiest he ever had.

"Excuse me, miss," came a voice behind her at the bar, causing Holly to turn around.

"How may I help you?" Holly asked.

"Is Michael Carlear is still staying here?" The lovely young woman asked politely.

Just who the hell is this and what the HELL does she want with her man, Holly thought. She was doing her best to control her temper; knowing she couldn't blow her up in broad daylight. Settle yourself down and get rid of her.

"I'm sorry dear, he has already checked out," Holly told her as nicely as she could, hoping her cheeks weren't getting flushed.

Apparently they were and the woman could tell.

"Please leave him a message just in case he comes by. Tell him Devona Thayer stopped by and said she enjoyed last night tremendously and would like to do it again." Devona said adding extra emphasis on the last word as she turned to leave.

"Yes ma'am, no problem. By the way where are you staying, in case he asks?" Holly asked, while using every last ounce of restraint not to get hostile.

"The Fulcrum Hotel," Devona said casually with a wicked grin and walked out.

She's damn lucky I have to be a good girl. Just calm down and go pay her a visit, Holly thought wickedly.

"I'll be back in a little while uncle; I have to run a couple errands," Holly told Valkriss when he came up with more supplies from the cellar.

"Do you remember what I told you?" Valkriss asked, giving her a stern look.

"Whatever; I don't have time for this right now," Holly said and started to leave, when he grabbed her arm.

"I asked you a question dear. It's not nice to disrespect your elders; now is it?" He said crisply.

Holly jerked her arm away.

"Look, ever grab me like that again and I'll show you exactly what Soladar taught me. You hear me; you old goat!" Holly said in a heated voice causing some of the other patrons to look their way.

"I'm sorry, Holly, I'm just trying to help you the best I know how;" Valkriss said in a tone of compassion.

"Never touch me like that again and we'll get along fine, okay," Holly said still angry at being grabbed.

"Holly if you mess up both of our heads will be on the chopping block. Have a little compassion, why don't you," he said solemnly.

"I'm sorry uncle, don't worry we'll both be fine. Besides Michael and I should be out of here in a couple days. I just have to take care of something before we leave, that's all, no worries."

"Well I've trusted you this far. I guess I can trust you to see this thing through to its bitter end, however it goes. Anyway I've lived my life.

You're the one I worry about the most youngin',"
he said.

With that, Holly walked out of the tavern.

It took her a little while to find it. She still
didn't know the city well. She walked inside the
Fulcrum Hotel to the front desk where a lanky
middle-aged man sat on a small wooden stood.
He stood up when he saw her walking toward the
counter.

"How may I help, miss?" The clerk asked
in a proper tone.

"My friend Devona Thayer told me to
come by. We are going out for lunch. Is she in?"
Holly inquired.

"Yes, she's in. Would you like for me to
get her for you?" The clerk asked.

"No, no don't trouble yourself dear. What
room is she staying in? I'll go up and see if she's
ready yet," Holly said sweetly.

"Let me see, ah here it is, room thirty-one,
it's on the third floor, first door on the left.
Anything else, ma'am?"

"No, you been extremely helpful. Thank
you so much," Holly said beaming.

Now we will see who the better woman is,
she thought heading for the stairs.

There was a knock at the door; wonder who that could be Devona thought getting up from her chair in front of the mirror.

"Just a minute, please," Devona said applying a last second touchup to her makeup; thinking Michael was stopping by on his way out of town. That brought a smile to her lovely face.

"I'm coming," she said hurrying over to open the door.

"It's you! What…"

"Oh yes dear. It's me. Now; is that any way to greet a guest?"

Were the last words Devona heard before the lights in the room went dim and finally black.

Chapter 3
All Hallows Month

It was noon and the city was getting crowded again with people coming in from all over the countryside to trade and enjoy all the attractions and activities happening at this time of year. There was an abundance of food at every turn. Farmers' carts piled high from a great harvest with pumpkins; squash, corn of all colors, beans, and many fruits and vegetables which Michael had never seen before. The aromas of all the food cooking drifted through the air were making him hungry again.

He was always willing to try different foods and had learned many things that look bad actually tasted good. Michael wondered what to eat, as he sized up a couple of food vendors in front of him. One had large clear glass jars filled with various pickled meats and other hard to identify foods. He walked up a little closer.

"What's your special?" Michael asked the young man.

"Pickled Pigs Feet, they're the best, we butcher our own hogs and make it fresh. Nothing artificial about these babies. We allow them to pickle for a full year, care for a sample?" The man asked.

Oh boy here I go again Michael thought.

"Sure, why not," he told the vendor.

The man reached him a small stick with a piece of what could only be described as raw looking meat with a clear jelly covering it. Michael put it in his mouth and chewed it; well it tasted like pickles and pork. The texture however would take some getting used to.

"Thanks for the sample," Michael said still trying to swallow the rest of it.

"Would you like some more?" The young man asked, hoping for a sale.

"I'm good; thanks though," Michael replied and went on touring nearby food carts.

Now where was the one he'd found the sausage at the day before, trying to remember. Maybe closer to the gate, no, damn they were too many people running around for him to get his bearings.

Oh wait, this one looks promising as he stopped in front of a wagon with a white washed sign on front advertising whole turkey legs for sale.

"Don't be shy sir, step on up. What can I get for you today?" A slim built man with a black handlebar mustache that looked like it was painted on almost comically.

"All our turkey legs are fresh from the butcher, slow roasted with salt, pepper, and our mouth-watering spices," he said in his best sales pitch, which were drawing others besides Michael.

"I'll take one with two pieces of black bread please," Michael said quickly, before the others started with their orders.

He always had to have some kind of bread with his meals. He never really thought about it, but a meal just wasn't a meal without bread of some kind. The turkey leg smelled fantastic, he couldn't wait to find a place to sit down and eat.

It was perfect weather to be outside; warm autumn days were hard to come by. Now if he could just find something to drink and somewhere halfway quiet. Luckily he got a cold glass of milk from one of the drink sellers and located a small stone bench by a large statue of some man on a horse.

Who it was, he had no clue until he read the small bronze plaque at the base, so this is the great Sir Lawrence.

Boy the milk was nice and cold. He didn't care how they kept it cold. He suspected they had a magical cooler box to keep it in. Magic does have some uses he thought. He heard of an engineering guild in Cinnibar that had been working on a refrigerator of some sorts. It was supposed to be able to keep things cold even in the summer months without using blocks of ice.

He had his doubts, truth be told it was most likely some mage contraption or they got help from them to build it. You're going to have to accept new ways and new things he thought finishing off the turkey leg washing it down with the rest of the milk. No stopping progress, like time, it just keeps going forward.

He had piddled around long enough. It was time to make up his mind; Holly or Devona? Wouldn't hurt to see if he could find the hotel where Devona was staying he thought. She said she was staying at the Fulcrum. He didn't know where it was, but surely it wouldn't be too hard to find. He went into a local shop on Main Street.

He learned whenever traveling and you needed directions, go in a local business and ask. Odds are they will give you great directions. He waited until the clerk had finished waiting on a customer and then walked up to the counter.

"Hello, what can I get for you?" The young man asked.

"I'm looking for the Fulcrum Hotel. Do you know where it's at?" Michael asked.

"Why yes sir. Just follow King's Way down three blocks; turn left onto Lubeck Street, then go two blocks. It's on the right, can't miss it. It's an old stone grey three story hotel, large sign out front." The clerk finished.

"Thank you. You've been very helpful. Here you go," Michael said and reached him a copper as a tip for the good directions.

He liked it when people took time to help, especially in cities where many people won't give you the time of day.

"Thanks sir," the young clerk said.

"You're welcome," Michael said already on his way out the door.

The air certainly had a crisp coolness to it for it to be midday; it was a little colder today than yesterday, but still a nice fall day. Soon old

man winter would wrap the land in a heavy
blanket of white, not relenting till spring.

At times that suited Michael just fine. The
icy chill of winter would match his heart which
had grown just as cold since losing Kara.

However since coming to Lawrence
something had begun working in him. He didn't
know what it was exactly. Maybe desire was
being rekindled somehow. Was he looking for a
replacement for Kara? Was he weak for doing so,
if that's what he was doing? Wasn't he man
enough to stand alone? Where was his strength?
"Be a man." Michael muttered as he picked his
way through the crowded streets.

He continued to chastise himself as he
walked down Lubeck Street. Life is what you
make of it, nothing more nothing less, deal with
it. "And for Honos sake stop talking to yourself,"
he mumbled under his breath. Good grief, damn
you're crazier than a loon. Okay get a grip man,
you're going to see a lovely woman.

He stopped in front of the hotel and stared
at it for what seemed an eternity; finally he made
himself go in. It was a nice hotel, a lot better than
the Golden Paw. He looked around at all the
plush furnishings.

Beautiful paintings hung on every wall, surrounding an extremely large fireplace. Two large chairs and a comfortable looking sofa faced the crackling fire. The walls were covered by mahogany paneling polished to a brilliant sheen. He walked up to the front desk, which was marble wrapped in bronze.

"May I help you?" The man in a blue jacket wearing a funny looking round hat of the same color asked.

"Yes, I'm looking for a friend who's staying here. Her name is Devona Thayer. Is she in?" Michael asked.

The man seemed to get nervous when he said her name.

"I'm sorry Miss Thayer checked out earlier," the desk clerk said, trying to keep his composure glancing around nervously.

"Did she leave any messages for me? My name is Michael Carlear."

"No, no messages sir. She just said something about sick family and she had to check out early."

He could tell the man was hiding something. Maybe Devona had changed her mind and didn't want to hurt his feelings or something. He didn't have much experience with women.

"Thank you sir, have a nice day," Michael said, turned and left without another word.

It was a slight blow to his ego. Win some lose some he thought walking back out into the fresh autumn air.

He wondered if he should bother with women at all. It didn't make sense to get caught up in another relationship with all that was going on in his life. His only real one had been with Kara.

They were other women of course, but nothing serious. One from Trayden and a couple others in various places he'd visited in his travels, mostly flings. Maybe that was what was going on with him now; desiring the company of a woman for a while. He was lonesome after all and there was nothing wrong with that. He thought heading back to the Golden Paw.

He arrived at the tavern a little after three. Thankful the lunch crowd had left already. He had enough of people for a while. One thing about staying out in the countryside you weren't around too many. It wasn't that he didn't like people; you just never knew what they were going to do.

Michael walked up to the bar where he joined two other men having drinks.

"Same?"

Michael heard the unmistakable crackling dry voice of Valkriss.

"Sounds like a winner to me," Michael smiled.

"Coming right up," Valkriss said.

"Here ya go youngin', awful early. Better pace yourself, I got special entertainment lined up tonight," he said with a smile.

"Thanks, I'll remember that," Michael replied faking a grin and grabbed the mead.

It tasted so good as he took a large drink. Maybe instead of trying to get a woman for a night, he'd get drunk. Unfortunately he wasn't in the mood.

He finished the mead quicker than he realized and with a glance to Valkriss, he came over to get the empty mug for a refill.

"By the way, is Holly working today?" Michael asked Valkriss as he reached for the mug.

"Yep sure is, though she's not here at the minute. I sent her to run some errands. She should be getting back before too long. Why?" Valkriss asked, raising an eyebrow.

"You interested in her youngin'? You know she's my dearest niece. So you be a gentleman."

Michael was caught off guard. He'd forgotten about Holly being his niece.

"Oh; yes sir, I wouldn't dream of treating her anything short of a lady," Michael said with the best straight-forward expression he could muster.

"This round's on me. Let me know if you need anything. I'm a little short-handed at the minute. My extra help comes on at five," Valkriss said and walked around the bar to serve another customer who just walked through the door.

The tavern started to fill up again before long. The place done a lot of business, Michael noticed drinking his mead.

"Delwen?" She asked breathlessly.

"Excuse me?" Michael asked the woman with the flaming red hair who was calling him Delwen.

"Delwen, it's me Asuvalia. I can't believe it; I know it's been a while. You still look the same. Don't you remember me?" She asked with trembling lips and tears in her eyes.

"Michael I'm so sorry. She comes in here at least once a week, telling some random guy he's Delwen," Holly said walking quickly up to them.

Then she whispered to him.

"Poor thing's got a screw loose. I'll see her out," Holly said as she grabbed Asuvalias' arm.

Before he could protest Holly was leading her out.

"Come along with me, dear. Now you know Valkriss told you not to come in here and bother our customers," Holly said loud enough to be overheard as she walked Asuvalia to the door.

Then she whispered into her ear.

"Enchantum silento," Asuvalia quit resisting after that. Holly looked into her glazed-over eyes.

"Do not return to this place. Now go," Holly said in a low menacing voice.

Damn it; what's going to happen next? I can't trust that brainless old goat with anything,

Holly thought hurrying back to Michael who was sitting on the bar looking bewildered.

"Michael I am so sorry. My uncle warned me about her, but I just got back from running errands," Holly said.

She could tell he was bothered by it, yet played it cool.

"What's wrong?"

"My father's name was Delwen. That's where I get my middle name from," Michael said with an edge to his voice.

"Oh dear, I can see how upsetting that would be for you. Certainly a dreadful coincidence, Valkriss told me that poor woman's son was named Delwen. She hasn't been right since he died two years ago. Now every man she sees around his age, she thinks it's him. As you can see, you look nothing like her," Holly said, trying to lighten the ominous mood which had come over Michael.

"Here, let me get you another round. What are you drinking?" Holly asked sweetly.

"Rockbite," Michael answered.

He was beginning to regret ever stepping foot in this damn city. He never liked coincidences. The sooner he got out of Lawrence the better, he thought as Holly sat the drink down in front of him.

"Here you go, on the house," she said smiling.

"I'll be right back," Holly said pleasantly and patted him on his shoulder.
She had a soft touch. It had been over a year since he's felt the touch of a woman.

His thoughts began to race again. He had always been told he looked like his father. Why did this strange lady call him Delwen? She seemed so sure. Was she that delusional to think he was her son, when he looked nothing like her?

She did look pretty rough, with disheveled hair, dressed in an old brown tattered dress and a well-worn gray shawl.
Don't dwell on it, you're crazy enough; he told himself and took a large gulp of mead.

"Uncle, can I see you for a minute?" Holly asked as he was taking an order at a nearby table causing him to jump a little in fright.

"You're back already."

"Why of course, dear," Holly replied.

"I'll be right back with your order," he told the people at his table; then walked over to the far end of the bar so they wouldn't be overheard.

"Why in the hell didn't you see Asuvalia?" Holly asked through clenched teeth.

"I was working in case you hadn't noticed. Besides, the last time I saw her in here was years ago. She used to come in here for a while after Delwen's death, but stopped coming around about five years ago," Valkriss retorted in his defense.

"Well, she was here just a minute ago and saw Michael," Holly said fuming.

Valkriss winched.

"That's right, she called him Delwen. He looks all freaked out now. We're going to have to move our plans up."

"We can't Holly. Everything's on a timeline; it will ruin our plans."

"Well it can't be helped now, can it? We'll have to do the best we can. I got to get back and repair the damage that's been done. By the way I made up some story about Asuvalia being crazy over the loss of her son named, Delwen and now she calls all guys that okay, just so we have our story straight."

"Got it," Valkriss said getting to his table's order as Holly walked back over to Michael.

Chapter 4
Seduction

"Michael, let me apologize again for the inconvenience. I'd like to make it up to you," Holly said in her light sweet voice.

Every time he looked at her she was more beautiful than before.

"What did you have in mind?" He asked unable to stop grinning.

"Now Michael behave yourself, I was thinking of a nice dinner. How about it? Seven sound okay? We have a small room just off the kitchen that is perfect for the two of us," Holly said flirtatiously.

"Sounds great, I'll go up and get ready. Would you have Valkriss send Mick up to get a bath ready please?" Michael asked.

"No problem," Holly said feeling better now that she had cheered him up. I know exactly what he needs, she thought with a wicked grin as she walked off.

Michael finished his mead and went upstairs to his room. It was nothing special, just a queen size bed; a dresser with mirror, nightstand with a porcelain washbowl and a pitcher of fresh water on top. He grabbed his pack put it on the bed, opened it and got his set of good clothes out. They were still neatly folded, white tunic with a drawstring, chocolate brown pants. He carried them for a night out on the town that never came.

A small white laced handkerchief fell off the shirt to the floor without a sound. He stooped down, hesitated then picked it up and gently caressed it with his fingers. It was the only thing of Kara's he carried with him. All of their other belongings he kept safely tucked away in their small cottage outside Odessa. Stop it Michael, he told himself, don't go there.

A light knock on the door brought him back to reality. He grabbed his sword before he realized where he was.

"Who is it?" Michael asked clearing his throat.

"Your bath is ready," a feminine voice called out from the other side of the door.

Wow talk about service, Michael thought when the door opened.

"Hello again, handsome," Holly said smiling mischievously.

She stood just inside the room and closed the door. Damn he got better looking every time she saw him.

"I forgot to ask what you would like for dinner." She said.

"Sure, sounds great," Michael said, his thoughts drifting.

"What sounds great? You haven't told me what you want to eat," Holly said with a teasing look.

"Oh; steak if you have it, cooked medium," Michael replied.

"My favorite, I'll see you downstairs," she said smiling as she closed the door.

Michael went to the bathroom where he found soap, washcloth, and towel laid out already and the tub already half full of water. He took his clothes off and climbed in when he heard a knock at the door.

"Come in," Michael said absent-mindedly thinking it was Mick. Yet it was Holly who walked through the door carrying water.

When she entered the room, it filled with a scent of the sweetest flowers he had ever smelled. He was enthralled by her charming grace while she poured the steaming hot water into the tub.

"I'll be right back with more water."

Unable to speak, he managed to nod his head, while gazing at her face looking into her beautiful eyes. Oh, what beauty she possessed; it was hard to believe someone like her could be pouring baths in a tavern.

While she was out of the room getting more water, he couldn't keep his mind from wondering about her. He was still preoccupied with his thoughts when another gentle knock at the door brought him back to reality.

"Come in," he said clearing his throat.

Holly smiled and entered with two more pails of hot water. She was very polite and asked before pouring the water into the tub. As she did Michael noticed her eyes going over every inch of his body, scanning it, as if reading a book.

"Is there anything else I can get for you?" Holly asked.

Michael had no idea how to ask her to stay with him and talk. He didn't realize he was so lonesome until now. He needed; no craved her companionship if only for a little while.

So he simply blurted it out before he could stop himself. "Would you please, sit and talk with me? It's seldom I have anyone to talk too," Michael said sadly, looking at the water in the tub, not daring to look at her.

"Don't mind if I do," she said.

"A beautiful lady like you should not being working in her uncle's tavern or any tavern for that matter. You should be at a king's side," Michael said smiling.

One thing she loved about Michael was his incredible white smile, black hair, and his hazel green eyes didn't hurt anything either.

She was smiling now, but he tensed when she stood up from the bench and approached him.

"Easy," Holly said softly and spoke some inaudible words as she took the wash cloth from his hands, lathered up the soap and began to wash his back.

She dropped the wash cloth and began to rub his shoulders, back, and neck, sending chills throughout his entire body. Gently but firmly, her hands moved from his back to his chest.

She leaned over in front of him with her hands on his chest, slowly going down to his stomach. His tanned chest and stomach muscles rippled in excitement as they tensed and relaxed to her gentle touch.

Not stopping there, she slowly moved her hands farther down. Then he reached out and pulled her into the tub causing water to splash over its side. Holly squealed in excitement as she fell on top of his wet, partially soaped naked body.

As he slipped the dress off her shoulders, her long wavy brown hair fell softly to her breast. Michael grasped it in his strong battle worn hands and gently let it slip freely through his fingers like flowing strands of silk.

Holly seemed to radiate beauty as the sun shining in its strength. A glow settled around her as light from a nearby window focused on her as if being drawn to her beauty as much as he was. Michael caught a gleam of light dance across her beautiful green eyes as each of them was consumed in the heat of the moment.

She gave herself to him and let him feel her passion for him and held him close.
Oh god he felt great, concentrate she told herself. Stay with your plan and don't fall for him.

Her body moved in rhythmic motion.
Wave after wave of pleasure shot through her

from head to toe. She always thought sex was great, but damn sex with Michael certainly showed her what she had been missing out on. The other guys she'd been with, which weren't many; held no comparison to Michael in the least. He was in a league of his own.

They embraced passionately, thrills of excitement rushing through him as he felt her bare skin next to his. Michael couldn't believe what he was doing, yet he had no fears or worries, only the pleasure of the moment.

It had been so long since he had been with a woman and it felt wonderful to be with Holly. She felt so amazing; it was absolute bliss holding her, kissing her, simply touching her sent him to the heights of ecstasy. He could feel the fire rekindle in his soul and well as his loins. Power and strength ran freely through his veins again, evoking similar feelings he shared with Kara before.

"That was incredible," Holly said breathing heavily.

"You were phenomenal," Michael said, kissing her neck as they lay in the tub caressing each other.

Keep it together he told himself, don't get caught up with her; you hardly know her. Take it easy it's not like you're going to marry her now, just enjoy the moment. He hated feeling torn about anything, yet he certainly had acted on the spur of the moment.

"What are you thinking about? You look so lost in thought," Holly asked, seeing different expressions wash over Michael's face.

He was never any good at keeping his emotions hidden. "I hope you don't think ill of me. I haven't been myself lately and I normally get to know someone better before well; getting physical with them, if you know what I mean," Michael said slightly nervous.

"I was thinking the same thing Michael, hoping you wouldn't think I'm a bad woman because of this. I am very attracted to you and I'm not ashamed of it. Are you?"

"No way, you're a fantastic woman and hell-of-a-lover. I have no bad opinion of you and it takes two to tangle," he told her smiling and gave her another firm hug which caused her to smile.

"As much as I hate to; I have to help my uncle get the bar ready for tonight's crowd. Are you still coming down for dinner?" Holly asked.

"Sure, I've worked up a heck of an appetite," he smiled as she climbed out of the tub and grabbed the towel off the bench, dried off and got dressed.

He watched every move she made, completely captivated by her. She was stunning, everything about her radiated beauty. Her smooth soft creamy white skin, even the way she moved conveyed a powerful presence of a woman who was unashamed of her body and not afraid to after what she wanted.

Too bad she had to go back to work, Michael thought. It would be nice to spend more time together. Soon after dinner, he found himself in his room heavy with sleep, tired from the day's events. It felt great to be carefree and happy, totally relaxed.

Early the next morning, he got dressed and headed downstairs to the barroom. He neared the bottom of the steps and saw two men trying to force Holly to go with them. The look in her eyes was enough to tell him she didn't want to go. His hand gripped his sword tightly.

"Leave her alone!"

"What's it to you?" The younger of the two growled back.

"If you value your life, let her be," Michael's deep harsh tone let them know he was serious.

"Aye, best leave well enough alone or you'll pay dearly," the other sneered.

Something snapped inside Michael's head and the scene changed. Holly turned into his beloved Kara, and the two kidnappers morphed into black devils.

With a howl of anger that seemed to shake the bar. Michael jumped down the stairs, his sword coming out of its sheath while he was still in midair.

It took a second for their initial shock to wear off; however the evil beasts were not going to be denied their prey. Growling with anger they charged at him, swinging their claws trying to cut him in half. He ducked when the larger one swung in hard from the right, while engaging the smaller more agile one with his blade. Michael jumped backward and was thrown off balance by a chair which nearly caused him to fall.

The smaller black devil took full advantage of this and lunged forward with its claws, trying to stab Michael. With one fluid swing Michael batted them away while slicing through its hide sending it reeling backward in pain.

With a wail of anger the larger beast came swinging fanatically at him. With a swift kick to its stomach, he sent it crashing into a nearby table and tumbling off onto the floor.

When he turned however, he felt a searing pain in his right side and saw the smaller black devil had taken the opportunity to make a last desperate strike at him. Little did the murderous bastard know it wasn't going to make any difference.

Michael was battle tested and once rage was ignited in him, nothing would stop him from defeating an enemy. Even mortally wounded he would continue to fight on until every last drop of blood ran out of him.

Michael saw the surprise in the creature's eyes when he swung his sword down hard across its chest. It fell backward arms outstretched with blood flying from the gaping wound.

Michael looked around for the second one and saw it was out cold, lying halfway out the front door. Evidently it was trying to get away once it seen its partner fall. Kara stood over him with a tight grip on the handle of a broken mug.

"Couldn't let you have all the fun now could I," she said grinning.

Then her grin changed to a look of worry. "You're hurt," her breath quickened.

"Kara, you're okay! You're alright! I saved you!" Michael spoke through clenched teeth, doing his best to cover up the pain ripping through his side.

"I'm fine, let's worry about you," Kara said running over to see how bad the wound was.

Bright red blood was staining his tunic.

"Can you walk?" Kara asked gently.

"Run Kara, there's more coming. I won't be able to hold them off. Please; run, they'll kill you. Leave me," Michael said with a spaced out look in his eyes.

"Michael, snap out of it. It's me; Holly. Michael; look at me," Holly said and then smacked him hard across his face.

"Damn woman, why'd you slap me?" Michael asked angrily.

"You were; never mind; can you walk?"

"Of course I can," he grunted.

"Good we need to get out of here. The town's guards will be here any minute asking questions," Holly leaned in and put her arm around him.

"What happened?" He started to object.

"We'll get to that later," Holly said urgently.

Michael got the feeling she didn't relish the thought of answering questions of why someone was laying on the floor in a pool of blood and another was out cold in the doorway.

They headed for the back door of the tavern. Just before they left Holly told Valkriss in a low voice.

"You know where we'll be."

An understanding nod from him and they were soon standing in the old alleyway running behind the bar. As they left Michael could hear Valkriss telling someone that it was a drunken brawl that got out of hand.

"Next time you'll be fined, you hear," one of the guards bellowed, evidently losing his temper.

"Well at least I knocked out the one who did it, didn't I? You should pay me for doing yer job," was the last thing he overheard Valkriss say.

Michael could feel himself growing weaker as the warm blood continued to ooze from the deep wound in his side. He staggered and held onto Holly even more for support, as she tried to get him up on a horse tethered to an old post. With what strength he had left, he pulled himself up onto the saddle and Holly mounted it behind him.

She took the reins, turned the horse and rode at a full gallop down the long alleyway. She only slowed to a trot after leaving it into the open avenue so they wouldn't draw attention to themselves.

"Hold on; I'll get us to safety," Holly whispered in his ear.

As soon as they were clear of the city gate Holly kicked the horse back into full gallop again. Don't die on me damn you; I've come too far to quit now, Holly thought in a panic. Michael remained conscience for a little, then sensing no more danger, blackness engulfed him.

Holly thought she would never get to the small cottage Valkriss owned on the outskirts of Lawrence. How in the hell did they find her? What else is going to go wrong? She had planned everything so well during her years of captivity; thankfully she always had back-up plans.

When they reached the little stone cottage, she could no longer hold onto Michael. He fell from the horse and hit the ground with a sickening thud. She jumped off the horse and knelt down beside him checking for a pulse. It was there thank heavens, faint but still there. No way was she going to be able to carry him inside.

"Arura Nominos," Holly said and waved her right hand in a half circle motion toward Michael. His body slowly lifted off the ground and began to float four feet in the air.

"That's better," Holly muttered.

"Now in you go," she directed him toward the house.

"Ostium Porta," she spoke and made a flick with her left index finger causing the front door to open with a creaking sound due to lack of use.

Once inside, she maneuvered him onto the black wrought iron bed in the bedroom off of the kitchen. The place smelled of dampness and had a musky odor to it. She had meant to air it out before they used it, yet with everything going on she hadn't had the chance. She would take care of all that later. Right now, she had to save Michael's life and her plans.

She placed him on the bed and ran to the kitchen to get clean bandages; medical kit, and water. Luckily she had already stocked the place. Back at his side, she rolled up his tunic to get a better look at the damage. She got a sickening feeling deep in the pit of her stomach. It was much worse than she thought.

She cleaned as much of the blood off as she could and stitched the wound neatly and dressed it with clean white linen bandages.

Thank goodness he was unconscious otherwise he would have been in terrific pain without the aid of anything for it. Her magical healing spells weren't the best. She specialized in death and destruction, not saving people.

Still, she had to do whatever she could to save him. If she just had Silverberry Licor, she thought. Had she been able to use her magic at the tavern none of this would have happened. She could have easily blown those stupid thugs to bits, like child's play, if she hadn't feared exposing herself.

"Consano Percuro," Holly said, moving both hands over Michael's side where the stab wound was. She knew he had internal injuries and bleeding.

"Damn, damn, damn," she muttered out loud.

"Michael, don't you die on me, damn you," she told him, gently wiping his forehead with a wet cloth.

"I need you too much," she finished covering him with a warm quilt.

Then she busied herself with getting firewood and cleaning up the place. In no time she had it warm in the quaint cottage and sat down in a comfortable chair close to the bed.

His breathing was steady, though his color was pale from the loss of blood. She would rest a while then ride back to the tavern under the cover of darkness. If she could get to the rest of her supplies, she had healing potions and salves at the ready.

She had to get back to Lawrence and make sure all her plans were not going down the drain.

Asuvalia had added yet another new dimension to her problem. They had to be more to her and Delwen than just a fling twenty years ago.

Thankfully the cottage wasn't very far from Lawrence; still Holly didn't mind the ride. She loved horses and the old spotted brown gelding was very gentle and used to being ridden, even at a gallop. She took it easy on the poor thing. He had certainly seen his better days, yet he was still strong with one of the purest animal spirits she'd ever seen. That in and of itself made up for any difficulties age put in his way.

The fog was so thick the stone gray walls of Lawrence didn't come into view until she was a hundred yards away. The night was nearly pitch-black with no starlight or moonlight. It didn't matter to her, thanks to a night-seeing spell she learned, she could see like it was daylight. However she wished she knew a spell that would allow her to see through fog like she could darkness.

The gates, she knew would be closed this time of night; hopefully she wouldn't have a hard time getting in. She stopped in front of the solid black iron gates and waited on the guard. A small hatch opened showing the face of one of Lawrence's guards.

"State your business, miss," he spoke with authority, like all soldiers do.

"My name is Holly Brackenthorn. I'm going to the Golden Paw Tavern & Inn to stay for a couple days for the Hallowed Month events," she said politely. Figuring it was better not to say anything about being the niece of Valkriss.

"That's no place for a lady after what happened; heard there was a man killed there today. Best be careful madam. The Fulcrum would be a better and safer place for you," the guard said courteously.

"Thank you, I've heard of that place. What street is it on?" Holly had no intentions of going back there besides; she already had her fun.

"On Lubeck Street just off King's Way, can't miss it," the guard said opening the gate to let her in.

"Thank you kindly sir," Holly said guiding the horse through the massive iron gates.

"You're welcome, miss."

She heard as she trotted off down the cobblestone street. Holly hoped there was no follow-up investigation. Valkriss ran a well-respected place, which should afford him the benefit of the doubt.

She tied the horse up behind the venerable old tavern and entered through the back door. It was near closing time. She looked around the bar area and didn't see him anywhere. Then walked towards the cellar, and saw a faint light coming up through the stairwell.

"Valkriss, are you down there?" Holly called out.

"I'm here," he answered from the bottom of the steps as she headed down.

"How is he? Is he going to make it?" Valkriss asked nervously.

"He's going to pull through, I think."

"What do you mean; you think? How bad is it?" Valkriss asked, his old voice sounding more parched than ever.

"It's bad, he's lost a lot of blood and suffered internal damage. I'm doing everything I can. The reason I came back tonight was to get my healing herbs. I used what healing spells I could on him, but they're not much. They're weaker than my others. Have the guards came back asking any questions?" Holly asked.

"No, they bought my story as far as I know," Valkriss answered.

"How'd they find me Valkriss? And where were you when the fight broke out?" Holly asked with a suspicious edge to her voice.

"What in sam's hell? You think I had something to do with this? I was in the cellar. I didn't hear it right away," Valkriss said sounding hurt by her accusations.

What she didn't know was he was in the secret room off to the side of the cellar which was sound proof.

She raised an eyebrow.

"You spend a lot of time down here, uncle," she said suspiciously before he cut her off.

"Why would I risk it? If he finds you at my place; if he evens thinks for a second I helped you. I'm a dead man. I have every reason to help you, not hurt you. Remember your family to me," he said trying to smile.

"You have to find out more about Asuvalia. She and Delwen must have had more than a fling. I charmed her so she wouldn't come back to the tavern," Holly added.

"I know Delwen was from Trayden and if Michael carries his sword, he must be a direct blood descendant. Michael is young enough to be his son. I have a friend who may know," Valkriss filled her in, and then asked. "Have you had any luck finding the whereabouts of Tiberious?"

"None yet, but I will. His last location was Odessa. I think he was trying to find Michael. That was last year when Kara got her fool-self killed and Michael left and hasn't returned since," Holly said.

"We need him Holly; Tiberious holds an important piece of the puzzle and without him, we may not have the ending we both desire. He was with Delwen and returned to the site. He must have recovered the sword. Delwen's body was never found; you know very well what that could mean," Valkriss said solemnly.

"I know, I know. One thing at a time uncle," Holly said irritated.

He couldn't tell her everything just yet, a little at a time he told himself.

"Is Michael still part of the plan?" Valkriss asked uncomfortably.

"Only if he lives," Holly grimaced.

"Is there another way?" Valkriss asked.

"Next to impossible."

"That's what I was afraid of; you better hope he makes it then."

"I know uncle; don't remind me of what I already know please. Do not become part of the problem; help me with the solution."

"I'll do my best."

"Now one more thing before I go. Get word to the Auckley Council of Mages in Sindara that Sir Lawrence will need their help come spring. His army will not be enough to handle what Soladar is getting ready to do," Holly said.

"What do you mean, getting ready to do?" Valkriss asked clearly worried.

"Just leave it at that uncle. Now I need my things, I have to get back. He may already be dead," Holly said and walked over to the far corner of the cellar.

"Invenio Nanciscor," Holly made a strange gesture with her right hand while she stood near the old stone wall lined with wooden shelves on each side. A small golden oak chest bound with bands of black spiraling iron appeared from nowhere.

"Ostium Porta," she spoke again and the little chest opened revealing Holly's special supplies. She didn't worry about Valkriss knowing or anyone for that matter. The enchantment hiding the chest would protect it from even the most skilled mage. The last word of the spell which reveals it could only be spoken accurately by its owner. To anyone else who listens, even standing beside her, the word would sound different.

"Invenio Nanciscor," Holly said again and the oak chest disappeared from sight.
"I'll be back as soon as I can with news. I won't use Aura candles, they're not safe anymore," Holly added as she headed back up the stairs.

Chapter 5
A Journey

He waited for a couple of minutes and heard nothing but the creaks of the old heavy floor beams overhead. Just groaning's of a building far past its prime, like him. He walked over to where Holly had stood earlier.

"Invenio Nancyio," nothing happened.

"Invenio Nankcio."

Damn it; he had seen her do it a hundred times, but it never worked for him. So much for learning any of her secrets; they were other ways he knew of. He headed back up to finish cleaning the bar and get ready for the day's customers.

He would have to get a hold of Arnette Glace and send him to Trayden to see what he could find out.

Who could he send to Sindara? Mick? No, poor kid wouldn't make it past Bentree. Sam's hell!

Holly was sure asking a lot. They were no way he could go. He had no one to run the bar and most importantly keep tabs on Holly and Michael. Sam's hell, fire and damnation, he swore, mulling over what to do.

He could do without Mick for a while. After all he was sixteen. His youth and stamina would certainly prove useful on a long journey. Mick had been working for him for four years now.

He practically adopted the boy ever since his parents had to leave him when he was only twelve. He let Mick stay at the inn, fed and clothed him, plus paid him a weekly salary so he would have spending money to make him happy. He was willing to do whatever Valkriss asked of him without question. Mick was always trying to prove himself or maybe attempting to repay him.

Would that be too much to ask? The road had its perils. He didn't want any harm to come to Mick; he was just a kid after all. However he had no one else he could send.

He would send him at first light. At least it would give him time to get Mick packed for the trip. It wasn't long before the sun was up. Yet another sleepless night for him, which bothered

him more now that he was older. At least he had
Mick packed up and ready to go.

"Mick, where are you boy?" Valkriss
hollered out from behind the bar.

He had just sent him to get more ale from
the cellar. I swear that boy moves slower than
molasses, I'm old and do better, he thought
crabbily.

Mick came up out of the cellar as always
carrying way too much.

"Here, let me help you before you drop it
and cost me more money than you already do,"
Valkriss said sternly.

He hated to be hard on him, but he knew
life was going to be much harder in the years to
come. He had to make sure he would be strong
enough for what lay ahead.

He promised his parents he would do his
best. After all, the boy was going to be the 'Arx
Sacramentum,' or 'The Oath Giver', one day. He
had already been chosen by Tiberious at the
tender age of twelve. Just as Tiberious had been
chosen by his predecessor and Valkriss had
raised him as well. And so it had been since the
formation of the Silver Knights.

He was one a dedicated few who secretly searched for the descendants of Glollas, hoping one day to restore them to their former glory.

Delwen was the only heir they found, yet Tiberious had been unable to administer the oath before he met his doom. Of course, Holly didn't know all he did, which was fine by him. He had to keep his cards hidden until he needed them.

Besides he wasn't sure Soladar hadn't tainted her mind during her years of captivity. Still the old man wondered how Michael fit into all this. Was he Delwen's son? Damn Tiberious for disappearing after Delwen's death. Without knowing; he was stuck between a rock and a hard place. He was sure Tiberious would have fought to the death right beside Delwen. Why didn't he? Did he blame himself? He heard a couple of stories that Tiberious left under direct order to get word back to Sir Lawrence. So why did he vanish?

Valkriss was a patient man and at the moment he had to get word out to all the others. This time he had no intentions of failing. A new Primericerus would be crowned, beginning a new rein of the Silver Knights and he would to live to see it.

He helped Mick get the boxes stowed behind the bar. Hallowed Month was going extremely well for the tavern despite the fact of the killing.

"Follow me; I have to talk to you, not here, in the cellar," Valkriss told Mick heading towards the cellar.

"Now Mick, I have a job for you; an important one. You listening?"

"Yes, sir," Mick answered quickly.

"I'm going to send you on a mission. It is a long one and you must be careful. Do exactly as I tell you. Understand?" Valkriss added extra emphasis on the word exactly.

"I'm your man!" Mick said enthusiastically.

"If you don't want to go, I'll understand," Valkriss said in a gentle tone.

"I'll go; I'll go," Mick said worrying Valkriss might change his mind.

"Okay then; I need you to go to Sindara. Take this scroll to the Auckley Council of Mages. Make sure you hand it directly to the chairman. His name is Vadis DeKalb. If you have any trouble getting in to see him, tell them that you were sent by Valkriss VaughBlair. Make sure you do not break the seal on the scroll. The enchantments on it will cause it to turn to ash unless it's open by Vadis. Do you understand?" Mick nodded silently.

"Speak boy. Do you understand? I want to hear you. Don't just stand there nodding like a dummy."

"Yes sir, I understand, sir," Mick said, his mind beginning to spin.

Finally; Mick thought to himself all my hard work has paid off and now I will show him that I am a man. I will be counted as someone and not just an object to be tossed aside when it doesn't suit them any longer. Like his parents who left him at the tavern when he was only twelve. He would show them how important he was and what a mistake they made by abandoning him. He would never forgive them for that.

"When do I leave?" Mick asked as calmly as he could.

"Right now; I have a good horse ready and already loaded with rations tied out back. Remember Mick, speak to no one! Do as I say and you will be fine," Valkriss gave him final instructions, along with a map and money for the trip.

"One more thing Mick, stay in an inn if you have to. Otherwise stay out of Cinnibar and the other local villages along the way. There is too much trouble in those places for you to get into youngin'; understand?"

"Yes sir, I'll do exactly as you have told me.

"Sam's hell, I almost forgot," Valkriss continued.

"I put a special Aura candle inside the right saddlebag. If you get into trouble and need me, light it and speak my name and we'll be able to communicate with each other. However, you must not use it unless it's an absolute emergency, got it?"

"Consider the job done; It is the least I can do for you," Mick said brightly.

"Now dang it boy, don't go getting' soft on me. Off you go," Valkriss said trying before getting emotional.

Before he could move, Mick grabbed him and hugged him.

"Now I told you, enough of the mushy stuff. Off you go now," Valkriss said showing a little emotion and hugged him back lightly.

"Quit lollygagging' for cryin' out loud. What are you waiting for? Go," Valkriss said, and with that Mick went bounding up the steps two at a time and hollered back down. "I'll get my stuff and be off."

Valkriss had forgotten how it was to be young and carefree. To Mick it must seem like an adventure of a lifetime, if he only knew what lay ahead.

The horse was a beautiful red mare. She looked no more than four or five years old. Mick patted her neck; she was soft under his young hand.

"I'll call you Jenny; yep that's a good name for a good horse," he whispered in her ear.

He put the money, pouch, and map Valkriss gave him into the left saddlebag, took the reins, placed his foot in the stirrup and swung up on its back. She was steady and made him feel very comfortable on her. He had ridden for three years now, so he was use to horses. Valkriss would have him ride to some of the farms outside town for supplies for the tavern, but half the time he was pulling a wagon.

Mick felt the best he ever had felt in his life; he was somebody now, someone who could be trusted and counted on. He was important, yet that did little to ease his growing fear of the long journey to Sindara. The weather was cooperating at least; it was warm with a bright sun shining high in the sky.

He didn't mind traveling so much except the time of year it was. Hallows Month always frightened him; hearing all the ghost stories about the winds of fall setting spirits free to roam the forest.

Just keep your mind off it and you'll be fine, Mick reassured himself. He had never traveled any farther than ten miles or so from Lawrence. You can do it, he said again in his mind, as he rode out of Lawrence's massive main gate. He never looked back, keeping his eyes focused on the road in front of him.

This would also show Holly too, that he was dependable. She always made him feel like he was just a boy, when she was only six years older than he was. Who was she to talk? She was just a girl and they don't know anything.

He rode until noon, when he realized he was farther than he had ever been from Lawrence. A mixture of fear and happiness raced through his mind. He was really doing this.

He stopped in a little clearing off to the side of the road. Valkriss told him to never get far from it, so he didn't. He tied Jenny to a small bush so she could graze on what little green grass there was left before winter.

One thing he hadn't thought too much about was taking care of the horse. His duties consisted of carrying water for baths; carrying liquor, and carrying supplies; come to think of it, he done a lot of carrying. Well at least now he wouldn't have to do any carrying for at least two whole weeks.

It would take at least one week up and then another week back. Two weeks on the road; wow he thought, this was going to be a grand adventure. Sleeping under the stars and living like a true explorer in the wild.

He ate very little from the dry rations Valkriss packed for him. He hardly had any appetite because of the excitement he felt. Jenny appeared to sense he was ready and looked at him expectantly. Maybe she could feel his energy and was excited as well.

He saddled up and was off again, enjoying the scenery. After a few more hours his enthusiasm had dimed slightly, but he was still eager about the journey ahead.

At the edge of dark Mick was nowhere close to Lawrence or anywhere else for that matter when he decided to find a place to make camp.

The skies were clear, which meant a cold frosty night. A chill hung in the air already. He was glad he had a small tent with thick woolen blankets. Valkriss certainly took good care of him.

He tied Jenny close by and build a small, but warm fire with firewood he managed to cut up with his short sword.

Mick knew Jenny would hear anything long before he did and alert him. He took out the money pouch to see how much he had for the trip, so he could budget what he could spend along the way.

Hopefully he would be able to buy a few souvenirs in Sindara and stop at Cinnibar on his

way back and see the sights. He heard so many
wonderful tales about it and the port of Calumet.
Oh the stories he would have to tell his kids one
day. Of how he traveled all the way from
Lawrence to Sindara all by himself when he was
only sixteen. Well sixteen and a half, but who's
counting, he thought.

The old man definitely gave him more than
enough for the trip. Mick couldn't believe
Valkriss gave him ten gold coins. That was more
than he got in two months of an allowance.
Regardless of what the old goat said, here was
proof he liked him.

He had grown rather fond of Valkriss too.
He had seen to it that he wasn't sent to an
orphanage. He took Mick in and kept him when
his parents outright disappeared one day. They
never said a word, just told him to stay there at
the tavern while they ran errands and never
returned. Some parents they were. Who in the
world would leave their twelve year old son with
a complete stranger, at a tavern of all places?

Yet Mick never let that get the best of him,
even though he had in run-ins with some of the
local bullies who liked to pick on him. He never

backed down from a fight, even when they got the best of him.

He would practice every night down in the cellar after Valkriss went to bed. On his days off he would go over to the guard's barracks.

That's where he met Lucerna. She was his age and the daughter of the captain of the guard. She knew a lot about fighting and showed him how to use a sword. It was her who gave him the sword he carried now.

"Damn, damn," he cursed out loud. Boy it was great to curse out loud and not get in trouble. Damn it, he forgot to tell Lucerna he was leaving. Valkriss would skin his hide if he had. Ah well, she'll skin it when he got back.

That thought brought a wide smile to his face. She was fierce when she got angry and could always best him in a fight, not that he would ever hit a girl. It wasn't the manly thing to do; maybe if he had too. He would have to cross that bridge if he ever came to it. At least he could tell her about his journey when he got back. He knew she was going to be so impressed.

Before long he was yawning and decided to turn in for the night. He had camped out once before when he was ten, except that was with his parents. That one thing upset him the most. Why had they been so good to him and then leave him?

He made up stories to tell his friends, well Lucerna anyway, about how his parents were away on business and got killed. That way she wouldn't know that they just left him and never told him or anyone as far as he knew why.

He tried spying on Valkriss whenever he talked to people, but so far nothing. Then Holly came to the tavern this past summer and he began spying on them when they were talking in the cellar. Although most of the time he couldn't make out what they were saying through the thick floor.

He picked up a few nuggets of information here and there. Like he knew they were planning something involving someone named Soladar. He also heard a few other names as well, something about a Michael and a guy called Dellween. One time he was listening he almost got busted and had to beat a hasty retreat.

Mick was so wound up; he was having an extremely hard time going to sleep. It must have been well after midnight. Thankfully the moon was three quarters full and lent a good deal of light.

He could see the shadows of trees waving in the winds though his tent. Then suddenly one of the shadows looked like a human one. Oh hell he thought, suppressing an urge to cry out. Someone was out there and was going to get him.

Get a hold of yourself man he chastised his cowardice and grabbed his short sword lying next to him inside the tent.

Slowly and carefully, he got to his knees, watching the shadow move closer to the front of the tent. He was going to have to charge it head on with everything he had, if he was going to survive.

"Okay here goes nothing," he prayed quietly and charged.

"STOP! WHAT ARE YOU DOING?"

It was the sound of a girl's voice; he heard when he tackled the shadowy figure to the ground.

"GET OFF ME!" she yelled angrily.

"What? Who are you?" Mick demanded.

"If you don't know my voice by now you're a simpleton," she said roughly.

"LUCERNA!" Mick said, clearly dumbfounded.

"Who else would it be?" She replied.

"Now get off me! Please."

"Of course; I'm sorry I didn't know who you were," Mick said hastily trying to get off her, when he accidentally touched her breast.

"SORRY!" He said scrambling.

"Never mind that just move please. There; finally, thank you. You're always so clumsy Micknia," Lucerna said.

"Put your ass on the ground, didn't I? So there!" Mick said teasingly.

"I was going easy on you. Didn't want to scare you," she scoffed.

"I wasn't scared; not for a minute. Your just damn lucky I didn't cut you."

Mick made a swinging motion with his sword.

"Yeah; yeah whatever big man," Lucerna mocked.

They dusted off and Mick rebuilt the campfire and sat down next to each other. "How did you find me?" Mick asked confused.

"Wasn't hard, my dad is the captain of the guard," she said smugly.

"Well how'd he know then?" Mick asked indignantly.

"One of his guards saw you ride off this morning. I stopped by the tavern and Valkriss told me you'd be gone for a while. I knew you were up to something. I thought you ran off to find out what really happened to your parents. I couldn't sneak off until later and you got a head start on me. That's why I'm so late getting to you," she informed him; crossing her arms and waiting on his reply.

"Lucerna I'm on a top secret mission. You shouldn't have come," Mick said trying to hide the fact he was happy she was there and he'd have a companion to travel with.

"What about your dad?" He asked, looking worried.

"I left him a note Mick; all he cares about is his damn soldiers. He doesn't care about me, ever since..." she hesitated.

"Ever since she died, all he does is work; work, and more work. It's like I'm invisible to him or something. He probably won't even miss me at all," she finished sadly.

"So; where are we going?" Lucerna asked.

"Wait a second. Who said anything about you coming with me? I told you I'm on a top secret mission. I haven't said whether you could go or not," Mick said crossing his arms.

"Oh so you're the head honcho now; huh? What if I beat your ass? How'd that be for starters?" Lucerna said in a deadly tone.

"Now don't go getting all hasty on me. I swear you should have been a redhead instead of a brunette with that temper of yours."

"Well then don't piss me off acting like a big shot when I know you're not," she said bluntly.

"I'm sorry Lucerna; it's just Valkriss has entrusted me with a very important mission to deliver something to someone someplace. You have to SWEAR you will not say anything to anyone! You swear?" Micknia asked gravely.

"I swear to all that is holy!"

"Come on Lucerna. This is important. Swear, seriously."

"Mick, I swear," she stated like she was giving a solemn oath raising her right hand.

"That's better; now I have to go to Sindara..." Was all he got out, before she interrupted him again.

"WHAT! What in the hell is that crazy old man thinking? I know he's a nut job now! No doubt about it! Sending you all the way to Sindara!" she started getting loud.

"Shhh; quiet down Lucerna; you're going to wake the whole forest if you don't shut up. Damn, girl," Mick scowled furiously.

"Sorry," she said in a lower voice.

"But Mick, it will take us two weeks to make the round trip."

"I know, but it's important to Valkriss. I have to do it for him; show him I can be trusted, that I'm a man," Mick said.

"I'm still coming with you Mick. You can't do this alone."

"What about your father? Won't he get worried and send his guards after you?" Mick asked beginning to get nervous, thinking about the retribution her father would exact on him.

Mr. Riner; who he never called by his first name Kyger, was a big man and being captain of the guard made it even worse. If he thought for a minute that Mick had anything to do with Lucerna leaving, he might as well stay in Sindara. If he didn't kill him first, he would lock him away in the dungeon until he was old like Valkriss.

"Mick it'll be fine, like I said he's out on field training. He won't even know I'm gone," she told him reassuringly.

"Are you sure?" Mick asked again.

"I'm sure; besides if you're not in Lawrence; what fun would I have?" she smiled, giving Mick a good feeling to have her along with him.

"Did you bring any supplies?"

"A little; I couldn't get away with much. It would have tipped them off, but I have some allowance money I've been saving. I brought that with me," she said proudly.

"Did you bring a tent; food, water, or anything?" Mick asked, getting worried.

"I told you already, I couldn't bring much. I have a change of clothes; soap, washcloth, towel, blanket, and some odds and ends. That's it."

"That's it?"

Mick repeated her last two words as if asking a question, but really making a statement. Where she was going to sleep, he only had the one tent.

"Well I only have the one tent and it's small," Mick said, obviously nervous.

"Oh; I see now, what you're worried about. Micknia; how dare you think…" she said accusingly.

"Lucerna it's not that; it's just, it's just," oh great, now he was stuttering.

"Oh hell with it, just make sure you stay on your side of the tent that's all."

"Don't worry Mick I won't bite," she poked him in the arm.

She never really looked at Micknia in that way before. True he was handsome in a rugged way with his dark sandy brown hair, bright blue eyes. He had a good body too, when it wasn't covered by the baggy clothes he wore.

They were both the same age and had met just after his parents left. Not long afterward her mother took ill and passed away. They were both two lonesome souls wandering the streets of Lawrence when their paths crossed and ever since, they were inseparable.

"Just make sure you stay on your side, okay?" Lucerna winked at him.

"Oh don't worry about that, I will. Well what are we waiting for? Let's get to bed. We need to get an early start if we're going to make any distance," Mick said standing up and heading for the tent.

"Right behind you," Lucerna said following him.

The tent which seemed roomy at first; now was crowded. He had never slept beside anyone before, especially a girl. Even though she was his friend and he didn't look at her in that way. It was still awkward.

"One last thing; we sleep clothes on; okay? No touching either," Mick added.

"Same rules for you too. Goodnight."

"Goodnight," Mick said.

The night passed quickly and peacefully.

When they awoke, Mick found he had rolled over in his sleep and put his arm around her, which he quickly moved once he realized where it was.

"Thought you said no touching, Mick?" Lucerna said with a grin.

"I didn't mean to. It's just; I'm not used to sleeping with someone, err I mean next to someone," he could feel the blood running hot to his cheeks, causing them to turn red.

"It's ok Mick; I know you like me," Lucerna said batting her eyelashes and smiling making it worse.

"Whatever, let's get going. I have some dry rations in my saddlebag we can have for breakfast," Mick said, trying to change the subject.

He did like her and his feelings were changing toward her too. They were different now than the use to be when they first met. He found himself paying a lot more attention to the way she looked more than he use too. He got angry whenever he saw her talking to other boys in town.

She was his friend, not theirs. Maybe that was childish of him, but he didn't care. He bet none of the other boys could make the trip he was on. They'd run home crying to their mommy before the first night was over. He was too tough for that. Besides he had no one to go home too, other than old Valkriss, and he was always grumpy.

At least with Lucerna was coming on this quest with him. He would be able to show her how much of a man he really was. Yep she would look at him in a whole new light once she saw how well he done on the mission.

Chapter 6
Wounds

It didn't take her long to reach the cottage. She decided it was best to simply charm the guard on her way out of town. That way, he would never know she left. She tied the horse up outside and went straight in to check on Michael. He was resting well enough.

"Santo Infirmus," Holly chanted and a soft white glow surrounded him lightly illumining the room. It was one of her best healing spells.

She went to the kitchen, unpacked her supplies and began preparing the Silverberry Licor that she knew would heal him. The only hard part was going to be getting him to wake up enough to take it. She made it thin enough to drink without having to eat it like you normally would.

She stopped what she was doing when she heard his voice from the bedroom and raced in there.

"What is it, Michael? What do you need?" Holly asked.

He started tossing and turning in bed causing the healing spell in shimmer and blink out.

"Damn it Michael, you have to stay still. It won't work right if you don't," she muttered impatiently and recast the spell.

The world went far out of focus as his mind settled into nothingness, yet he could hear distant sounds echoing somewhere far away. Then his surroundings changed. He was outside in a field of golden yellow wheat and there she was walking toward him.

"Kara," he reached for her, yet she was too far away.

Oh great, he's dying; I've lost him. Or maybe not, Holly thought.

"I've missed you so much, come to me. I'm glad it's finally over. I'm free, free to be with you forever."

"Michael I'm so sorry," Kara said in an other-worldly voice.

"Don't be, it was my fault. I couldn't save you. I failed you. Please forgive me Kara. I love you so much. I've never loved anyone as I have you. I have nothing to live for. No one will miss me. I have nothing without you, nothing but heartache, pain and suffering since the day you…you left."

Tears rolled down his cheeks.

"But now I have you again. I don't have to be sad anymore. I don't have to see your beautiful face in every passing woman. We are together for eternity. Please come to me. Let me hold you as I once did. I've waited for this day," he said.

"Michael not now; you have things to do," Kara said gently as she walked closer.

"You must understand what happened to me was not your fault. Michael you must understand that."

Finally she was in front of him. She placed her hand on the side of his face. It glowed warmly.

"You have to go on with your life, for me," Kara looked into his watery eyes.

"I want you to go on with your life, grow old and start the family we never had a chance to. I always thought you would make a great father. Do this and make me happy," she told him as she wiped away his tears.

"Kara, I have no life without you."

"In time you will heal Michael, if you are strong. Be strong for me; stop being hard on yourself. What happened wasn't your fault," she spoke firmly.

He reached up and ran his hand down her beautiful face. This one simple touch he would have given anything, moved heaven and earth for it. And now she was telling him to go on without her. He didn't know how, but if that's what she wanted, he would do his best. Kara smiled as if she read his mind.

"Thank you. Remember Michael I'll always be a part of you. You will always carry me inside your heart," Kara said smiling as she faded from sight.

"I know," Michael said sadly and watched until she was gone. Then blackness swallowed him.

Before long he woke into the cruel grip of pain.

"Michael, I need you to wake up and drink this. Michael can you hear me? Please; I need you to hear me, wake up." Holly said panicking at the thought he wasn't going to come out of it.

"What? Leave me be."

"I need you to wake up; please," Holly said gently caressing his cheek with her free hand.

"Where am I?" He asked through clenched teeth, doing his best to overcome the pain ripping through his midsection.

"We're safe; it's me Holly. Now drink this; it will make you feel better," she said holding the cup to his lips.

He struggled to drink the bitter tasting liquid.

"Drink it all; you must," Holly told him firmly, not moving the cup until all of the foul drink was gone.

"What in the world did you make me drink?" Michael asked with a disgusted look on his face.

"Never mind what it was. Medicine never tastes good," Holly said in a motherly tone.

"Now sleep; we'll talk more later, you need your rest now okay," Holly ordered.

"Okay," was the last thing he remembered saying before falling into a very restful sleep.

Holly fell asleep in the chair next to the bed. She woke every couple of hours to check on him and then dosed off again.

She woke up cold and stiff from her uncomfortable sleep in the old chair. It was earlier than she usually got up. She always liked to sleep in whenever she could.

Holly looked out the bedroom window to see what the weather would be. The sky was gray and overcast, which meant cold rain, would be falling shortly. She stood up and allowed the thin brown woolen blanket to slide down to the floor.

She raised her arms and stretched, letting a little moan. When she looked over at Michael, he was watching her and smiling.

"Are you feeling better?" Holly asked gently and stepped closer to check on him.

The healing spell had already worn off, and he never noticed a thing. She knew he distrusted magic, even if it was for his benefit.

After hearing the way he talked last night, she wasn't sure if he would be happy waking up or not.

"Thirsty," Michael said barely audible.

"Of course, just a second and I'll get you something to drink. Be right back," Holly said, much happier now that he had come around.

She went into the small kitchen, poured him a glass of water, and returned.

"Here you go. Now don't drink too fast, or you'll get sick," she told him handing the glass to him and steadying his hand as he took a drink.

"There you go," she said sounding like a nurse at the bedside of a patient.

He managed to take a couple of drinks before reaching the glass back to her.

"Thanks," Michael said, his voice sounding stronger.

"You're welcome dear," Holly replied smiling.

"Oh now it's 'dear,' huh," he said with a grin.

"Why of course. You saved me from being kidnapped at the tavern. Heaven knows what they would have done to me," Holly's tone was grim.

"Why on earth would anyone want to kidnap you?"

"Beyond me, but I don't know my uncle that well. Maybe he has enemies and they wanted to settle an old score or ransom me, thinking he's got money. Times are hard," Holly said with the most honest look she could muster.

"True, times are hard," Michael agreed.

"Don't worry about them anymore. One is dead and the other one is in prison."

"Are they looking for me?" Michael asked.

"No; Valkriss told the investigating guards it was a drunken brawl which got out of hand. And he knocked out the one who killed the other when he tried to run. Besides the one who lived isn't going to say what his true reason was for being at the tavern, now is he?

What's he going to say, me and my partner went to kidnap Valkriss' niece and a Good Samaritan stopped us? No he'll keep quiet," Holly said.

"I see your point."

"Now let me take a look at those bandages," Holly continued pulling down the cover.

"Just admit, you want to see my hot body again, don't you?" Michael grinned.

"Oh baby, you're so right. I want you badly," Holly said laughing out loud while thinking, damn boy you are sexy as hell even if you are hurt.

Well, at least he still had his sense of humor.

She rolled up his tunic so she could check the bandages. Damn it; they were soaked in blood again.

"I need to change these. Be still while I go get more from the kitchen."

"Yes, ma'am," Michael said and coughed a little causing it to hurt like hell and send pain shooting through his midsection.

She returned with fresh sterile dressings to replace the old ones. When she got them off, the wound had finally stopped bleeding. The stitches were holding quite well, despite of her lack of skill.

It had taken over twenty to fully close the wound. She knew he'd be fine as long as infection didn't set in. She covered it well with healing salve before redressing it.

"There, that should do for now," she said satisfied with her handy work.

"Thank you for all you're doing."

"Michael, it's the very least I can do. It was my fault you got hurt in the first place," Holly said rolling his tunic back down and covering him with the checkered quilt.

He grabbed her hand and gave it a gentle squeeze. "Did I say anything last night while I was out?" Michael asked looking worried.

"What do you mean?" Holly asked, playing dumb.

"I was having a weird dream or something, that's all."

"You never said a word, just tossed a little," Holly patted his hand.

"Now; do you feel up to eating anything this morning?" She asked brightly.

"Not right now, maybe later."

"Well you get you some rest and I'll make myself useful around here. This place needs a good cleaning," Holly said.

Michael didn't need much coaxing. He was back to sleep within minutes.

She busied herself carrying in plenty of wood so it would stay dry. She wished she could use magic to do the chores, but she was afraid of Michael waking up and catching her.

She would have to get around to telling him about her talents soon. However it would have to wait until the right time and place; otherwise he would never understand.

"I see you have a nice fire going for us," Michael said watching Holly adding more wood to the fire.

It was after noon when he woke up.

"Anything for you, my darling," she said, acting overly dramatic.

"Well I am special after all," Michael said trying not to laugh because it hurt like hell.

"Hungry yet?"

"A little."

"I prepared some chicken soup."

"Yum my favorite," Michael said and winced.

"Liar," Holly said with a short laugh.

"No it's my new favorite, I swear," Michael said smiling.

"Sure sure," Holly mocked as she walked to the kitchen and returned with a steaming hot bowl of chicken soup.

She sat it in the chair and helped him sit upright, piling pillows behind him and then sat the food down in front of him on a small table.

He ate nearly all of it and felt better afterwards.

"Good boy," Holly said as she took the tray away to the kitchen.

Michael ate again that evening and seemed to be doing well. The bandages were no longer getting soaked with blood and his color was slowly returning.

The days were shorter, and the nights longer now that autumn was in full swing. Before long, Michael was asleep again just a little after it got dark

She had to think of what to do. She would wait a few days before going back to find out what Valkriss found out. She hoped he would turn up something; they were way too many loose ends. The one thing she hated was loose ends. They only brought trouble when you least expected it.

Finally she got sleepy she resigned herself to the chair again. As much as she wanted to sleep in the bed, she didn't want to take a chance on accidently hitting his wound.

Chapter 7
A New Face

Thankfully Glollas' brother Elias had devised a communication system. He used Indocite Orbs to tap into the earth's natural lay lines and use their energy. Whereby allowing them to talk over vast distances.

They were only twenty-four installed before his death and they still worked. Their use and location were only known to the inner circle. Each orb is a perfect twelve inch sphere and glows blue and can only be activated by the touch.

Messages could be stored inside the Indocite Orb for a particular knight and then retrieved at any time. No other person could see it or hear any message that came through it unless it was for them.

Little did anyone know an Indocite Orb had been placed in a small rural village, beneath where the present day Golden Paw Tavern and Inn was. Valkriss learned its location as a young man working for the previous owner who ran it as a general store. He uncovered it by accident one day working in the storage cellar moving crates

At the time he didn't know what it was or its uses. He kept it a secret and after years of studying Silver Knight lore and reforming the Inner Circle. He learned the true value the orb.

He made the silver rings they now used to locate the orbs. Each ring had a small blue indocite stone inset with a tiny silver sword. As soon as the knight's name was spoken to the orb in the stone would glow and the sword would turn in the direction of the nearest orb. Only oath sworn inner circle members were given one.

"Why have you called for me, Valkriss?" The man with the piercing blue eyes asked.

Valkriss always had a hard time looking Arnette in the face; dark tanned leather-like skin, coal black hair and two new scars running all the way down both sides of his face.

"I have a job for you," Valkriss swallowed hard.

"What is it this time? Come on, out with it Val," Arnette's voice was solemn, dispassionate.

Valkriss knew not to play games with him.

"I need you to go to Trayden and find out if Delwen had a son named Michael."

"Wouldn't Tiberious have told us if he had?" Arnette asked.

"He should've, but if I'm right Tiberious hid it from us and you know what that means," Valkriss said frowning.

"Has he turned against us?"

"I don't know; that's another reason I activated the orbs. I hope he will re-establish communication with us. In the mean time we cannot afford to wait any longer. If Michael is the heir, he must be given the oath soon. Soladar is planning something major," Valkriss said concerned.

"Any information from Adrelia?" Arnette asked.

"A little, not very helpful though. I'm sending Micknia to Sindara to get word to the Ackley Council of Mages," Valkriss said gritting his teeth.

"So you told him?"

"Sam's hell no!"

"Then why are you sending him for?"

"I need you in Trayden and word must reach Sindara fast enough so the alliance can be in place," Valkriss said defensibly.

"While Tiberious is alive, Micknia will not have the gift; you know that. And yet you send him on a dangerous journey," Arnette said tapping his right index finger on his chin.

"My judgment is sound old friend. I haven't failed us yet, have I?" Valkriss said trying to lighten the mood in the small dark room where the orb floated above its silver pedestal.

"How did you get the new scars?" Valkriss asked, trying to change the subject. Also curious what he had been up to.

"Been up north hunting," Arnette grimaced a little.

"What?"

"Our old nemesis is back," Arnette told Valkriss just to watch the color drain from his old face.

"Sam's hell; are you sure?" Valkriss asked in a shaky voice.

"You asked where I got the scars from. You know what they do to the dead or captured," Arnette said and made a cutting motion along his chinbone.

"They have been rumors of course," Valkriss said scratching his head.

"You can't believe tavern talk."

"Well it's true they're back and growing in numbers. I've heard they have made a pact with Soladar," Arnette said smiling.

"What in the world are you smiling for Arnette? Have you lost your mind?"

"Valkriss while you sat studying history I've been gathering information. As a matter of fact the Vorlocks have reached sufficient numbers and now plan to try to resurrect Kavanaugh."

As soon as Valkriss heard this he sat down on a small wooden chair beside the orb's pedestal, looking defeated.

"Cheer up old friend; I said try, didn't I?"

"I'll get word to everyone as soon as you leave. We must begin rapid recruiting immediately and speed plans up for Blacen."

"For what?" Arnette asked a little surprised.

"Besides studying history as you say. I've been busy with other things Arnette."

"Really?" Arnette said raising an eyebrow.

"To the north of here between the Tug and Lavisa rivers we are building the new home for the Silver Knights and it will be called by Glollas' last name, Blacen in honor of him. We already have the bridges build over both rivers and working on the stronghold now," Valkriss said.

"What does King Galanar say about it?"

"Since when do we answer to him? Anyway we have the support we need. The new city will be a boon to the kingdom; with goods being transported down the Tug and Lavisa rivers to the port at Blacen. That will connect Calumet and Sindara ports with the western Carrillion coast. Perfect to increase the king's coffers as well as funding what we need," Valkriss finished clearly impressed with his plans.

"None of this can wait till spring?" Arnette asked.

"The temple can wait until the fortifications are done, but you said yourself their growing in numbers. We must have enough to fight and if something happens to Michael then we need alterative plans," Valkriss said.

"What do you mean?" Arnette asked in an edge of anger.

"They may be a way around the bloodline. If they are no living heirs to Glollas then his sword is able to go to The Oath Giver, who can then become the Primericerus," Valkriss explained.

"Heresy! I will not hear such talk!" Arnette said with a growl pulling out his silver sword.

"Easy Arnette; I will not harm Michael or any Silver Knight. I am oath sworn, remember that!" His voice rising.

"However we must have a way to once again bring the Silver Knights out of the shadows and into the light of glory once and for all time to come!" Valkriss was standing now, radiating a powerful presence completely unlike him.

"Agreed *old one*; forgive my doubts, I've lost my sense of trust fighting those evil bastards up north," Arnette said re-sheathing his sword and extending his right hand.

"Forgiven," Valkriss said shaking his hand.

"I must be off, if I'm going to get to Trayden," Arnette said turning to leave.

"By the way, Kelsa is overseeing things in Blacen. It's on your way to Trayden if you care to stop in and see our progress," Valkriss said.

He had been savoring this last bit of information, so he could enjoy watching Arnette's reaction, which remained as stoic as always. Sam's hell, Valkriss thought before wishing him safe journeys.

"Godspeed," Valkriss told him as they left the secret room.

Now that was over with he could get busy on letting the others know and checking on the progress of Blacen.

Kelsa was a day late on her reports which was unlike her. She had an eagle eye for detail and kept to a tight schedule. He would have to make sure they made the outer fortifications priority and get them completed before spring.

Valkriss went up to the bar making another check on things before heading down to the secret room again. He walked over to the Indocite orb and gently laid his right hand on it and watched it glow. "Kelsa," was the only word he spoke.

It was the only one he needed too. He knew her ring would illuminate and she would contact him. Now he could tend to other matters.

Arnette decided to make a stop on his way out of town. He would have to bring Orndoff up to speed.

Orndoff could feel someone watching him. He looked up from his anvil and saw someone standing in the shadows of his old smoky forge.

"If yer here for de horseshoes, there not ready yet," Orndoff grumbled.

"Why not?" The man asked without moving.

"Cause if you want them right it takes time."

"Wait is that?"

"Arnette; you ol' bastard," Orndoff said gruffly throwing his hammer down on the anvil with a clang.

"For Honos sake laddie, I figured you for dead."

"You should know I'm too stubborn to die."

"True enough; I'll have the Mrs. get us a drink."

"Thanks old friend; I can use one before heading to Trayden."

Orndoff stopped in his tracks.

"So I was right."

"That you were."

"Then why are you going to Trayden for?"

"I have to make sure."

"You know no one can carry de sword without bein' an heir."

"True; however I have to find out why Tiberious kept this from us."

"How can I help?"

"While I'm in Trayden I need you to find out all you can about Asuvalia Lyndhurst."

"Who's she?"

"A woman here in Lawrence that Delwen may have had a relationship with before he was killed."

"I see."

"Anything else I can do?"

"Valkriss is activating the inner circle and we will begin rapid recruiting soon."

When Orndoff heard this he smiled broadly.

"So de time has come."

"So it has my friend."

"Here," Orndoff said and pulled a dusty old bottle of whiskey out of a nearby cabinet.

"Been savin' this," he said and poured each of them a large shot into two small silver goblets.

"To de Silver Knights," Orndoff toasted.

"The Silver Knights," Arnette repeated.

"Mrs. won't let me drink nothing but damned ol' wheat ale. Says it's good for me, blah," Orndoff spat on the blackened floor.

Arnette smiled.

"I must be off old friend."

"So soon; you just got here."

"Time is short; I'll return within the week with news."

"I'll have de information you be needin' on Asuvalia."

"Thanks," Arnette said and extending his right hand.

Orndoff shook it firmly.

"See you still have your grip," Arnette smiled.

"From my hammer," Orndoff said looking over his shoulder toward his anvil.

"Godspeed."

"Be well," Arnette said and was on his way.

He rode from Lawrence until dusk before finding a place to camp. There were no places in between Trayden and Lawrence, only a small logging camp he knew of.

However he had been away a while and things change. Valkriss was getting ambitious, maybe too much. One thing for certain now that he was back, he would have his work cut out for him.

The last piece of information Valkriss told him hurt. Not enough for him to show it and give the old goat the satisfaction he desired. Valkriss knew how he felt when he made Kelsa a member of the inner circle. He knew they had a relationship and yet he still recruited her.

Arnette confronted her about it, but she was hell bent of joining the cause and right the wrongs of the world; if she only knew. Try as he might he could not bring himself to tell her the whole truth. She simply thought he didn't want her to join because she was a woman. He could not reveal the true nature of why he didn't want her to join.

He would in time, when he had eliminated the danger; the very one which resulted in the murder of Glollas' brother. One little fact of why he didn't tell Valkriss he'd been fighting the Vorlocks in the north.

They had some kind of tie between them and the Silver Knights. A traitor who went undetected and may have left behind others to carry out future work. Things would never be safe until the truth was known. Arnette bet his life that's why Tiberious hid Michael, was to protect him. But what did he know? He had to find out.

First he would make a quick stop and see the progress of Blacen. That would save him from having to ford the river at the logging camp to the east and hopefully run into Kelsa. Maybe she'd cooled off and forgave him. After all, it had been two years since he last saw her. Although she had a hell of a temper once you got on her bad side.

He still remembered every detail about her; her beautiful wavy black hair, tall and slender; with the most incredible blue eyes. The thoughts of her warmed his cold heart and caused him to smile despite the harsh weather setting in.

Chapter 8
An Old Nemesis

Three days had passed before Holly decided to ride back to Lawrence. She told Michael she needed to get more supplies. He was in no shape to travel even a short distance. Mercifully he didn't object and made her take some of his money for the goods; which were the last thing on her mind. At least in the daytime the gates would be open, and she wouldn't have to deal with any guards this time.

Before long she was at the tavern again. As she entered through the front she saw Valkriss tending the bar as always. It was midafternoon with only a few patrons looking to get of the rain.

Valkriss saw her as soon as she walked in. "Good to see you again," he greeted her like an old friend.

"Come on over and I'll fix you up something that will knock the chill out of yer bones," he beckoned Holly to sit at the barstool closest to the cellar.

As soon as she sat down, he placed a large clear shot glass in front of her and poured her a double Cinnigin.

"There you go dear," he said before lowering his voice.

"How is he?"

"He's going to be fine," Holly said and could see instant relief wash over the old man's face.

"So; have you found out anything? Have you sent word to Sindara? Has Arnette reported back?" Holly asked, trying to keep her voice down.

"Sam's hell; one question at a time, girl;" Valkriss snapped in his old crackling voice.

"I sent Arnette to Trayden to see if he can find out anything for us. He hasn't returned yet, but he should be back any day now. As for Sindara, I had to send Mick," he said frowning.

Holly almost spilled her drink. "You sent who? Valkriss; how could you. He's only sixteen."

"He's a good lad Holly and besides I had no one else to send. Arnette's in Trayden and you told me to get word to Sindara. If I couldn't use an aura candle to talk to them, someone had to go in person. I didn't want to send him," he continued.

"I would have gone myself, but I have to be here to run this place and get the information we need," Valkriss said flatly.

"You're right; you know Mick better than I do. He's just so young; I'll worry about him," Holly said.

"Do you think I won't? He's like a grandson to me," Valkriss said sadly.

"Well, what's done is done. We can't change it now," Holly said firmly.

"I need more supplies," she told Valkriss.

"I have anything you need right here," he said.

"Give me a bottle of Cinnigin, will you? I need something for this weather, also some Rockbite for when Michael's feeling better," Holly said and couldn't help but smile.

Damn it, get a hold of yourself and stop acting like a schoolgirl, she scolded herself.

Valkriss helped her carry out the supplies and tie them to the horse.

"Thanks again, I'll be back in two days," Holly told him as she put her foot in the stirrup and saddled up.

"You're welcome dear; just be safe; if anything comes up before you get back, I'll send word," Valkriss added as she turned and rode off.

The rain set in again halfway back to the cottage. She had a good cloak which kept the water from soaking her. Still her face and legs were getting soaked when the wind blew. It seemed the weather mirrored her emotions, she wasn't feeling very positive about things at the moment. Too many loose ends she thought again coming up to the front of the cottage; she would have to make the best of it though.

Michael was sitting up when she went to the bedroom to check on him.

"Glad you're up," Holly said.

"Feeling better," he replied.

"Well don't get too excited, big fella. You still have a ways to go before you're a hundred percent," Holly said smiling.

"Now lie back and let me check that bandage again."

"Whatever you say doc," Michael said as he slowly laid back.

She lifted up his tunic and saw that the bandage was dry, which made her breathe a sigh of relief.

"Are you hungry or thirsty?"

"I don't want to trouble you."

"Nonsense; what are friends for? Besides I'm in your debt; remember?" Holly smiled.

"I'm thirsty, if you wouldn't mind, but I'm not hungry yet."

"Be right back," Holly said and hurried off to the kitchen to get him some water.

"I'm afraid you'll have to wait a little while before you can drink the Rockbite I brought back for you," Holly grinned.

"Oh, I knew I liked you for a reason," Michael allowed himself to laugh a little, which didn't hurt as badly as before.

"Now I'm in your debt."

"It's okay; I'll let you work it off," Holly replied with a wicked smile.

"Now if you'll leave me alone for a minute, I have work to do. If you don't mind, your highness?"

"You may be excused, lowly servant," Michael said and laughed again. This time it hurt like hell and made him wince in exquisite pain.

"Oh now look what you went and did. You're hurting again; lay back and take it easy and that's an order; got it mister?" she said in her sternest voice.

"Okay okay, I give up. I'll just lay here and be a bum," Michael said this time making sure he didn't laugh.

Holly certainly had a way about her that made him relax and feel so peaceful, and it felt great.

Another two days passed; he was feeling much better, though she still insisted he stay in bed. The weather had faired considerably, yet it was still cold at night.

"Oh, dear?" Michael called out for Holly.

"Yes dear, I'm coming," Holly responded politely, thinking men are worse than kids when they get hurt. However he was her main weapon, so she had better take care of him.

"I was wondering if I could get up and on my feet. I'm feeling much stronger, and the wound has fully closed."

"If you must, but let me help you. You'll be weak though, you lost a lot of blood," Holly said concerned.

He sat up and swung his feet over to the cold floor beneath.

"Here, put your arm around me for support; there you go," Holly said helping him get to his feet.

"See, I told you I'm fine as can b... whoa," Michael said getting lightheaded.

"I told you; here back on the bed, I can't hold you long. You're too heavy," Holly said straining to keep him from falling in the floor.

She managed to angle him back onto the bed without letting him fall.

"There you're okay; better?"

"Yeah," Michael said, sounding a little winded.

Damn he couldn't believe how weak he felt, he needed his ointment; the stuff burns like hades, but works wonders. He didn't like feeling helpless.

"You'll get your strength back in no time Michael. You lost a lot of blood, it's a miracle you're alive," Holly stroked his black wavy hair.

He took her hand and kissed it, "thank you."

"I told you..."

He cut her off before she could finish. "Come here."

"What?"

"Come here," he cradled her face in both his hands and kissed her soft lips passionately.

She kissed him back and gently leaned back with him on the bed.

"But Michael, you're hurt," she protested.

"Not bad enough to stop me from this," he spoke with a deep baritone voice seducing her with every whisper; every kiss, every touch. She drew closer to him until they became one, united in an all-consuming passion.

Holly rolled over carefully on her side afterward, still breathing furiously; "you okay?"

"Never better," Michael lied; his body was between sheer ecstasy and phenomenal pain.

Still he didn't give a damn. That was incredible, though secretly in the back of his mind he worried he was using her as a substitute for Kara. Give yourself time, he told himself lying there next to her.

"Could you help me sit up please?"

"I thought you were okay," Holly looked worried.

"I was until you hurt me. Now I have a sex injury to go with my sword injury. At this rate, I'll be lucky to survive," Michael said laughing, causing his side to hurt even more.

"Oh you're impossible," Holly said and lightly smacked him on his shoulder as she raised him up on the bed.

"There you go, hitting an injured man. What kind of person hits a man who's injured?" Michael said smiling, trying not to laugh again.

Soon it was dark again, but this time Holly was curled up next to Michael in the soft warm bed and slept like a baby.

Now instead of being alone, he had a companion again, at least for a while. Life was pain; he had dealt with it in the past and will again in the future. He gradually regained his strength under Holly's skillful care. Little did he know what lay ahead; nor did he care so long as he had her.

He remembered part of an old book he read long ago:

'The piercing arrow of love cut by the shearing edge of the sword of truth; neither can coexist, so yet one must fall to the other. Which shall it be?

None can foretell for each must decide, when the time arrives; though when no love is lost, no emotion can be felt. For when loss comes; feelings are born, seeped in sorrow. When the last rays of despair depart like the morning dew; a heat of undying passion arises, welling up in the heart like the noonday sun.

Knowing we have loved and what it truly means and not to be told by another. The power of emotion takes us to the heights of heaven and to the depths of hades!

Feeling mighty when we are weak, humble when we are proud; illuminating our soul with the divine light of love. Human we could not be; neither man nor woman would exist without feelings. Yea if they slay us, yet we would welcome them!'

He finally found happiness again and would fight the demons of hell itself to keep it.

Holly woke really early that morning. She planned a trip into town to see if Valkriss had any news and get Michael's things and a little surprise too. It had been such a long time since anyone had shown her any kindness, yet she was still fearful after her latest round at the bar.

Holly hoped her uncle Valkriss would be

okay through all of this. He was the only family she had been able to locate and that had taken over a year to do. She was using the fake name they'd thought up for her, Holly Brackenthorn, instead of her real name, Adrelia VaughBlair. She wondered if she should tell Michael about that too. That would have to wait; they were still too many questions going through her mind. How did they manage to find her again?

She had been on the run for nearly two years and had always been careful in every place she stayed. Had her former captor hired mercenaries to kill her, or just to take her back into his cruel evil grasp? She loathed thinking of that horrid place that reeked of filth and death; no happiness only misery. She remembered the day of her capture all too well.

She was almost twelve when the Scarious found her playing in the woods and took her ten years ago. Days of endless torture designed to break her will and years of magical training in the dark arts followed.

But there remained something inside of Holly, a spark of goodness, which could not be extinguished; however evil it may be. So she learned all she could in hopes of one day escaping her hated master.

That was all behind her now, or at least she had thought, until now. She came around a sharp bend in the road, not far from the cottage, when the sound of rustling leaves snapped her back to reality.

As soon as she looked towards the forest, she saw them. She knew their black shadows anywhere. She jumped from her horse; there was no way she was going to lead them back to the cottage and Lawrence was too far away.

Quickly she focused her mind and chanted; "Mobilis Agilis."

That would give her the agility she needed for fast spell casting. It wasn't much, but at least it would give her time in battle. No sooner than the words of the spell were uttered, they were on her.

Thinking quickly, Holly called forth another spell; "Auruas Luminous."

The closest beasts went shrieking in terror blinded by the tremendous burst of light. More rushed in to fill their diminished ranks, yet Holly had another trick up her sleeve now that she had a few more precious seconds. She had been well trained in fast combat magic at the citadel.

"Ilire Illum Exploria!" Searing yellowish fire exploded from Holly's hands as she spoke, killing four of the devils.

They were too many; in another heartbeat she was surrounded being restrained.

Michael woke early as he usually did, allowing Holly to sleep in a bit. He rolled over to get out of bed and noticed she was up before him. He still felt a little weak when his feet touched the floor. He glanced around the quaint cottage bedroom; got dressed and made his way slowly toward the kitchen, still stiff from the bed rest. He noticed a piece of small parchment lying on the kitchen counter and picked it up and read it.

'Went to town; be home later with supplies, Love Holly.'

No sooner than the smile appeared on his face, he heard something in the distance that made him drop the note on the counter. He grabbed his sword, and dashed out the front door.

The noise grew more distinct as he ran in the direction it was coming from. His heart raced wildly. It sounded like a woman's scream, that made him redouble his pace, forgetting his pain. He ran as fast as he ever had in his life.

He came to a sharp bend in the road a

ways from the cottage when he saw Scarious dragging bodies of their slain into the nearby forest.

His eyes quickly darted from one to the other. Damn it! No Holly! Michael glowered.

It never entered his mind how many they were. It didn't matter; he would kill them all or die trying. Yelling with rage; he ran straight into the middle of them, slashing; hacking, kicking, whatever he could do to squeeze the life right out of the filthy black beasts.

Most ran when they saw him brandishing the hated sword they knew so well; the sword which had slain so many of their kind.

Afterward Michael stopped and looked over the scene and noticed one of the black devils moving slowly on the ground. He walked over to it and grabbed it up by its grimy hide.

"Where did you take her?"

The creature just moaned. Michael held his sword in front of its red eyes and watched it squirm under his tightening grip.

"I'll ask you once more. Tell me, and you'll die quickly or don't and you will die a slow agonizing death. Where did you take her?"

The beast began muttering violently. "Not

matters anyway... we have her; our master will reward us well."

"Who's your master?" Michael demanded, shaking it violently with anger.

"He is, in den of madness... you shall meet him soon...he's comin' for you… So…La...Dar," with a faint gasp it died.

Michael threw its lifeless body to the ground. He came to himself and surveyed the aftermath focusing on the area leading into the woods. They were no paths or roads heading into the forest, only a couple of broken branches on a small evergreen bush.

He investigated the area more and saw four of the beasts lying dead not less than a hundred feet from the woods. He had defiantly under estimated Holly's abilities; she could hold her own. Most men would flee at the sight of one Scarious, yet somehow she had managed to slay four of them.

There was magic used here; powerful magic, not just potions or parlor tricks. What in hades had he gotten himself into he wondered? He didn't have time to stand around and debate though; he had to move fast if he was going to catch them.

Michael returned to the cottage to get some supplies before going after Holly's kidnappers. He knew he wouldn't get far without provisions and warmer clothes. As he walked through the small wooden door of the gray stone cottage, he felt a familiar pain deep in his heart.

"Just like Kara," Michael whispered to himself.

Yet it was a small comfort Holly had not been killed, just kidnapped. Those beasts work for Soladar; now he knew for sure. For what reason, he didn't know, which meant Soladar wants her alive.

Why had the Scarious taken Holly? Were they going to use her in a trap for him? Was this his fault? He would never forgive himself if something happened to her because of him. And now he knew for sure who the master of those bastards and in that; the one ultimately responsible for Kara and his father's death.

In time he will feel the cold steel of my blade, Michael thought angrily stuffing supplies into a brown leather pack. The sun was high when he entered the forest. It was an unusually warm autumn day, however he knew good weather would not hold out long. Winters in this region came early and were long and harsh.

He picked his way through the forest carefully to avoid disturbing tell-tell signs left behind by those he was pursuing. Michael saw no signs of Holly's footprints, only those of the foul beasts.

They must be carrying her, he thought and a little smile played at the corner of his mouth, when he thought of her fighting all the way.

She had spirit, he gave her that. Michael only hoped she wouldn't anger them too much; those damn beasts are not very smart and highly temperamental.

He journeyed until the sun began to dip below the horizon. He would have gone on through the night, but he knew it would be useless because he would easily lose their trail in the darkness. Against his determined will, he made camp in a small clearing.

The few brown leaves left hanging on the trees rustled noisily in the wind. He lay there gazing up at the bright stars twinkling in the heavens above; his mind was filled with tormented comparisons of Kara and Holly. Sleep would come, no doubt, but it would be a troubled sleep indeed. Yet he had to focus on rest so he would have the strength to take the fight to the enemy.

The next day began gray and overcast, and soon snow began to settle in, drifting lazily at first as if performing a dance on its downward trek. Steadily it grew worse as the wind whipped the dazzling white flakes in every direction. It was mesmerizing to watch, and Michael could feel the bitter cold seep into his bones; they were something purifying about it. The glistening white powder coated everything in sight sealing in what lay beneath.

The air felt crisp and clean; renewed and refreshed through the magic of winter. But soon enough, the grey skies overhead darkened as nighttime came upon the land. Soon there would be no light left to find his way, knowing he must camp he had to fight the urge to go on in spite of the impending blizzard. The falling snow extinguished all the hope he had of finding Holly.

Michael knew the snow would quickly cover any visible tracks and he would be hard pressed even with his tracking skill to locate his prey. The black devils hardly left any signs to follow under normal conditions, let alone foul weather.

His one hope lay in the fact that they had not gotten much of a head start. Knowing this would afford him a little comfort while he made camp for the night.

Soon Michael had a small comfortable shelter that would keep him out of the snow and cold wind during the night. After a few attempts, he had a small but warm fire. He knew a larger fire would draw unwanted attention and give warning to Holly's captors. So he chose the driest wood he could find that would give off the least amount of smoke. Michael settled in as best as he could under the small canopy of interlaced branches he had thatched together.

He sat in front of the small crackling fire and dug into his pack for rations of baked black bread and strips of dried pork. He held a small piece of meat close to the fire to warm it before eating it, in hopes it would stave off the cold a little.

One thing that sent warmth streaming through him was the thoughts of Holly. Yet why had she kept her magical ability to herself and not told him about it? Maybe because she didn't know him well enough.

They were plenty of people distrusting of anyone who used magic, not just him. He couldn't help but smile a little when he thought of how well she did against the devils. He sat chewing the hardened bread, thankful he brought along a flask of aromatibus mead, it was a treasure to have. Just a small sip was all that was needed to restore a person's vitality.

He learned long ago the herbs needed to make his own, how to carefully seep each herb in the mead to get its full effect. Once it was concocted the slight alcohol in the mead was overpowered by the herbs which by themselves could sustain a man. He showed Holly how to make it just yesterday. She loved learning new things, always full of questions.

Darkness cascaded over the land like drawing curtains on a window. The night was pitch black, thick grey clouds covered the heavens like a woolen blanket. Neither moonlight nor a twinkle of starlight could be seen.

If not for the fire, he would not have been able to see his hands before his face. Mercifully sleep came quickly thanks to a generous helping of aromatibus mead; he spent the entire night in dreamless slumber.

Dawn came early and cold. The snow had slacked off a little during the night, but now began to pick back up. The weather was against him too it seemed; damn it was everything always against him? Michael fought many perils, and weather was the least of his fears.

His desire for Holly and answers would keep him searching to the ends of the world; if that's what it took. Another innocent person would not be harmed over him; not again, not after Kara.

He was a damn fool to ever believe there would be any happiness in this life for him. Why did he think he could ever be happy? He would hunt down and kill Holly's captors and set her free and then continue his vendetta. Even better now that he had a name to who was behind the damn Scarious.

He packed camp quickly and set out through the snowbound forest; deep within he was losing hope. He knew the black devils were nearly impossible to follow, even for the most experienced tracker. Yet his resolve was set in stone, nothing would stand between him and Holly. He found himself half running at times through the forest; it was easy for him to cover a lot of ground fast with his powerful legs.

To his surprise, the sword wound from the tavern fight didn't bother him in the least. Holly was a remarkable healer; a person would have to look close to even see the scar.

The storm grew more intense by noon, completely burring out the sun, making it more like night than day. Hour after bitter hour Michael went on half running at times. No tracks were visible now; they had been completely obliterated by the growing storm.

He hoped Holly's' captors hadn't changed course and that was his one hope. Michael had to slow down to keep from missing signs left by the black devils or Holly. He paused a second to take in the wide expanse of forest that lay before him. The falling snow had done its job in concealing their foot tracks. Luckily for him there were still minor signs; broken branches and a small piece of fabric torn from Holly's clothes hanging on a nearby oak branch stripped of its leaves by the harsh wind. He knew Holly had placed it there, having torn it from her clothing as a sign for him to follow.

He knew the worsening snow storm would

impede Holly's' captors as well; he hoped he could use this to his advantage. Scarious were quite adapted to cold weather with their thick hides and layers of fur. Over the years, he learned many things about the beasts.

However one thing he didn't know, was Soladar created them after going insane trying to destroy the Orb of Chaos. Soladar in his madness gathered all his followers who believed in his power and thought they would help him bring in a new rein and begin a time of unprecedented chaos. The most remarkable fact was the great white mage Soladar had been corrupted by the very thing he sought to destroy.
The Orb of Chaos twisted Soladar's mind and bound his soul deep within it, unable to break free, yearning one day to escape the prison of chaos. Yet no one powerful enough had come forward to fight. Those that did died, or worse captured were tortured and turned into Scarious. Unbelievable as it was, many of his followers chose their fate willingly. Thinking they would share in his power and in the end become nothing more than beast of burden to an insane master.

Michael had learned well through the years spent fighting them; how their hide was so tough normal arrows could not penetrate it. Their razor sharp claws could slash through the hardest steel and long fangs that could sever a man's arm in one bite. Just one Scarious had the strength of four men.

One question remained however. Why did Soladar want Holly? After all she was just a niece of a tavern owner; or was she? She must be more than that, he thought. Did this have something to do with him? Was she the bait to lead him into a trap?

Chapter 9
Partial truth

Holly had her own plan of escape. While as she was being carried by the black devils she was bidding her time; time to strike out with full force with all her might and power. Physically she could do little; her power lay in her magic which she kept hidden from Michael.

She knew he was already beginning to be curious to the point of near suspicion about her past. Still she hadn't mustered the courage to tell him. What if he didn't believe her? She couldn't bear the thought of losing his help. She had lost so much in her young life and she wasn't about to lose again. She just had to plan it out right and make him understand, feeding him just enough information to keep him on her side. And well, if that failed, she would just have to use other methods of persuasion.

Holly knew she would have no future while Soladar lived. She knew Michael hated the Scarious and that knowledge comforted her some. But would that same hatred extend to Soladar? Surely if she told him that Soladar was behind the creation of the beasts, he would go after him and help her defeat him. Then she would be free at last. She had to keep telling herself Michael was nothing more than a tool; nothing more.

Coldness began to sink into every joint in her body; she was growing numb and nearly lifeless. Her devilish captors also sensed this and stopped. The one who had been carrying her, dropped her to the ground roughly, the deepening snow softened the impact a little. She opened her eyes a little and saw the leader, guessing by his size, ordered another one to give her something to drink from a dirty flask.

The beast loosened the rag which bound her mouth and forced the smelly flask to her lips. She forced herself to drink in spite of the bitter taste; she knew she had to keep up her strength.

Holly had been well prepared for an opportunity like this. As she sipped, she stared into the dark eyes of the beast and spoke softly, "Illibrum Enchantenum."

Her eyes glazed over for a second while the beast was held spell bound.

She whispered, "loose me."

With one quick motion of the beasts' sharp claws, her ropes were cleanly cut.

She wasted no time and uttered one word, "kill."

Her newly charmed Scarious lunged forward and attacked his fellow beasts. They were stunned at first by the shock of fighting one of their own. The charmed beast fought furiously against the others, killing two before being jumped by the other three.

Yet this was all she needed; she could handle three now that she was loose. Just as they finished killing the one she charmed, Holly began to chant one of the most powerful spells she knew. Working her hands in a loop motion, she spoke with such a powerful voice it echoed throughout the forest, "Ilire Illum Exploria!"

She invoked a white hot boiling fire, growing larger as she worked her hands. With a swift forward motion of her palms out shot a consuming fire incinerating her enemies and leaving nothing but ashes

Suddenly Michael stopped; the wind carried a faint sound of a woman's voice just above its roar. It came from straight ahead. His heart beat rapidly; in an instant he was running in the direction the sound came from.

He came to was an expanse of grassland in the forest. Thankfully the snow wasn't too deep and he made his way across quickly. Entering the woods again he was stunned at what he saw. Burn marks as least twenty feet high on the trees and the bodies of three black devils. Ashes sprinkled over them littering the ground as well.

No average woman could have done something like this; hell no average man could have done this.

A sound of a twig snapping nearby brought him back to reality; within a split second Michael's gleaming sword was out of its sheath and ready for action. He glanced quickly around, eyes wide.

Something move twenty yards away off to the right. In seconds he closed the distance ready to attack whatever it was.

With his sword raised he charged it. However when he got within a few feet; it slumped and fell forward to its knees. No longer sensing a threat he lowered his sword, keeping it at the ready just in case. Face down it fell in the snow and he quickly re-sheathed his sword. He knelt down to roll the cloaked figure over when a sickening pain gripped the pit of his stomach as the hood fell back revealing Holly's face.

She was pale, covered in sweat; deep red lines bored down each side of her cheeks where she'd been gagged. With tender fingers of a tender lover Michael felt for life. There was a weak pulse and shallow breath, however she was so pale and her clammy. She would die without warmth and proper care.

He had to get her to a safe place and that was Stonebrook, which was too far away. He would have to make a shelter if he was going to save her; then they could travel once he had her well enough.

The storm seemed to have a will of its own; unrelenting, trying to bury the land in white ice. He took off his heavy fur cloak and wrapped Holly's frail body working fast to build a warm shelter. The snow itself would help some, as he cleared a small area and heaped snow up into a ring shaped mound with the center hollowed out.

He cut down evergreen branches off some nearby pines with his sword. After a few minutes the task was done and snow had already begun to seal the small structure.

He gently pulled Holly through the small opening and laid her upon a soft thick bed of pine needles. It would do for now until he could find better. He placed spare branches across the entryway to seal them in against the weather. Michael knew he had to get her warm. She was beginning to shake uncontrollably.

He undressed as quickly as he could; then undressed her being careful to keep her underneath his cloak. Then he covered both of them with his clothes and cover on top. Michael put both his massive arms around her and pulled her in close to his warm body, hoping it wasn't too late to save her.

He concentrated his mind on making his body come alive with heat, an old trick he'd learned years ago during the long brutal winters in Trayden. He focused all his energy in forcing the warmth out from his chest to radiate outward to all parts of his body.

She didn't stir or make any sound, but Michael saw she was breathing easier. He gently reached for his flask of spiced mead; uncorked it, put it up to her lips, and tried to give her a small sip, but it just trickled down her chin. He repositioned her limp head better and opened her mouth to allow the drink to enter. If he managed to get a little down her, he knew it would help her and him. So he took a small drink and set it aside.

Michael had them covered so completely that even their heads were covered. After what seemed hours, he finally felt warmth return to her limbs, feeling encouraged he fell asleep.

Was she dreaming or drifting between worlds; everything was so blurred. She remembered escaping the clutches of the foul beasts, yet the powerful spell she cast drained her already weak body to the breaking point. She fell into soft white cloud and was picked up by someone or something.

When she awoke, she had no clothes on and it was dark. She rolled a little and felt a warm naked body beside her. In her confusion and the dimness, it startled her, until she realized it was Michael.

Relief flooded through her and she took her hand and gently caressed his soft wavy hair. His hazel eyes slowly opened and he raised himself up on one elbow. Using his other arm to wrap around Holly and pull her in close. They kissed with the electrifying passion of a love reunited. Words weren't needed to communicate what was needed to be said between them, it was spoken heart to heart.

Neither Holly nor Michael wanted to leave their small comfortable shelter, but they knew they had too. They embraced each other one last time before getting their things together. They sat across from each other smiling and forgot the outside world for a while.

Michael they should not to head back to the small cottage and instead travel on to Stonebrook. It was farther north and a well-fortified city.

It was on the southern border of the Northern Wastes, one of the most inhospitable places known. The lowlands teamed with all manners of beasts. The highlands were snowcapped year round due to the tremendous height of the mountains.

Many famous explorers had met their doom in the wilds of that miserable place. Only a few hearty souls who managed to come back; told stories of perilous adventures of how they cheated death, searching for untold riches in that barbaric land.

Just outside the stone wall of Stonebrook,

sat the home of Garian; Michael's one hope. He was renowned for being an exceptionally powerful priest with no love for Soladar. Both were counting on that in their quest against Soladar; his power was too great to fight alone.

Stonebrook was exactly the place Michael wanted to be. Somewhere they wouldn't attract the attention of Soladar's minions. Garian had known his father and was a loyal friend to his family in any time of need. He had trained Michael in the ways of making various healing salves he used through the years of fighting. Now, Michael hoped to enlist his aid once more, this time in a much greater capacity.

Michael and Holly walked under the forest's canopy to avoid the deep snow that piled up during the storm. He held a firm grip onto his sword's handle, prepared for whatever danger lurking ahead. As they walked, Holly placed her soft hand on his and spoke in a low gentle voice.

"We're safe now."

Michael looked over at her and smiled; unconvinced, but relaxed his grip a little.

"It will take us about two days from here to reach Stonebrook if the weather holds,"

Michael told her.

That would include a stop at the Bubbling Springs, he thought. He heard about it on his trips to Stonebrook, but never had a chance to stop.

It had many hot water springs bubbling up from deep within the earth. The water came up through natural soapstone, found abundantly in that part of the region. Huge iridescent spheres wafting along on the soft breeze.

The Carillion region was a vast region spanning thousands of miles with the largest cities Sindara and Cinnibar along the southern coast. Silverheart was northwest of Cinnibar and was quite large as well.

Stonebrook was the largest, most northern city. They would have normally traveled just east of Bubbling Springs to reach Stonebrook. Yet Michael planned to make a stop to relax and enjoy the wonderful hot springs. Not only did the waters have cleaning ability, they were also reputed to have healing ones as well.

Regardless, he wanted a reprieve from the cold and to rest from their travels. He also knew that there wouldn't be any danger. The black devils despised the Bubbling Springs and being close to Stonebrook, they would be afraid of being caught.

Holly and Michael made their way through the woods, being cautious of what they could encounter. The black devils weren't the only thing to be found in the vast forest.

Thankfully the fierce early snow storm had abated and the temperature was rising some. Even with the summer foliage gone from the hardwoods; the canopy of the scattered evergreens was thick enough to stop a lot of the snow from hitting the ground unlike the open areas, where it was knee deep.

"Do you think Garian will aid us?" Holly asked just above a whisper.

Michael thought for a second. "He was there for my father and for me when my father wasn't. By no means is he any friend of Soladar's."

Yet Holly was really thinking about how to feed him more information about her past. Even if he didn't care, it was important so her plans would work out like she wanted. She was growing fond of him.

Fear stabbed her; how much should she tell him? What if he got angry and left her on her own; what then? It would wreck all her well laid plans for Soladar's demise. Should she chance it, she thought? Yes she had too, if she didn't, things go would wrong. If they did, she would have to continue on alone. However she would wait and chose the right time and place and little by little, feed him information that would make him hate Soladar.

Michael's thoughts too where drifting back to his youth. The hatred raged in his heart for those responsible for the death of his father and his beloved Kara. How could he tell her about his past? He barely knew her and already they had been through so much together. He was torn because to want a life with Holly, he would have to bury Kara's memory forever and kill Soladar. Once again his past was interfering with his future.

Then he realized Holly was watching him intently.

"What are you thinking about?" She queried.

"Nothing, I was trying to remember the way to Stonebrook," an obvious lie and which Holly could tell, but said nothing, which he was thankful for.

They continued walking in silence until the sun sank low to the horizon. The number of daylight hours were dwindling as winter's approach drew ever nearer. They stopped to prepare to camp for the night.

Michael gathered evergreen branches to build a shelter with. While he was busy, Holly quietly slipped away into the forest after firewood and possibly dinner. She walked slowly through the woods and spotted a rabbit about twenty paces off to her left.

"Killdaum," She cast with a quick flick of her right hand.

A small jet of green light struck the critter, killing it instantly. Satisfied with her kill, she gathered it up along with some firewood and headed back to camp.

Michael was just putting the finishing touches on the shelter. He turned around and noticed her standing there with a grey rabbit in her left hand and firewood in the other.

"You're full of surprises, aren't you," he said, with a broadening smile.

"If you only knew," she replied.

Before long, they had a small comfortable fire going. Michael cleaned the rabbit and placed it on a split over the fire. Soon they were both enjoying a hot meat with spiced mead. Both sat quietly eating when Holly broke the silence.

"I think it's time to… tell you about my past."

Michael started to interrupt her, but she went on telling him how Soladar killed her parents and kidnapped her at the age of twelve. How he tried to brainwash her, teaching her dark magic. She pretended to fight back tears as she continued to tell how she managed to escape Soladar's clutches using the very magic she had learned. Damn you're a great actress she thought wickedly, and then continued.

"My name isn't even Holly," she muttered red-eyed.

"It's… it's… Adrelia… Adrelia VaughBlair. My uncle and I thought it up while I was staying at his bar."

Michael didn't know if this made things clearer or confused him even more. All he knew was, he cared for her; although he wondered if she would be as accepting of his past as he was of hers. One thing for certain, Soladar was as intertwined in both their destinies as they were to each other.

Before Holly knew it, she was sobbing. Michael moved over to where she sat and put his arm around her. When she turned to him with her head down, he placed his hand gently under her chin and lifted her head up.

"I accept you regardless of your past or your name," he said in a warm soft voice.

"But, there's more," Holly said, hanging her head again.

"Okay, out with it," Michael said sounding concerned.

Did he really know Holly, or whatever her name was, as well as he thought he did?

"At the tavern I charmed you in the bathtub and took advantage of you." Holly started to sob again until Michael laughed.

"You think it's funny," she said upset.

"I'll remember that the next time and play along," Michael said smiling.

"What do you mean, 'play along the next time'?" Holly asked clearly annoyed.

"What I mean dear; is magic doesn't work on me and never has."

"But; what about the tavern then?" Holly asked.

"It was what it was, two people needing each other," Michael said.

"Care to put that theory of yours to a test?"

Holly asked with a grin.

Now she would get a chance to see if Valkriss was right or not.

"So long as you promise not to hurt me," Michael said and winked at her.

"If you're immune to magic like you say you are, you have nothing to worry about from little ol' me."

"Hardly," Michael chuckled as he got to his feet.

"Where would you like me to stand my lady?" Michael said in a proper tone, bowing low as if in front of a queen.

"Right where you are should do just fine," Holly said and began to walk away, getting about ten paces before casting her spell.

"Be gentle," were the only words Michael could get out before he felt himself flying twenty feet backward from the force of Holly's spell, which hit him square in the chest.

Thankfully he landed in a pile of leaves that softened his landing a little, but still knocked the breath out of him. He lay there momentarily stunned by the sheer power of her spell.

Holly let out a squeal of delight over her ability and then fear swept through her when she didn't see him get up. She ran in the direction she saw him flying backwards, yet he was nowhere in sight. She was just trying to teach him a lesson she didn't want to actually hurt him.

"Michael where are you?" Holly called in a panicky voice.

Suddenly two massive arms shot up through the leaves and grabbed her, pulling her down on top of him. She screamed a little before she realized it was Michael and smacked him on his shoulder.

"What's that for?" Michael asked.

"That's for scaring me," Holly smacked him again.

"And that one was for making me think I hurt you. I thought magic couldn't hurt you?"

"The essence of magic such as enchantments, magical fire, ice, and other types can't, but the force of a spell can," Michael said earnestly.

"And since you hurt me, now you're going to have to kiss me and make it all better," Michael said in his best pouty face.

Holly never could resist him; he leaned in, kissed her soft lips and pulled her close.

"Now about your name, I never liked it

anyway," Michael grinned. Holly buried her face into Michael's chest, feeling the happiest she had ever felt.

Everything was back on track now. They agreed she should keep using her fake name wherever they went to hide her true identity. Then they retired to their little shelter for the night. The night passed in a dreamless bliss for Holly and Michael. Before long the morning sun was peeked out of the over the eastern hills.

She awoke first and smiled when she looked over at Michael who was still in deep sleep. She gently kissed him causing him to stir slightly and then when she kissed him again, he grabbed her with a sudden movement. She let out a quick squeal of surprise and laughed as they embraced.

"I have a little surprise in mind for you," Michael said smiling when they were finally on their way.

"What is it? How did you get a gift out here? Where is it?" she asked.

He wouldn't answer any of her questions. He figured they'd arrive at the springs late that afternoon and camp there and then head for Stonebrook the next morning, arriving there before sundown.

He also remembered a special herb that only grew at the Bubbling Springs. It was Clovian and he sorely needed it to replenish his stock of healing salve. Garian would certainly be thankful for it, not having to use his own stock to make it. Michael knew how to make it, yet it still must be blessed by a priest for it to be truly effective.

It was around midday when Michael and Holly stopped to rest, sip on the spiced mead and snack on some of Michael's baked bread, rejuvenating them both. Holly noticed Michael looked slightly worried.

"Don't worry we'll have enough to get us to Stonebrook. Besides there are always more rabbits," Holly said smiling. This made Michael laugh in spite of his worries.

Soon they were walking again; each lost in their own thoughts. Michael felt a warm breeze and knew they must be nearing the Bubbling Springs.

"Remember the surprise I told you about?" Michael asked Holly.

"I do."

"Well, it's not much farther."

"What is?"

"Just wait and see," Michael answered with a grin.

They walked on a couple hours more. Finally the woods gave way to a huge clearing where there was no snow and as they drew nearer, gigantic iridescent bubbles floated around everywhere. As they walked farther into the Bubbling Springs, the sounds of bubbling water filled the air.

Hot water springs were dotted throughout the entire area as far as one could see. It was a lot warmer in this area as well. The springs created its own weather pattern, staying nearly the same temperature year round, varying only a few degrees. Michael smiled as he saw Holly taking it all in and was reminded of the first time he saw it.

"Would you like to soak in one of the springs?" he asked.

"Could we? That would be wonderful!" Holly sounded excited.

"Sure," Michael answered.

"We just have to check and make sure the spring isn't too hot. Many are, but some are great for bathing in."

After checking a few they found one that was just right. Soon they were undressed and soaking in the hot soapy water. Holly was intrigued by the natural soapstone; it felt so smooth to her touch yet hard.

The spring was shoulder deep; bubbles became smaller and more frequent. Holly slid over to Michael urging him to move forward a little so she could get behind him. As soon as she did, she gently caressed his back. Then she began to massage his thick muscular neck making him groan in pleasure.

He reached up and took hold of her hands, kissed them lightly then moved her to the front of him. He passionately kissed her soft lips while his hands stroked her breasts.

She cradled him and took him deep inside. With almost no secrets between them, she could now give herself fully to him. That made for the most passionate sex they had shared with one another.

In the hot water spring they totally relaxed, unaware of the outside world, curled up inseparable in each other's arms. Unwillingly they got out and dried off and put their clothes on. It was nearly dark when they finished. They decided there would be no need for a shelter since they could sleep in the Bubbling Springs and leave out in the morning for Stonebrook.

Michael spread out his large bear hide; then he and Holly sat down, neither ready for sleep. Every so often a huge bubble would float by with an insect trapped inside, riding it until it burst.

Even though it was getting dark, the land had a pale white glow about it making it as easy to see, as if it were a night of a full moon. Holly was so glad Michael had brought her here.

With that thought, she looked over and noticed he was already fast asleep. She sat watching for hours; then she finally curled up beside him and fell into a peaceful slumber.

The morning came so swiftly it seemed they had hardly slept at all, yet both felt rested. Michael was the first to awaken. Holly woke up to find him gently caressing her cheek.

After finishing the last of the baked bread and washing it down with a drink of spiced mead, they prepared to leave.

Chapter 10
Safe House

Michael found a nice cluster of Clovian on their way out.

"What's that"? Holly asked, unfamiliar with the plant.

"Clovian, it's used in healing salves." Then he went on to explain its uses to her.

"Besides Garian will be grateful he doesn't have to use his supply."

Before long they were well into the forest again; suddenly Michael stopped. Holly knew immediately he sensed danger.

"Everything's too quiet," he whispered.

They stood still and scanned the forest in front of them, when they heard the sound of a twig snapping. In seconds they were surrounded by beasts that were four to five feet tall and just as wide.

They were covered in filthy brown hair and tattered pieces of sewn leather clothing. They were incredibility strong, with large powerful jaws fully capable of severing an arm or leg in one bite.

Holly and Michael stood back to back as the snarling creatures closed in.

Holly struck first, shouting, "Killdaum," killing one of the foul brutes instantly.

Michael jumped forward, sword in hand fighting two that came in from the left. With a few expert swings of his deadly sword, the beasts fell lifeless to the ground.

"Ilire illum Exploria," shouted Holly.

Yellowish white hot fire exploded in front of her, incinerating three instantly. Unafraid of Michael knowing her magical abilities now, she fought eagerly and fiercely.

She caught a glimpse out of the corner of her eye; a beast was running toward Michael's back. He was fighting two in front of him and didn't see it.

With no time to warn him, "Protectum," Holly yelled, sending a shimmering stream from her hand. A glowing shield formed behind him seconds before the creature's strike causing it to bounce off harmlessly.

The next instant Michael swung around

catching the beast right across the chest. He glanced at Holly with a smile of thanks. She winked back wryly and continued the fight. The beasts began retreating into the forest. Holly and Michael let them flee, killing two who lingered behind.

Then they surveyed the scene making sure nothing else was going to attack them and then made sure each other were okay.

"I'd hate to be on your bad side," Michael chuckled, causing her to smile.

"Then don't argue with me," she said with a short laugh.

"What were those things?" she asked.

"They're called Bullyworgs. They run throughout the forest, and as you've seen; they're ferocious little bastards."

They knew they had to get a move on if they were going to make it to Stonebrook. Nightfall was fast approaching and they wanted to avoid any more encounters. They began walking again after finishing off the last of the aromatibus mead.

The rest of the way to Stonebrook was quiet, which both were thankful for. It was nearing dusk when they arrived. The city was impressive with its well-fortified huge stone wall encircling it. It had two mammoth wooden gates that could be barred from the inside in times of war.

When they arrived at Garian's house; they saw the soft glow of a candle through one of the two front windows.

"Should we tell him who I really am?" Holly asked, a little worried, as they approached the door.

"Of course; I'd trust him with my life and have," Michael replied when the door opened before he could knock; startling them a little.

A distant voice within welcomed them to enter. They hesitated a moment before the voice spoke again.

"Do not fear, Michael. It is I, Garian. Come in and be welcome."

When they went inside, the door closed behind them on its own. Once inside, they looked around. At first they saw no one, but then in the flame of a candle they were surprised to see a small image of Garian's face.

It spoke again, "please make yourselves comfortable while I am away."

"Thank you," Michael replied.

"You'll find a well-stocked pantry for you and your lovely friend," Garian said.

Michael smiled, "her name is Holly."

She stepped forward a little and curtsied.

"A suitable name; yet Adrelia is much prettier," Garian's face lit up with a smile, glimmering in the candlelight.

"How did you…" Holly began to ask before Garian spoke again.

"I know many things; besides I wouldn't be much of a priest if I could not tell someone's true name," then he continued.

"I have set protective enchantments around my house knowing friend from foe. You will be quiet safe within its walls, for the barrier cannot be breached. I've been looking forward to your coming."

Michael thanked him again, and with a departing smile, Garian's face vanished from the aura candle flame leaving it glowing softly in silence. It took a minute for Michael's amazement to leave him, while Holly seemed right at home with the magical surroundings.

"There is old magic at work here," Holly said breaking the silence. Michael nodded in agreement.

The crackling fire provided glowing warmth radiating throughout the room. It was a pleasant retreat from the cold winter's night cascading over the land. Holly was quite intrigued by the fire in the large fireplace, intently staring at it.

"What is it?" Michael asked.

"The wood's not being consumed by the flames," she replied, taking a step toward the fireplace. With her right hand, she made a clockwise circular motion.

"It's everlasting fire," she spoke, half to herself.

"What is that?" Michael asked.

"It is a special fire that can only be started from a spark, from the Great Ardor Mountain in the Solum Lands. Only thought to exist in legends and myth," Holly said clearly impressed.

"Garian's full of surprises," Michael replied.

"Let's find that well stocked pantry; shall we?" Michael said rubbing his stomach, indicating his hunger.

After their long journey both of them had a terrific appetite. Soon they were seated across from each other at the kitchen table enjoying tasty dried meat with dark brown wheat bread that was as fresh as if it was baked that day.

Holly found some exquisite brambleberry jelly and fine light ale to wash everything down with.

After they ate, both full and went to find the guest room, down the hall from the kitchen. To their surprise they found the huge bed was already turned down.

"He really was expecting us," Michael said surprised.

Sleep came easily for both of them in the warm soft bed. Michael still felt a twinge of uneasiness about all this magic as he drifted off to sleep. Never trust magic he told himself and went to sleep.

Holly was curled up next to him with her head lying gently on his left shoulder. They slept soundly that night, waking up late the next morning. They lay in bed enjoying the respite from their travel in the protection of Garian's home.

It was far more spacious and elegant than the outside appearance led one to believe. Neither one was in a hurry to get out of bed, preferring to cuddle close and forget the cold harsh winter day outside. They could see through small circular glass window, it had already begun to snow again.

After dosing for a while longer, Michael was the first out of bed only putting on his pants and boots with his undershirt. He didn't bother to fully dress. He had no intentions of going outside.

He made his way to the kitchen looking to make a breakfast for Holly and something to drink for him, since he wasn't hungry yet. He returned to the bedroom with a tray piled high with bread; jelly, honey, butter, and dried ham along with two goblets of sweet nectar he found rummaging through the pantry.

Holly was sitting up in bed when he walked in the room. He smiled as he walked slowly toward the bed, being careful not to spill the nectar.

"You shouldn't have," she said with a warm smile.

"Okay then," he said and made a gesture to leave and then turned back to Holly laughing.

She gave him a cross look and laughed as well. He sat the tray down on the bed and she ate while he sipped his nectar smiling.

"What are you smiling at?" she questioned.

"Nothing," he replied.

Holly gave him a disappointing look.

"I can't remember being happier," he said, giving into her question.

She stopped eating, sat her goblet down and reached forward and wrapped her arms around him nearly tipping the tray over. When he hugged he could feel her hot tears running down his neck. They held one another for a long time; wordlessly, content with silence. Buried deep in his mind however; was fear. Fear this happiness would be taken away just like before.

After washing up, they decided to go into Stonebrook and see if they could hear of any news. Holly also hoped to do a little shopping too.

She had to find a way of contacting Valkriss. Not being able to trust aura candles was going to make it difficult. Maybe she would hire a courier to take a message to him. He knew where she was going after the cottage, but she was supposed to go back to Lawrence and check in with him first.

It was killing her not knowing what information Arnette had found out in Trayden.

Patience, she kept telling herself. For now shopping would help distract her. She could definitely use a new robe and a wand to replace the one she lost during her escape.

By the time got to Stonebrook's huge wooden gates, the snow had quit, though a cold wind was still blowing.

Michael looked at the city, "this place has grown a lot since I the last time I was here," he told Holly as they walked through the gates.

The main street now covered the stream that use to run straight through the middle of the city. Small shops and street vendors selling their wares to passersby now lined both sides. There was a surprising array of goods in the marketplace.

Stonebrook had a healthy trade with Cinnibar and traveling adventurers making their way south. Then of course there were the local tradesmen; farmers, and traveling salesmen which made it a bustling haven of activity.

Holly made her way into one of the clothing shops that had a beautiful robe displayed in the front window. Michael entered behind her, keeping an eye out for potential trouble.

The shopkeeper was a plump friendly

woman with round wire frame glasses resting on the tip of her nose. Her hair rolled into a tight bun, she appeared quite stern, yet greeted Holly warmly.

"Come in child; do come in out of the cold. My name is Mrs. Harkens. How may I be of service?"

"Pleasure to meet you; my name is Holly and this is Michael."

Michael turned and nodded at Mrs. Harkens with a smile, "pleased to meet you," he said before turning to look back out the windows overlooking the street outside.

"I bet you could use a new robe; couldn't you dear?" Mrs. Harkens asked, beaming at the prospect of a sale.

"Yes and also a pair of boots good for traveling, something warm and rugged."

When Michael overheard Holly's reply, he had to suppress a little laugh. If Mrs. Harkens only knew Holly the way he did, she would sell her the toughest boots she had in the store.

After a little while and a promise from Mrs. Harkens the robe alterations would be completed by tomorrow. They walked back outside onto the main street.

The wind picked up noticeably and the clouds grew dark again. Holly moved closer to Michael's side as they walked down the street. She was longing for the warmth of Garian's house, but not enough to stop shopping. She wanted to see what the other vendors offered. They wandered further on and ended up at the last cart, which looked interesting.

It was ran by an older man wearing a thick brown woolen cloak with a hood that obscured nearly everything about him; except his crystal blue eyes that glowed with an unnatural quality. His rugged traveling cart was piled high with a wide array of exotic looking items.

Michael fingered a sword that caught his attention. Holly asked the traveling salesman if he had any wands for sale. The salesman disappeared into the wagon for a moment, returning with a small leather bundle. He placed it before Holly on a small table, unfurled the leather and revealed a wand nearly sixteen inches long with a thick handle tapering down to a point. It was an ordinary looking wand as far as Michael could tell, but he didn't know much about magical things. He let Holly haggle out the details with Murt.

210

He was keeping an eye for trouble and
unable to fully enjoy his time out with Holly. He
always had a hard time relaxing whenever he was
in public, let alone the way things were now.
Then too, there was something about this 'Murt'
character that made him uneasy. He would not
look him in the eyes. Michael figured it was
because salesmen rarely do.

Holly and Murt finally agreed to a price,
she paid him and they headed back to Garian's.
By now the snow began to fall slowly again, but
by the time they reached Garian's, it was falling
steadily. They were glad to have a chance to get
out for a while, yet it was nice to be back inside
the comfortable home. Warmth slowly crept back
into their cold limbs. It was so relaxing they
dozed off while sitting on the couch in front of
the crackling fire.

In the middle of the night, Michael woke
up and stirred slowly, trying not to wake Holly
up. He got up and went to the bedroom to get a
blanket for her. When he walked back into the
living room; he paused to look how beautiful she
was lying there sleeping peacefully.

Michael walked over quietly to where she
lay and gently covered her. Still something kept

nagging him in the back of his mind about that street vendor. Maybe he was just overly worried; these where dangerous times.

Not long after he had dosed off beside Holly on the couch again. War cries and men yelling woke them. They jumped up and quickly ran to the front door. They opened the door and saw Stonebrook was under attack by a massive force of Scarious joined by bullyworgs.

He tried to get her to stay behind in the safety of Garian's house, yet she ran straight into battle behind him.

The gates were holding against the onslaught, but some of the enemy broke off and were now scaling the walls using long ladders. Michael ran for the ones trying to scale the walls, while Holly went at the ones ramming the gates.

Just as soon as she flew into action, they suddenly stopped and turned on her. That's when she got a sickening feeling in her stomach, realizing she and Michael had just walked right into an ambush. It wasn't Stonebrook they were after, but them.

The fake attack was used to draw them out of Garian's house. They knew, or where told they couldn't penetrate its defenses. This fueled her anger and now properly equipped with a wand; she bent down slightly and gripped the wand tightly. Holly began to chant her most powerful spell as the fierce beasts closed in around her. "Illumium Exploria," she chanted and again and then a third time, "ILLUMIUM EXPLOROIA!"

She worked feverishly before they were on top of her. They were so close, she could smell the stench of their reeking breath by the time she completed the spell. Glowing red lines encircled down the wand as her fury was unleashed and all hell broke loose.

Michael swung his mighty sword hard, catching a black devil trying to climb the ladder in front of him. It was dead before it hit the ground, yet something was wrong. Now they were turning all their focus on him and not the city. His thoughts quickly turned to Holly.

He looked toward the gates and saw a swarm of beasts closing in on her. He took off running as fast as he could in her direction, cutting down anything in his way, fearing he wouldn't make it in time. He couldn't see her for the devils and bullyworgs.

Suddenly an explosion of light and fire erupted from the center of them, sending beasts flying in all directions. Stunned for a split second by what he witnessed. He continued running toward Holly as new waves of beasts came running out of the forest to take up the fight.

When he reached her, she was still bent down and rose up to full height as he drew near. She was glistening with a reddish glow.

"I'm okay," she said in a low voice like someone else was speaking through her.

No time to discuss anything further, they were fighting for their lives again. Holly and Michael stood back to back. He focused on any creature that got close, while she took the distance ones. As the fight drew on, their hope seemed futile. Wave after wave crashed down upon them like a raging sea. Mercifully the archers on top of the walls cut many of them down as soon as they stepped into range, yet their numbers were overwhelming.

Michael was knocked to the ground by three Scarious and two bullyworgs. He fought to get free, bashing one with the hilt of his sword and kicked one. He punched the other trying desperately to get to his feet. Finally he regained his footing and realized Holly was nowhere in sight.

Anger; rage, and hatred exploded in him all at once. He planted his sword in the ground, lowered his head, and spoke in a pulsating echo.

"Father; father of my father, ancients of old, grant me the strength to slay my foes!"

His eyes gleamed with shear power when he pulled his father's sword from the earth. Now glowing pale white and extending around him as well. He charged his enemy with a ferocity born of hate and fueled by love, killing anything standing in his way. Blood ran freely staining the snow covered ground crimson red.

The ground shook like an earthquake was taking place beneath his feet. The creatures looked bewildered, yet Michael was unfazed and used the distraction to cut even more down.

The ground suddenly began to move in unexplained ways, rippling like waves of water, knocking his enemies off their feet. He struggled to maintain his balance. Seconds later he spotted the cause of it. Garian stood at the forest's edge, staff in hand. Now he had hope of finding Holly again.

The creatures, sensing defeat scattered in all directions, running for the cover and protection of the forest. The battle was over as fast as it had begun.

Once the enemy had fled, Garian made his way to Michael.

"Looks like they weren't playing fair," Garian said looking at all the corpses littering the ground.

"Did you see if they took Holly in your direction?" Michael asked breathlessly.

"They never came my way," Garian said grimly.

They searched the area for any signs, when they heard a muffled voice coming from their right near the tree line. Both approached cautiously.

They could see the corpses of three bullyworgs lying face down with arrows in their backs. The muffled voice was coming from underneath them.

Michael grabbed the one lying in the middle and rolled it over. And to his instant relief there laid Holly, very unhappy, but otherwise unhurt. He pulled her to her feet and hugged her so tightly it almost took her breath away.

"Easy; I was okay, but if you keep that up I won't be."

He loosened his grip little and she hugged

him back.

Garian cleared his throat.

"Oh," Michael said remembering they weren't alone.

"Holly; this is Garian," Michael said.

"Pleasure to finally meet you in person," Holly tried to smile.

"Pleasure's mine," Garian replied.

"We had better get back. It's still unsafe," Garian said and turned back toward the city.

Holly and Michael followed closely, looking back to make sure they weren't going to be attacked again.

Once back they began assisting the injured with Garian taking charge. He directed people where to take the wounded and bury the dead.

They quickly set up a make shift infirmary in one of the guard barracks. There were at least a couple dozen injured and almost as many dead.

Holly went to work on the injured right away. She was an amazing woman, Michael thought, watching her binding soldiers' wounds.

It was near midnight when they headed back to Garian's house. Now that the excitement was over, each was drained and ready for a good night's rest.

Garian was the first to speak. "You two make yourselves comfortable, while I make a final check of things. We'll have plenty of time to talk about the day's events in the morning after we've had a good night's sleep."

Both Michael and Holly were too tired to argue otherwise. With a thank you and goodnight, they were off to bed. One last thought went through Holly's mind before she fell asleep.

Her wand she just bought acted funny. She didn't know much about them, but she knew that most didn't glow when used. Magic was channeled from within a mage, so even without a wand or staff they can still use spells.

Wands; staffs, or artifacts, act to focus the mages' magical energy making the spells more powerful. Only rare ones have special properties themselves. Most simply serve as a vessel for the mage's power to flow through. Surely the merchant would have known it was much more than a simple wand.

Finally too tired to think, she gave into a fitful sleep. They slept late the next morning, comfortable in the thought of being safely behind the enchanted walls of Garian's home.

Holly woke first and quietly got up, taking

care not to wake Michael; he was resting so well.

She made her way from the bedroom, walking down the stone gray floor well-worn from years of use. Garian was already sitting in the living room on the couch in front of the fireplace. He was staring at the blazing fire. Holly could tell his mind was somewhere else.

"Good morning," she spoke at last, thinking it would be rude to stand there staring.

"Mornin'," Garian replied, half absentmindedly before turning to face her.

She could see Garian's eyes where cloudy, yet cleared to their usual blue within seconds. She knew he was digging deep into his memories trying to remember something. She had seen that same look before; a slight shiver went down her spine at the thought of it.

"Come; sit my dear," Garian said pointing to a nearby chair.

Garian had indeed been using his magical abilities to delve deep into his mind. Bringing up memories as though they were moving pictures; recalling every word, regardless of how long it had been. Many thoughts roamed through his mind.

Why was Soladar so intent on capturing

Holly? What about Michael? Did he simply want him out of the way so his plans wouldn't fail; killing him as he had his father?

All these questions and more were going through Garian's mind when he noticed Holly studying him. She had an air of confidence about her and a timeless beauty; like one before her.

Could it be? Garian thought, his mind racing back into the past again. He had known both of Adrelias' parents and knew Soladar had loved Ezmora deeply before his fall. Yet Ezmora fell in love with another.
That same unattainable love drove him to his doom. Could Soladar think Adrelia is his? The timing was right.

Chapter 11
Orb of Chaos

Holly studied Garian intently in the daylight streaming through the window. He looked much older than he did last night with deep thought lines on his brow. He had a full head of straight wispy silver gray hair and fine narrow eyebrows to match. However there was a subtle sense of strength to him. She could tell that, even though he was small in stature, just a little taller than her and almost as slim, he radiated a powerful magical presence.

"Sleep well?" Garian's voice sounded musical when he spoke, surprising her a little when she snapped back to reality, having been lost in thought herself.

"Yes quiet well, thank you," she replied.

"It seems Michael is, too," Garian's tone changing to a more fatherly one.

She could tell he was very fond of him.

"You must be hungry," he said getting up and heading into the kitchen.

"Care for a late breakfast?"

"I'm a little hungry," Holly confessed when her stomach made a grumbling noise at the thought of food.

She followed him to the kitchen, which was quite spacious considering he lived alone. He went to the cabinets above the white porcelain double bowl sink. He opened the old wooden doors and pulled out a mixing bowl. Then opened a small bin in the corner and took out a scoop of flour.

"Anything I can help with?" Holly asked.

"No need," he replied as he made a quick circular motion with his right hand in a causing a spoon to appear out of thin air and begin stirring the flour while he proceeded to add water.

"Comforts of magic," he added smiling as he turned to Holly and sat down at the table with her.

"It seems you and Michael have had a challenging journey; or so I hear," Garian said raising an eyebrow.

"Yes; a little," she said, curious how much he knew.

"Ah humility and beauty, a rare combination indeed," he said thoughtfully.

"Well the important thing is you're here now, in one piece, where you'll be safe."

Soon Michael joined the two, just as Garian was putting the finishing touches on breakfast. Holly stood and gave him a hug and a gentle kiss on his cheek. Soon they were eating the extremely good meal Garian had cooked.

"I think it's time you two learned more about Soladar," Garian began.

With those words Michael and Holly's attention were captured.

Garian continued, "In ancient times, a great battle took place. Long ago magic was divided into two schools. Those who practiced the white form called Lysetus and those who practiced the dark form called Noxerium.

The dark ones probed deeply into the dimly lit recesses long abandoned by the very ones who brought it into existence. Even its current practitioners know little of how; that even in its infancy the malevolent power eventually consumed anyone who used it.

They never realized its very source; its nature was to corrupt and destroy anything or anyone. The dark power neither cared; nor had any feelings whatsoever, as to who or what it hurt. The reason it exists is to destroy and one day unravel all that has been created. The dark power in doing so will recreate its own essence; which is complete destruction and chaos.

"Rumors abound about its nature and where it's fabled home lies. The best theory speaks of a place in the Neither Region. There lies the fabled resting place of a great Orb of Chaos floating in the middle of a huge black expanse of deserted lands.

There has been much conjecture and many wild tales about the place through the ages. Many think it lays north of the Great Barrier; the impenetrable wall at the edge of the world. It's rumored years ago the greatest of the white mages Soladar, actually made it through. His fate was never fully known; some say the Orb of Chaos consumed him upon crossing the barrier.

Others say he made the perilous journey across the black expanse to the center. There appeared a gaping chasm and in the middle a small island. Above floated the Orb, emanating all of its chaotic power in every direction.

"Soladar fought valiantly for days against it, yet all his power was not enough. He even invoked the power of the god Vehementer, the very source of the White Mages' power. However the Orb could not be destroyed.

He never understood the Orb of Chaos is neither good nor evil. It is what gives everyone and everything freewill; the freedom to choose what they want in life. He thought the Orb was the source of the black mages' power and why evil existed. There are three laws in the universe; good, evil, and neutrality, with the last one the least understood.

"The Orb changed Soladar into a raging lunatic who inhabits the Lair of Demens located inside the Citadel of Dolor. Little is known about the lair or the area it's located in, except what's been told by a few raving madmen; of which little has been deciphered.

Those who have been to the Citadel and returned have been changed from brave men into sheer lunatics. Current maps show its location far to the northeast of here in the Northern Wastes.

"The few maps that exist with any detail come from those who survived. They used their knowledge and made rough maps of the area. Current ones are mostly copies and some are outright forgeries, leading anyone who relies on them to certain death."

So much information, yet so few answers thought Holly after Garian finished speaking. It was hard to hide her aggravation. She had the feeling he knew far more than what he was willing to tell them and didn't know why. She didn't have any choice, she needed Garian's help and so far he had provided it.

One thing that began to stir in her mind, was Michael's past. Now that she'd thought about it; she only knew about his reputation as an incredible warrior who killed countless Scarious. She knew the reason behind Kara's death; still she didn't have all the pieces to the puzzle.

She would have to get word to Valkriss soon and find out if Arnette had come up with any information.

Then there was that damn Asuvalia woman. There was a missing link somewhere that tied Delwen and her together and she intended on finding out what it was.

She looked at Garian with questions of her own.

"How did you know we were coming?" she asked.

Holly was never one to beat around the bush and Garian could sense it.

"I have friends in many places, even as far away as Castle Lake; which was where I was, retrieving something," Garian answered, then continued.

"Whenever I am away, my enchantments protect my home from thievery, but they cannot tell me who's coming to visit. It was a Sapling who told me."

"But they usually hate humans, because of what we've done to their homelands. Why would one be so far from its home?" Holly asked surprised.

"Let's just say I've helped them a time or two and they keep tabs on things for me," Garian said with a wry smile.

"What's a sapling?" Michael asked bewildered.

This time it was Holly who answered.

"A Sapling is a devilish little creature that takes on a small human form with greenish skin when seen; although rarely. They have the ability to possess any living plant and use it. Saplings are neutral, concerning themselves with nature. They go about the forest and grasslands tending to their own business.

They are very fierce when angered and will disburse into nearby vegetation and make grass tangle the feet of their enemies or a tree limb to pound them into the ground or rip them to shreds. It's not known how many they are. They prefer to dwell in the wild lands, which for the most part are uninhabited by humans."

"Very knowledgeable my dear," Garian praised her knowledge.

"Let me put to rest any fears about my allegiance," he said and stood up.

"Appello," he spoke in a voice much younger and deeper than before.

The floor quivered a little and a staff came up through it like a little tree sprouting forth from the earth.

"Is that?" Holly sputtered.

"Yes dear, the very Earth Staff itself fashioned by the Terrenus; the ancient race of dwarves who love and faithfully served the earth goddess Dal'ya. In return for their undying loyalty, she granted them the opperite ore used for the cord that winds around the staff, found only in the deepest and hottest parts of the earth.

"The quartz crystal is the finest and purest one ever found and blessed by Dal'ya herself.

The willow wood came from a tender young tree growing beside the living waters in the far off lands beyond the Murky forest.

"At least that's one of the stories. The truest tale I know, is the one of the Keeper of Time and Fate. He was too powerful causing the other gods to become jealous. So they plotted and stole the Parca staff from the him and divided it into three and in doing so, created the Orb of Chaos which gave free will to mankind, thus ending the Keeper's control.

The earth staff went to Dal'ya, who then gave it to her faithful dwarves. Exuro the sun god gave his staff to his followers. Cerea, the moon goddess gave hers to her cult.

In reality they feared the Keeper would find out they had broken his staff into three and would not stop until he once again united it again.

"This was the downfall of Soladar, when he fought the Orb of Chaos. In all of his wisdom did not know the Orb could not be destroyed while the Parca Staff remained apart. Only when the three become one could the Orb be destroyed using it. Free will would end because the wielder of the staff would have control." Garian answered getting caught up in the story himself. He enjoyed epic tales.

"How did the dwarves lose the staff? Do they still exist? Wouldn't they want their staff back?" Holly asked excitedly.

"One question at a time," Garian said smiling.

"The Noxerium mages stole it; yes they still exist, and yes they want their staff back," Garian finished matter-of-factly.

Then he related the story of how they lost it.

"Long ago a mighty king built his castle on a large island in the middle of Castle Lake as a retreat and an impregnable fortress in time of war. Or so he thought, until the Mage War broke out. When he would not take their side, the Noxerium mages feared he would side with the Lysetus mages.

"They used the earth staff they had stolen from the dwarves and used its power for their own purposes. Surprised by how strong the king's defenses were. In the heat of the battle, the Noxerium mages, fearing defeat, invoked their most powerful spell using the earth staff to channel their energy.

"They sunk the island the king's castle was built on; thus defeating him. In their victory they lost the staff, because being used for evil; the staff buried itself deep within the earth, not to be seen again, until now.

"Is that what you used last night during the fight?" Michael asked remembering how the earth moved as if it were waves of water.

"Yes," Garian replied.

"And it's the reason behind my recent trip to Castle Lake. I finally found its location and went there after it," he finished.

Holly, who had been quietly thinking, spoke softly. "Soladar was looking for the earth staff too."

Garian smiled and then asked; "how did you know?"

"I was his prisoner for ten years. I learned a few things," she said biting her lip, not knowing how much to say.

"I know; he hopes to unite the three staffs once again, Tellus the Earth Staff, Noctila the Moon Staff, and Solaris the Sun Staff and rule everyone's destiny once he destroys the Orb of Chaos.

"With them united, no one would be able to oppose him. Each staff has incredible power on its own. However when all three are put together, they become the ultimate weapon," Garian finished grimly.

"Does Soladar have any of the other staffs?" Michael asked.

"I believe he has Solaris and maybe getting close to finding the location of Noctila," he answered in an ominous tone.

"Do you know where the Noctila Staff is?" Michael asked.

"It's hidden northwest of the Samaramoon forest in the Concubius Temple fiercely guarded by the moon cult Lunaris, forerunners to the Rune people.
We will have to take ship from Calumet to get there," Garian added.

Holly thought she saw him shutter slightly.

Michael knew a lot about Cinnibar, known for its wild cinnamon trees. On warm breezy days, you can smell soft hints of cinnamon drifting in the air.

Its commercial center was the Port of Calumet, located on the interior shore of the Saline Sea. The port itself lay at the head of a long wide inlet and lent great economic wealth to the city.

Ships came in laden with spices; fur, and exotic goods from all over the seven realms to trade in the open-air markets of Cinnibar. At least they might be able to see some of the sights Michael thought, not really relishing the idea of a sea voyage.

"Why can't we use magic to get there?" Holly spoke up.

"Unfortunately the island of Kemlah lies across the Saline Sea and has such dreaded enchantments that teleports of any kind will not work. The ice packs that surround the port of Kilar make it impossible to reach it in the winter and that's the only port in that forsaken place. We will have to wait until spring to travel to the port on the island. From there we will travel through the heart of Samaramoon Forest to reach the Concubius Temple," Garian finished in a foreboding voice.

They talked late into the day, making plans for their spring voyage and waiting for winter to release its icy grip and the new buds of spring to flower forth. Garian agreed to teach Holly all about white magic in the coming months.

Holly and Michael soon found themselves cuddled together on the old brown couch in front of the roaring fireplace. It was so mesmerizing to watch the flames dance in chorus to some unknown music.

Fire was intriguing to Holly; the pure unadulterated heat burned away all impurities, leaving behind the true essence. It represented flames of undying passion; of love searing its way into ones soul.

They lay on the couch late into the night enjoying each other's warm embrace. It was nice being intimate, she thought and dosed off into a blissful sleep.

The next morning Garian headed off to god knows where as he often did. Holly coaxed Michael into going with her to Mrs. Harkens shop to pick up her robe, hoping the alterations would not be forgotten in all the commotion of the attack.

They walked side by side through the thick iron-bound wooden gates. An uneasy air hung heavy over the city. People were hurrying to and from the local shops with worried looks. It was bad enough to be at the end of the Hallowed Month, but with the recent attack, many feared the last supply caravans coming up from Cinnibar would be disrupted.

Traders would not want to brave the hordes, along with superstitions of wandering spirits set free by phantom winds. On midnight began the first day of October, the Hallowed Month, which is the tenth month on the calendar.

A special night begins the month long event when the two worlds co-mingle. The spirits of the dead roam the land. The Keeper of Time and Fate open the curtains of heaven and flood the earth with untold horrors in retribution against the other gods.

Since ancient times, it has always been a time of unprecedented mystical events. Phantom winds rage across the land, taking on lives of their own, eerily whistling through the dark corridors of the forests.

It is said the winds sets the spirits free to roam the land. Michael's people have priest consecrate the tomes of their dead with holy water to keep them from being set free.

Chapter 12
Friends

They sat and ate in silence before Mick spoke.

"You sure you still want to go, Lucerna? You know you can still turn back," he said gingerly.

"How many times do I have to tell you Mick; I'm going with you all the way there and back. I'm not afraid of anything," she stated bravely.

He was more afraid of Lucerna's father finding them, than anything they might meet on their journey.

"Well if there's no talking you out of it, let's saddle up and get going. We have a long ride ahead of us," Mick said doing his best to tell himself everything would be okay and Mr. Riner wouldn't kill him if he found out.

They rode a little while before speaking again. Mick kept looking over his shoulder expecting to see Mr. Riner charging up behind him with a dozen guards. And haul him off to the dungeon or cut him down and bury him beside the road.

Lucerna could tell he was worried.

"Ahh Mick, cheer up. I told you, he won't even miss me. I heard him saying something about going out on field exercises with some of Sir Lawrence's units," Lucerna said cheerfully.

It made him feel a little better, at least they had a good head start on anyone coming from Lawrence. They would be hard pressed to catch them now.

"I was just making sure we're not being followed, that's all," Mick said trying to hide the real reason he kept looking back. He was never was a good liar. Lucerna didn't push the matter and instead changed the subject.

"So what did you think of this year's start to the Hallowed Month festivals?"

"Don't know, I was busting my ass in the tavern. I swear, every year it gets busier," Mick said grumpily.

"You're just mad you couldn't get out and look at all the pretty girls who come into town, aren't ya?" she teased, batting her eyelashes at him.

"Why Mick; am I not pretty enough for you?" now she was laying it on thick.

"I don't look at you like; you know, like that. Me and you are friends," Mick said his voice cracked when he said friends.

"Hum! Well you wouldn't know a good woman if you saw one; Micknia Trebelius!" she scowled angrily, her face turning three shades of red.

Oh hell, I've made her mad now, Mick thought.

"Lucerna you're pretty; very pretty. If you weren't my friend, I'd ask you out, but you are, and you know, friends can't ask other friends out; can they?" actually he wasn't sure what the hell he was talking about.

He just wanted to ride off like the wind and leave her there, before he said anything else that would make her more upset.

"What? Aren't you going to say anything?" Mick asked after a few minutes of silence.

"No," she replied.

"Oh great; now comes the silent treatment. I didn't do anything, Lucerna. Well fine, two can play that game. I'm going to give you the silent treatment, too!" Mick huffed.

"How do you like that? And that's the last thing I'm saying to you until you talk to me first," he finished.

They rode in silence for what seemed hours. The countryside was full of gently rolling hills. The road was well worn being the main route between Cinnibar and Lawrence.

Mick slowed and turned Jenny off to the side of the road a little ways and stopped. Lucerna followed, still silent. He got off Jenny and tied her to a low tree branch so she could graze a little. He dug through his saddle bag for something to eat. After finding something, he sat down on the ground and started to eat. Lucerna sat down in front of him looking expectantly.

"What? I can't read your mind. If you want something you will have to ask," Mick said boldly.

"Well at least I wasn't the first one to talk," Lucerna said smiling.

"Now if you don't mind, I'm starving and I'm thirsty," she said.

"Here you go," Mick said handing her a handful of dried beef and the canteen.

"Thanks."

"Welcome," Mick mumbled with a mouthful.

They ate and drank their fill before hitting the road again. It wasn't long before Lucerna started chatting nonstop about everything under the sun again. After thirty minutes Mick was beginning to wish she was still giving him the silent treatment.

Why do girls like to talk so much? And about the most mundane topics; what he said, she said, someone told them this, they told someone that. It was enough to drive a wooden man crazy.

He heard men talked about their wives in the tavern and now he understood what they were talking about. Women were certainly hard to figure out. Just when you thought you knew one; they up and change on you.

"According to the map Valkriss gave me, we should be coming up on a small village soon. He told me not to spend too much time in any place, 'get what I need and get out'," Mick said trying to mimic Valkriss, causing Lucerna to laugh and stop her endless babbling.

"You're getting better at your impressions of him."

"Sam's hell youngin,'" Mick said, trying out another phrase Valkriss said at least ten times a day.

"Oh that's my favorite," Lucerna giggled.

"You're pretty good at talking like him. God help you if he ever hears you making fun of him though. He'd skin you alive," she said laughing even harder.

"I'm not afraid of that old man," Mick said sticking his chest out, acting like the man she knew he wasn't.

"Sure sure, whatever you say," Lucerna looked over at him with a wink.

"I ain't scared of anything or anyone," Mick proclaimed, brandishing his short sword.

"Why are you so worried about my father then; big man?" Lucerna asked.

"Because he'll throw me in the dungeon, that's why! And I won't get out till I'm an old man. Have you seen that place? It's filthy and dark," he said and glanced over his shoulder again.

"Dad never let me go near that place, says it's no place for a lady. Ugg, I wish he'd just let me grow up," Lucerna said crossly.

Mick thought of telling her that she was certainly no lady and her father should let her see the dungeon, but was afraid it would start another fight.

"How much allowance money do you have?" Mick asked trying to get his mind off Mr. Riner.

He always made him nervous, even more so now that his sixteen year old daughter had run off with him to Sindara. He was going to die, no doubt about it. If the trip didn't kill him, Lucerna's father certainly would if they made it back.

"Forty two silver and fifteen coppers; why?"

"Just making sure we have enough in case I run low on money, that's all," Mick answered.

"I'll pay my own way. Just worry about yourself and we'll both be fine," Lucerna said sternly.

Damn, there she goes again, stubborn as a mule. The girl just doesn't know what's good for her. Let her have it her way and keep your mouth shut, he told himself.

"No worries here. It's a long trip that's all. We may want to stay a night or two at inns along the way if the weather turns bad. This time of year you never know what it's going to do from one day to the next," Mick said casually.

"That's true," Lucerna agreed.

Finally Mick thought, something she agrees with me on and smiled.

"Why are you smiling for?" Lucerna asked.

"Nothing; something funny Valkriss said one time. It's nothing," Mick said.

There was no way he was going to tell her what he was really thinking.

"If the ol' tight wad didn't give you enough money, we can share a room if you want," she said shyly.

"You know you want to get me alone. You want me," Mick said with a fake laugh.

"For that mister, you can sleep outside in the snow," Lucerna said with a sour look.

The sky grew darker as they rode. They met few travelers this time of year; most were already in whatever town or city they were going to for festivals.

With crops in, farmers stayed closed to home making ready for the long winter to come. Luckily for them, once they reached Cinnibar and began traveling the Old Coastal Road, snow shouldn't be much of a problem.

Warm air off the sea currents gave that region fairly good weather throughout most of the year. It only got bad for a couple of months in the dead of winter, or so Valkriss had told him.

"Mick; look up ahead," Lucerna told him, bringing him out of his thoughts.

Outlines of structures appeared in the distance.

"Damn, I forgot to tell you our story in case anyone asks. We're a young couple heading to Cinnibar to help our sick family. And once we're there, we'll use the same story and say we're traveling to Sindara," Mick said.

"But Mick; why not tell people were just going to Sindara from the start," Lucerna asked confused.

"Because from here, that would seem like too long of a journey for us. If we change our destination after we get to the next point, people will think were not traveling too far, get it?" Mick said confidently.

"Let me guess, you came up with that?" Lucerna asked.

"Yes I did, so what?" Mick rebutted.

"Well, if you ask me, I think we should tell people were sightseers from Odessa and just traveling around seeing the various Hallowed Month festivals. What do you think?" Lucerna asked.

What Mick wanted to say, was no one asked you, so keep your mouth shut and do what you're told. This was his mission and you invited yourself on it, but in the end he didn't.

"Sounds good, Lucerna. After all we don't want people knowing our final destination," Mick said, putting on his best smile.

"Why thank you Mick. For a minute I thought you would be pig-headed and say something mean," Lucerna said in a genuinely warm voice, which made him feel like a heel for thinking what he did.

"You're welcome; now when we get up here, let's watch our backs, okay? Did you bring a weapon?" He asked in a lower voice.

"Of course, never leave home without it," she smiled and lifted her cloak revealing a shiny handle of her favorite raptor blade. It was a special sword her father presented to her on her fourteenth birthday.

They had fought many pretend battles with it and she beat him in every one. It's a wonder she hadn't accidently cut his throat.

"Let's keep our head down, get what we need, and move on. And remember, tell no one what were really doing," Mick said seriously.

"Okay Mick, will you please for all that is good stop worrying and trust me? You've known me long enough by now, surely," Lucerna said getting aggravated.

"You're right; I'm sorry Lucerna. I really want to show Valkriss I can be trusted, and not getting us killed would be nice too," Mick said meekly.

"I'm sorry; I'll be good, I promise. I won't cause any trouble."

"Okay," he said.

They were close enough now to see the several of the buildings in the village. It wasn't a large one; still this would be the first place he ever visited outside Lawrence.

Axum was the name of it on his map. It was small; if you rode through too fast, you would almost miss it. In another day's ride from there, they would be in Bentree, leaving them two days ride to Cinnibar with no towns in between.

At least there was a general store; livery, and a few other shops. It would suffice to get the supplies they needed. They rode up to the general store side-by-side and tied their horses up to the old wood post in front. Many of the buildings were gray stone. The rest were wood frame structures like the store.

Lucerna and Mick glanced at each other briefly, took a deep breath, and walked into the store. There wasn't anyone in there when they went in. It was tended to by a clean shaven older gentleman. He wore a white long sleeve shirt under a funny little black vest and tie with a black semi-circle hat. He even had black pants on. This guy must like black, Mick thought.

The store was well stocked with a variety of items, except for one thing; a larger tent, Mick thought grumpily looking around. It didn't take them long to get what they needed and hit the road again.

The clerk was very helpful, even pleasant, though he was funny dressed. It was exciting for Mick to meet new people from different places. After packing their goods in their saddle bags, they rode out without so much as a strange look from anyone. Mick hoped the rest of the trip was as easy as this; maybe they would pull it off after all.

"Did we do okay?" Lucerna asked in a low voice when they neared the edge of town.

"Yes, you did fine," Mick congratulated her.

"You did good too," she smiled at him. It always made him feel good whenever Lucerna said good things to him. He didn't know why he craved her approval so much. He wanted to prove himself more and more to her lately, to show her how strong he was or how good he was at something. It really didn't matter what it was.

A short ways out of Axum, the weather turned for the worst. The cold rain started as a drizzle at first, then grew steadier. They pulled their cloaks around them to shield them from the soaking rain.

"Mick, we have to get out of this rain. We'll catch our death," Lucerna told him through chattering teeth.

"I see a small stand of pines up ahead. We'll set up camp under them. It'll help keep some of the rain off us," Mick felt the numbing coldness to.

There weren't many, a half dozen or so white pines, but they were large and would provide ample room under them. After struggling with the tent, Mick finally had it up. Lucerna unsaddled the horses and put blankets over them to keep them warm.

"I don't think I can get a fire going, Lucerna. Everything's too wet, even with my flint and iron," Mick said grimly.

"It's okay," she said lightly.

"What do you mean; 'it's okay?' It's not okay; we need to dry off and get warm," Mick spouted angrily.

"If you would give me a minute, you impatient man. I will show you what I mean," she snapped back.

"Here let me show you; make yourself useful and get some wood," she ordered.

Mick gathered up as much deadfall as he could and broke some of the lower branches off the surrounding pines.

"Now watch this," she said, huddling down over the firewood she heaped together and poured a thick blue liquid over it from a small metal flask.

"Now strike your flint and iron over it and watch," she told Mick.

He did as instructed and to his amazement; it lit on fire the instant the sparks flew off the flint.

"Wow; what it that stuff?"

"It's called Ambustio. I got it off one of the street vendors in town; like it?"

"Love it," he said cheerfully.

"They told me it would make a fire even in the wettest conditions. Guess they were right. I haven't had a chance to try it out until now. It's too expensive to play with. This flask cost me a half of a week's allowance," Lucerna said recapping the flask and stowing it away inside her cloak.

"Well I'm glad you brought it. It's certainly handy to have at a time like this," Mick said, thankful for the warmth coming from the blazing fire's flickering blue flames, which were beginning to turn bright red.

"Here, let's put more wood on it, so it won't go out," he told her.

The large white pines shielded them from much of the cold rain, yet the sky didn't look promising.

"You hungry?" Lucerna asked.

"Sure, I'm always hungry," he replied.

"Here you go," she said, when Mick reached out his hand; he saw she had his favorite food.

"Oh thank you! Valkriss didn't pack any, and besides I doubt he would even know what my favorite is," Mick told her earnestly.

"You're quite welcome; enjoy," she said tenderly.

That's the way Lucerna had always been to him. She understood him when no one else did and knew everything about him.

Well except one thing, which he would never in a million years tell her. He was a virgin. He always acted like he had been with several girls. He didn't know if she believed him or just played along so she didn't hurt his feelings. Either way, he didn't care. He avoided the subject of sex at all costs with anyone, but most importantly her.

She would certainly laugh at him if she knew he was a virgin. Over the summer, he had tried to kiss a girl in the alley behind the tavern, which was a disaster of epic proportions. He completely missed her mouth and kissed her forehead, which made the girl laugh at him.

He was so embarrassed, he ran into the tavern and avoided her for two weeks. She tried to tell him it was okay, but things weren't the same with them after that. Needless to say Lucerna knew none of this and never would, if he had anything to do with it.

"Mick what are you so lost in thought about?" Lucerna asked.

Apparently she had been watching him intently for the last few minutes while he ate his barbequed turkey jerky.

"What? Who me? Nothing just trying to remember everything Valkriss told me that's all," he said completely lying.t.

These damn feelings he kept having toward Lucerna weren't helping matters any either. It was becoming more and more difficult to control himself around her. He hoped he wouldn't do anything embarrassing.

All he needed was for her to find out how unskilled he was with women. Holy Honos he would have a heart attack if she ever saw his trousers when he got turned on; which was happening every damn hour. Oh great now that he was thinking about it, he was getting turned on again.

"Well I'm dry now. I'm going to turn in for the night," another lie, but he had to get away from her before she found out what was really wrong with him.

"I'll be in, in a minute," she said distracted.

He climbed into the small dry tent; spread out the blankets and laid his cloak aside to dry. The inside of the tent grew darker as night came. He listened to the pitter patter of tiny rain drops hitting the tent and fell into a troubled sleep.

Meanwhile Lucerna was caught up in her own thoughts. She had started to think of Mick in a different way. He was no longer a scruffy twelve year old who she had pretend sword fights and conquer the castle with. He was becoming a man. Other boys around town had asked her out, but she always said no. They never interested her in the least, not like Mick did.

He knew almost everything about her. She sat by the fire a long while wondering about him.

Had he ever been kissed? Was he a virgin, like her? Would he want to be her boyfriend and not just a 'friend'?

The trip would give her an opportunity to find out some answers she thought sleepily. She made sure the fire was out and crawled into the tent beside Mick, who was fast asleep. She slowly got under the blankets trying her best not to wake him.

God he felt so hot lying next to her. She started off with her back to him, then rolled over gently and slid her arm over him and snuggled close.

It felt so good, laying there next to him. She buried her face between his shoulder blades. He smelled good too; little did she know he managed to buy some cologne at the general store in Axum. She tried not to move much, so she wouldn't wake him. This would be a good trip indeed; closed her eyes and went to sleep smiling.

"Mick," Lucerna whispered.

"Mick," she whispered again, this time shaking him gently.

"What do you want?" Mick asked irritated by being woken up.

"I hear something outside," she said her voice barely above a whisper.

"Can't be much it would spook the horses. Now go back to sleep; we need to get an early start tomorrow and make up the time we lost today," Mick said and stopped talking, when he heard something too.

"See I told you; there's something out there. Get your sword."

"Right here with me. Stay inside and let me deal with it. If anything happens, get the scroll out of my pack, and follow the directions it has with it. Whatever you do don't open the scroll. Just do what the letter says; okay?" Mick told her deadly serious.

"There's no way I'm going to let you go out there without me. We're in this together; remember?" Lucerna said stubbornly.

"Lucerna, one of us must complete the mission. It has to get done. Now let me get out there and find out what it is before it jumps both of us," Mick said putting his cloak on and crawling out of the tent.

"Okay, be careful," she said.

Yet she had no intention of letting him get his fool self-killed trying to play the hero. She could fight better than he could any day of the week. She waited for him to get outside and then followed right out behind him.

"Damn it girl, I swear you won't do a blasted thing I tell you," Mick glared.

"Shhh, whatever it is, it's coming from over there," she said pointing to the right.

"Don't worry about me I'll stay behind you. Now go, before it gets us."

"Okay, be quiet; let's go," Mick said walking slowly to the right of the tent.

They could hear growling coming over a small hill in front of them. It sounded like something fighting and rolling around in the forest. Mick's heart was beating so hard against his chest it nearly drown out all other sounds. He felt Lucerna's hand on the small of his back reassuring him, which gave him the courage he needed to take another step forward.

Chapter 13
A What You Say?

When they got back to Garian's house Holly heard a noise coming from beside it. She immediately drew her wand. Michael's sword was already in hand.

"What do you think it is?" Holly whispered.

"Don't know, let's see," he answered.

They made their way slowly around the house and saw a stack of hay quivering.

"Come out of there, whoever you are," Michael said sensing little danger.

Still no one came out, but the haystack started shaking a little more vigorously.

"Okay, I'm going to give you till the count of three to come out of there; one," was as far as he got.

"Please, please no hurt Livies! I mean you no harm! Ravis is hurt. We need help. Please, please no hurt Livies," she continued in a little high-pitched, animated voice.

"Easy there little one; we won't hurt you, will we Holly?" Michael said gently.

"No we won't," Holly repeated.

The little creature which was less than three feet tall ran over and grabbed Michael's right leg in a death grip.

"Easy now; what's wrong?" Michael asked.

"My wolf is hurt; them mean ol' beasties hurt him last night out in the forest," Livies squeaked out in a little girlish voice, making them pity her.

"Is he under the hay Livies?" Holly asked.

"Yes yes, he's under there. I keeping him warm till I find help. Will you big on's help?" Livies asked with a pouty look.

"Will he bite?" Holly asked; she had never met a nice wolf.

"No no, Ravis never bites unless Livies tells him too," Livies said reassuringly.

Holly approached the hay stack and moved the hay off Ravis.

"There there boy; you'll be fine, just need to have a look and see how bad you're hurt," Holly spoke softly.

She didn't know if he could understand her or not. All she hoped was not to get bit while trying to doctor him. Yet somehow when she looked into Ravis' big brown eyes, she knew he understood.

"I told him you are going to help and not bite you," Livies chimed in confidently, her voice having a light musical quality to it.

"How did you tell him Livies? You didn't say anything out loud."

"Silly big on's," Livies said pointing to her little dark brown colored head.

"Up here silly, with my mind."

Holly nodded, unsure what to say.

"Let me see how bad he's hurt." She bent over Ravis and saw two large wounds running down the wolf's left side. They were coated with some sort of sticky brown substance that had got mixed in with all the blood.

"What's the stuff on his wounds, Livies?" Holly asked as she gently touched it.

"Gamuca."

"What in the world is Gamuca?" Holly asked looking puzzled.

"It's mixtures of mushroom healing spores, why of course," Livies answered, as if everyone in the world should know what Gamuca was.

"We need to get him inside. Will you help me carry him?" Holly asked Michael.

"Oh great, leave the hard stuff up to me," Michael grimaced.

Livies, mistaking the look as a refusal, started begging again.

"Please; please help Livies! Ravis hurt so bad. Oh Livies should have never talked Ravis into the trip, Livies sorry, please; please help. Wait, I know, I know, I pay you, I have…" She started looking through her little bag, pulling all its content out, consisting of half eaten mushrooms and child-size clothes.

"No, no little one, we don't need any payment. I was only kidding. Here, I'll carry Ravis in," Michael told Livies softly.

"Put your things up Livies. There's no need."

He put away his sword; reached down, placed both arms under Ravis, and lifted him up as gently as he could. Ravis howled in pain.

"It's okay, boy. Take it easy. We'll get you better in no time. You have the best healer in the realm. Trust me, I know from personal experience," Michael said, smiling at Holly.

He carried Ravis into Garian's house and placed him on the thick rug in front of the fireplace. Holly went to find medical supplies she could use. Unable to find much, she returned to the living room.

"I have to go to town and get a few things to bandage him up. I can't find any of Garian's remedies. I'll be back as fast as I can; meanwhile you two make sure he's comfortable till I return," Holly ordered and covered Ravis with a blanket.

"There there boy, don't worry. I'll be back soon," she said softly stroking him on top of his head, feeling his soft grey fur.

Michael had no idea what to do for Ravis or for that matter how to entertain Livies, so he decided to just talk. She seemed to like that anyway, sitting over there on the rug chattering away beside Ravis.

"So; Livies," he hesitated, "I don't believe I've ever come across your kind before," Michael said trying not to be awkward.

"Livies is a Kruckle," she said proudly in her squeaky voice, turning around to face him.

"Exactly what is a Knuckle?"

"No no big on'; I'm a Kruckle, not knuckle. You calling me names? You big ol' meanie," Livies said, crossing her arms with a big frown on her face.

"Sorry Livies I meant to say Kruckle, no offense," Michael apologized quickly.

It was difficult to understand her, because she talked so fast with a squeaky high pitch voice.

"Livies be right back, big on'," And she was at the front door before Michael knew it.

"Where you goin'?" Michael called after her.

"Be back," was the last thing Michael heard Livies say as the front door closed.

In less than a minute, she was coming back through the door dragging what looked to be a small horse saddle and a bag slung over her shoulder.

"Well are you just going to stand there, or are you going to help Livies, big on'," she said sounding winded.

"Sure," Michael walked over; stooped down, picked up the little saddle, and carried it over to where Ravis was laying. It felt like leather, but much lighter, having an organic feel to it. It even had two extremely small stirrups for tiny feet and a saddle horn with a billet strap so it could be used on the wolf, he guessed.

Livies was already sitting by Ravis eating; having dug out some mushrooms which she was enjoying rather happily.

"So Livies back to what we were talking about," Michael began again, determined to learn more about this fascinating little creature.

"What was that big one?" Livies chirped out, talking with a mouth full.

Not only are they fast Michael thought, they're forgetful too.

"Where are you from?" he asked.

"Goshen," Livies answered.

"And where's that?" Michael asked a little impatiently.

Livies stood up and shoved another piece of dark mushroom in her mouth. She put down her little bag and walked over to where he was now sitting on the couch.

"Look big on', the less you know, the better off you'll be," she said looking intently into his eyes.

He could tell she was being sincere.

"You can call me Michael, Livies. I prefer it to 'big on' okay? You can tell me about what kind of trouble you're in. Like you said I'm a 'big on,' and I can take care of myself; trust me Livies," he stated confidently.

Livies climbed up on the couch and sat down close to him. She placed her little hands in her lap and hung her head.

"Livies talked Ravis into coming here from our home; it's on the island of Kemlah. That's where Goshen is. We stole away on the last ship out of the port of Kilar before winter set in and have our adventure.

"Ravis my wolf is from the Sitka Wolf Clan of Samaramoon forest. We freed them from the mean ol' culties and they serve us now. We protect them and treat them good in return. Except for Livies; Livies is mean to her Ravis, made him come so far from home. He told me we shouldn't, but Livies wouldn't listen to him," she managed to say before she started crying.

"There there little one, it's okay don't cry," Michael placed his hand on her tiny shoulder and patted it gently.

He was never good at dealing with anyone crying, especially girls.

Livies stifled. "It's okay, big on'. You don't have to call me 'little one'. You can call me Livies," she attempted to dry her tears on Michael's shirt sleeve, which he didn't mind until she blew her nose on it.

Holly came through the front door and saw Livies wiping her eyes.

"What did you do to her Michael? Why's she crying? You better stop upsetting our little guest here," Holly said with a very disapproving look.

"What? Me? I didn't do anything; I swear," Michael said, caught off guard by her accusations.

"Livies was just telling me about where she's from, that's all. I didn't do anything."

"Ok then I believe you I guess, but I'm keeping an eye on you mister," Holly said playfully.

"Now, get over here and help me get Ravis bandaged up," she sternly ordered.

Michael lifted Ravis as easy as he could, while Holly took the dressing and wrapped his ribcage.

"There that should do for now. I got a few other things that will help as well," Holly said as she went into the kitchen, followed by Michael and Livies.

She unloaded the rest of the supplies she purchased in town onto the table.

"Now let's see," she mumbled to herself quietly, while crushing up what looked like green moss into a large bowl and adding a thick white liquid to it.

"Just glad I'm not the one you're giving that to. It smells awful," Michael said jokingly.

"And who's to say I didn't while we were at the cottage dear," Holly winked.

"Oh, you are evil," Michael said smiling.

"Healed you didn't I," Holly shot back.

"Can't argue with that."

"Then don't, if you know what's good for you. You two get out of here, and let me work, will you? Or I'll never get anything done."

"You don't have to tell me twice. Let's go Livies," Michael said, and they went back into the living room and sat on the couch.

Livies was endless entertainment, showing him all sorts of neat little tricks. He learned a lot when she didn't talk too fast and he could actually understand her.

Holly reappeared from the kitchen carrying a bowl half filled with the concoction she made.

"Now, let's see if Ravis will eat any," Holly said and walked over to where he lay in front of the fireplace.

"Here boy, eat. It will help you get better," she said gently, holding the bowl down low in front of his mouth.

He looked up at Holly then the bowl and snarled his nose at it.

"Livies, tell him that he has to eat this. It will help," Holly said without turning around.

Livies didn't say anything out loud; however her little brow furrowed and she wagged her little index finger at Ravis.

"Okay; he'll eat now or he better if he knows what's good for him," Livies squeaked.

With that Ravis turned his head back to the bowl and began to eat, half snarling his nose in between bites.

Holly almost felt bad for the poor wolf, yet she knew that the Silverberry Licor would heal his internal damage and set him on the mend.

"Now we can rest Livies, I'll check on him through the night. He'll be fine,"

Holly said pulling the empty bowl away from Ravis.

"If you say so, big on'," Livies said satisfied.

"You can call me Holly, if you like."

"Okay big on'."

"It's getting late Livies," Holly continued.

"Do you want to sleep on the couch? I don't know if Garian has another guess room. He's gone off somewhere."

"No no, I Sleep with Ravis. You two big on's go on," Livies said.

"If you need anything, we're just down the hall, first door on the right. The bathroom is down the same hall first door of the left," Holly instructed.

"Livies just fine; I find stuff, no worries, night," Livies said and got out her little blanket and curled up beside Ravis.

"Goodnight," Holly and Michael said in unison.

They turned and walked down the hallway to their room.

"Think we better leave the door open in case she needs anything?" Holly asked.

"Yeah, probably a good idea," Michael answered taking off his shirt and climbing into bed.

"Certainly been an interesting day," he added and was fast asleep as soon as his head hit the soft pillow.

"It was," Holly said as she climbed into bed only to find him already asleep.

She reached over and kissed him gently.

"Sweet dreams," she whispered and went to sleep.

She was up several times throughout the night checking on Ravis to make sure he was doing well. She knew he had broken ribs and was bleeding internally.

Yet she didn't say anything to poor little Livies for fear she would get too upset. Thankfully Ravis seemed to be responding well to the Silverberry treatment and with any luck would pull through just fine.

Instead of going back to bed, Holly retrieved a blanket from the closet in the hallway and got comfortable on the couch. She didn't want to wake Michael; he was a light sleeper.

Michael stirred early and walked into the living room where Holly was asleep on the couch and Livies was curled up beside Ravis.

"Morning, big on'," Livies said.

"I'm sorry if I woke you Livies," Michael apologized.

"Why don't you call me Michael, Livies? It sounds better than big on'."

"Ok, it's just Livies don't trust too many big on's. Look what they done to my poor ol' Ravis," Livies said in her little girlish tone.

"Well I promise you Livies, we're not anything like those other big ones. You can trust us," Michael said reassuringly.

"Well okay, if you say so, Mickall, Michelle...Mitchel," Livies said trying her best to pronounce Michael right.

"It's okay, you can call me Mitchel; just don't call me Michelle," Michael said smiling.

Holly would have a field day if she heard Livies calling him Michelle. He would never live it down.

"You won't get mad at Livies if I forget and call you big on', will you Mitchel?" she squeaked.

"Not at all little one," Michael said softly.

"Don't patronize me, you big ol' mean on'; name is Livies, not 'little one', got it?" she said looking serious.

"I'm sorry Livies," Michael said apologetically.

Then she rolled over laughing in a little fit of high pitch giggles.

"I made a funny; I made a funny. It's okay, if you call me 'little one.' I don't care. Fooled you didn't I; you thought Livies was mad," she said laughing again.

"What are you two going on about this early in the morning?" Holly asked with one eye open looking at them.

"Uh oh Livies, we did it now. We woke up the other big on'," Michael said.

"Sorry dear, we didn't mean to wake you. Would you like to go lay down in the bedroom?" Michael asked.

"No I'm good, I got some sleep last night," she said yawning and sat up on the couch stretching her arms.

"How's Ravis doing this morning?" Holly asked as she walked over to where he was laying, apparently asleep.

His breathing was less labored than it had been through the night. Livies put her tiny hand on his shoulder and gently caressed him.

"Is he okay? He won't talk to me," Livies looked extremely worried.

"He's fine Livies. He's just sleeping. The medicine I gave him will make him sleep so he can get better," Holly told Livies smiling, putting on her best face so she didn't worry the small creature.

"If you say so Olly," Livies said.

"Why thank you Livies; you called me by my name instead of big on'," Holly said surprised.

"You help Ravis; you a good big on', Olly," Livies sat down next to Ravis and started looking through her little brown bag.

"What are you looking for?" Michael asked.

"Livies hungry," she said bringing out what looked like an orange mushroom of some kind.

"What kind of food is that?" Holly asked.

She was always interested in learning about things she had never seen before.

"It's Luteus mushroom, good vitamins. Livies doesn't have any of her good ones left," she said and took a bite of the orange mushroom.

"May I have a piece Livies?" Holly asked politely.

"Yep, but big on's seldom like our food," she said and broke off a piece and handed it to her.

Holly held it up to her nose, it smelled like citrus. Then put it in her mouth and rolled it around with her tongue before chewing it up. It tasted nothing like what it smelled however.

"Livies told you," she giggled.

Holly's eyes watered. It didn't taste too bad; however the strong cinnamon and clove flavor made it bitter and hot.

"Excuse me a minute," Holly said and made her way to the kitchen for a glass of cold water.

Livies rolled on the floor holding her stomach giggling.

"Whew; I'll have to think twice before I try anything else Livies has," Holly said.

"Would you like some regular food, dear?" Michael asked making his way over to the cabinets.

"That would be wonderful. I've had my fill of mushrooms for the morning," Holly said crossly.

"Let's see," Michael said looking through the pantry.

"Ah, here we go," he said grabbing the honey, bread, jam, and trying to get the milk all at once.

"You're going to drop it; here let me help you," Holly said taking the bread and honey out of his hands.

"Livies, would you like anything to eat?" Holly asked.

"Have any black truffles? Livies loves them. Yes she does."

"No dear I'm sorry we don't have any. They're hard to come by. When I go out later, I'll see if I can find some at the market, okay?" Holly said in an upbeat voice.

That made Livies smile.

"Livies has payment, she does," she said and went to get her bag from the living room and joined Holly and Michael at the table, which she could barely see over.

"Mitchel, look at what I got," Livies squeaked excitedly.

Holly looked over at Michael. "I didn't know you changed your name, Mitchel is it?" she said with a smile.

"It's a long story," Michael said.

"Look big on', look," Livies said holding up some kind of thin brown leathery cloth.

"What's that Livies?" Holly asked.

"Tella Cloth; it's what we buy things with," Livies said as she eyed the piece like she was appraising it.

"If you get Livies some black truffles, I give you this piece. If they're real good, Livies may give you more."

Neither Holly nor Michael had any idea what Tella Cloth was, or if it had any value whatsoever to anyone other than to a Kruckle.

"Livies, I'll do my best to get you some black truffles," Holly said while she sat at the table eating breakfast.

"Oh that would make Livies very happy; very happy indeed."

After they finished breakfast, Holly made one more check on Ravis. Then headed to town; promising Livies that she would try her hardest to get her some black truffles.

"You two have fun," Holly said as she closed the door.

Great Michael thought, stuck in the house again. There were so many things he needed to be doing, for one finding out information on what was going on.

Garian left the day before without saying where he was going or how long he'd be gone. One thing about Garian he kept his business to himself and which suited Michael just fine.

However he hated being the last one to know and still could not fully trust magic.

He had to admit staying at Garian's was nice, with the magical enchantments doing the dishes and providing hot baths without having to heat water. Or for that matter carrying wood for the fire, which was one job he hated.

"So Livies, do you have a middle name or last one; or is it just Livies?" he asked as they returned to sit on the couch.

"Just Livies, that's all, Mitchel," she answered.

"I know you want to be called Livies, but do you have a last name?" Michael asked gently.

"If I can trust you; I'll tell you, but you have to promise to only call me Livies?"

"I promise," Michael said earnestly.

"It's Avaina Le'laya Livies Trellis. Where I come from we all have four names, but we pick which one we like to be called. You call me Livies okay," she said.

"Okay, Livies it is," Michael said.

"How old are you?" He asked.

"I'm one hundred fifty nine years old," Livies said proudly.

"I'll be one hundred and sixty soon," she smiled.

"Wow; Livies you are old," Michael said in amazement.

"I know; Livies will be sixteen in human years next month."

"What do you mean, Livies?" Michael asked confused.

"To Kruckles, one human year equals ten of ours," she answered.

"Oh I see; there for a minute I thought you were really old," Michael said amused.

Then her thoughts turned back to her wolf.

"You think my Ravis will get better, Mitchel?" Livies asked in a sorrowful high pitch tone.

"Father will be so mad at Livies," she started to cry little tan colored tears that ran down her smooth dark brown cheeks, which were beginning to turn burnt orange.

"There there Livies; Ravis will be fine and we'll see to it, that you both get home. We just have to wait until spring so we can get a ship to Kemlah. You're very lucky, little one. We were going there anyway," Michael finished trying to smile to cheer her up, which apparently was helping.

Her little eyes dried and she brighten and scurried closer to Michael and leaned her head on him. He lifted his arm and gently hugged her as she sat there quietly humming to herself. After a few minutes Michael looked down; she was asleep, still humming. He grew drowsy and nodded off, listening to the sound of her humming.

Holly walked into the living room and found them asleep on the couch. They looked so cute, Michael with his arm around Livies who was snuggled beside him.

She crept into the kitchen and unloaded the supplies. She had picked up more food and luckily had found a couple black truffles in

Strathbane's Apothecary where she had bought the Silverberry.

For a small city, Stonebrook had a great selection of everything a person needed. She would have to remember Strathbane's from now on. The owner had been very nice and helpful. Holly fixed another bowl of Silverberry Licor and hoped she could get Ravis to eat it without waking Livies for help.

"Here you go boy; come on. Wake up and eat," she urged gently, stroking his head with her right hand, holding the bowl in her left. He stirred a little and opened his eyes.

He looked up at Holly and she could swear he knew she was trying to help him. "Ravis, you're one smart wolf."

He put his nose to the bowl, smelled, and then turned his nose up at it.

"I know it doesn't smell good, but you have to eat it. It will help you. I promise. I'll get you a big fat juicy steak when you're feeling better, okay?" Holly told him smiling.

With that Ravis put his nose back down to the bowl and began to eat.

"Good boy, that's it, eat it all," Holly encouraged.

"Ravis, you're awake," said an unmistakable squeaky voice behind Holly.

Within a second, Livies was standing at his head, stroking his ears with her small hands.

"You do? That's good. I will," Livies said.

"What's that Livies?" Holly asked.

"Ravis says he likes you and tells you thanks," Livies said.

"Tell him he is very welcome Livies. He's going to be fine. The worst is over now. He'll be back to his old self before you know it."

As soon as Livies heard that, she started doing a strange little dance waving her arms in the air and going around in circles, saying something Holly couldn't understand.

The commotion woke up Michael. He started laughing as soon as he saw Livies dancing.

"Someone's happy; I take it Ravis is doing better," he said turning his neck to get the stiffness out.

"Holly, I think we need to make you a veterinarian," Michael said light-heartedly.

"Yep, I could take care of men and dogs, since they are the same species," Holly broke out into laughter.

It was nice to see her cheerful.

"Livies don't get it. Men walk on two legs, and dogs walk on four. How are they the same species?" Livies asked with honest sincerity, causing both of them to laugh even harder.

"Just an expression; that's all Livies," Holly said after she quit laughing.

Then she remembered the surprise she got for Livies and went into the kitchen to get it.

"Guess what I found while I was shopping in town, Livies?" Holly asked teasingly.

"What, what, Livies loves surprises. Loves them, loves them. What'd you get Livies?" She rambled so fast she was barely audible, dancing from side to side.

Holly opened her hand and in the blink of an eye. Livies sprang from where she was by Ravis and was at Holly's feet with her little hands out begging.

"Please; Olly a good big on', give Livies the black truffles; please," Livies begged.

"Okay okay; here ya go," Holly said beaming and reached them to her; at which point Livies went into a fit of some kind.

"Oh these Livies favorite; most favorite in the whole world. Ooo they so good, so good," she said dancing around holding the mushrooms up in the air.

The next second she was sitting by Ravis appraising the truffles like a jeweler appraising precious gemstones. She looked at each of them closely and then put each one up to her nose and smelled it.

Holly had eaten black truffles before and knew they were good, but never seen someone go this crazy over them. Yet seeing Livies enjoy them so much made her happy.

Livies took a small bite off one. "Hmm, umm, solid grade two," she mumbled and took another bite.

"Yep grade two; no doubt about it. Not bad; not bad at all! Thank you Olly. You made Livies very happy."

"You're very welcome, Livies. I'm glad you're enjoying them."

"Oh yes, oh yes," Livies said and put one of the truffles into her pouch for later.

"What's that Ravis? Now you be a good boy. Livies likes him and that's all that counts," she told him out loud.

"Likes who Livies?" Michael asked.

"Well, don't get mad Mitchel, but Ravis don't like you. He likes Olly though," Livies answered.

"What do you mean he doesn't like me? Did I do something to make him mad at me? If so I'm sorry," Michael apologized. He didn't want Livies crying again.

"No no Mitchel. Ravis is a male wolf. They like protecting us girls' better, that's all. If he was a girl wolf, then she would like you. Girl wolves like protecting boys, nothing personal," Livies said like it was the most logical thing in the world; however it made no sense at all to Michael.

Just go with it he told himself, although something about an idea of a large male wolf not liking him and being within arms distance didn't seem right.

"Ok Livies I'll take your word for it. Just as long as he doesn't bite me," Michael told her.

"No Ravis, you can't. No means No!" Livies told him.

"Livies; why are you telling Ravis no?" this time it was Holly who asked.

"Nothing," Livies answered.

"Livies what was it?" Holly asked again sternly.

"Ravis was asking if he could just bite Mitchel one time, but I told him no. No worries big on's. Ravis does what Livies says; okay?" she said confidently.

"If you say so Livies," Michael said with a worried look.

Chapter 14
A Sapling and a Wolf

It was one thing to play storming the castle or sword fighting with someone you knew wouldn't hurt you, but it was a whole other story to face the unknown.

"We have to surprise it; stay here while I sneak around the bank and jump it. Run if you have too," Mick whispered to her.

"Mick I told you..." was all she got out before he threw up his hand and snuck around the small earthen bank in front of them.

"Be careful," she whispered after him, staying put for the moment.

She had her own plan of course. She was going to go around the other side and attack from that direction.

"Arrr, grrrr, arrr, grrrr. Atttt, git, git; out of here!"

A little boy's voice was screaming in the darkness, trying to scare a wolf away. Mick, thinking the wolf was attacking a kid, jumped in front of it waving his sword like a madman.

Which made no difference to the large snarling wolf.

It sprang like a coiled serpent, knocking him to the ground and causing his short sword to fly out of his hands. He used all his strength to hold the wolf by its throat to keep it from tearing him apart.

Its hot steamy breath blew small poofs of clouds into the cold night air. White foamy saliva oozed from its iron jaws of death. It was doing its best to make Mick its next meal.

"Atttt, git, git, git out of here!" the little boy screamed and beat it with a stick.

Mick could feel the muscles in his arms burning like fire, they were nearing failure. His right hand slipped too close to its snapping jaws.

Instantly pain rocketed through his hand as the wolfs' canine teeth pierced his flesh. He hoped Lucerna would finish the mission he couldn't.

It would be over any second now, he was sure of it. The wolf would tear out his throat out and he would be done for. Then suddenly the beast let out an earsplitting howl and went limp on top of him.

"MICK! Oh god! Mick! Are you okay?" Lucerna screamed.

"I'm okay," Mick gasped; rolling the heavy predator off him.

"That was close; I thought I was done for," Mick said finally catching his breath.

"Thanks Lucerna; you saved my life."

"It was nothing; you would have done the same for me."

He felt kind of angry that she hadn't followed his orders. Although, if she had, he would have been toast for sure, so he couldn't be too mad.

With all the adrenalin surging through his veins, he didn't realize how bad his hand was until he stood up and felt the throbbing pain.

"Where's that little boy the wolf was attacking?" Mick said looking around confused.

"I don't know. I thought I heard a little boy too, but in all the commotion I don't know where he went," Lucerna said, checking him for injuries.

"You sure you're okay? It didn't bite you anywhere, did it?" she asked concerned.

"Just my hand," Mick told her, braving the pain and brushing her hands away.

"I'm fine; let's find that kid. He must be around here somewhere."

They looked around in the darkness, yet it was hard to see far.

"I'm here," the little voice called out.

"Sorry to disappear on you like that. I thought about running away after I saw you were okay, but I had to say thanks for saving me."

Lucerna pulled out a short piece of wood with a bulb-shaped end and shook it, it lit up as bright as a torch.

"What's that?" Mick asked amazed.

"Lumen wood."

"Another street vendor purchase?"

"Not funny Mick," she frowned.

They looked over to where the little boy stood, only to see a small greenish boy-like 'thing' standing there. Lucerna screamed before she could stop herself and Mick's mouth dropped wide opened.

"Why are you screaming, and what are you staring at? Good grief, you two act like you never saw a sapling before. For crying out loud, get a grip already!" The little guy told them.

Yet both were at a loss for words.

"Well, spit it out. You two look like morons. I've met smarter piglings than you," the sapling said in a boyish tone, though with very clear speech.

"What's a pigling?" Mick asked, before he could help himself.

"They're half sized pigs who walk on two legs; they talk, and have hands with four fingers and feet with three toes. They live in the Allegheny Swamp. They're fairly smart by simple standards I guess," the sapling informed him.

"What's your name?" Mick asked.

"Isom; and yours?"

"Mick, and this is Lucerna. We're glad to meet you," Mick said reaching his hand out.

"Sorry saplings don't like to touch humans. Germs you know; can't be too careful," Isom told Mick.

"Well that's okay; are you alright? Did the wolf hurt you?" Mick asked.

"No, I'm fine. He wouldn't have had me on the ropes like that, if I could have got to a tree in time," Isom said, poking the dead wolf with his tiny stick.

"Hello Isom," Lucerna said brightly.

"Would you two mind if we get back to camp instead of standing out here where his friends may come wondering to see where he's at?" she asked.

"Oh, good idea Lucerna," Mick said and turned and followed her with Isom in between them.

The rain had stopped by the time they got to their camp and rebuilt the fire. Lucerna was the first to speak breaking the awkward silence.

"So, um Isom. Why are you out here all alone, when you're so young?"

"Well dear, just so you know, we saplings don't count time like others do. I am three hundred fifty-one years old by your count. I guess, but we could care less about things like that. Time is but a season and a season is but a time; is our saying."

"Wow you're really old, then," Lucerna said astonished.

"If you say so," the little guy said lightly and smiled showing leafy green colored teeth with pointy shapes, which looked frightening in the fire light.

"Are you like a forest nymph?" Mick asked curiously.

"Now look, just because you saved my life, doesn't mean you can call me names. Besides, I had that wolf on the run. Another minute and I'd had him," Isom said bravely.

"Another minute and you'd been dinner," Mick sniggered.

"Don't get yourself in an uproar. I wasn't calling you names. I've just never met a sapling before; or for that matter, heard of them," he finished.

"Well, I accept your apology for comparing me to those nasty varmints of the forests," Isom said disgustingly and spat a foul green spit into the campfire, where it sizzled and turned the flames green for a few seconds.

Getting a closer look at him, they noticed he was wearing no shoes and short pants that looked like they were made from some kind of tree bark. His shirt was woven maple leaves and had some kind of green spiraling designs that wound around his arms up to his neck.

"You two are curious buggers, aren't you?" Isom said, not liking to be starred at.

"Sorry." They both said in unison. Then Lucerna saw Mick's hand.

"You told me you were alright Mick; look at your hand. Damn it boy! I swear!" Lucerna said angrily and grabbed Mick's hand to look at the damage.

"Here hold it by the fire light so I can see better. Oh, that's looks bad. We're going to have it looked at when we get to the next town. I can clean and bandage it till then. Let me get my bag. You better hope that wolf didn't have rabies, or you're going to be foaming at the mouth," Lucerna said getting to her feet.

"Sit still young lady. I can help Mick better than any human doctor can," Isom spoke up.

"After all, it's the least I can do for him saving me."

Lucerna sat back down with a huff, clearly aggravated that she wasn't the one to take care of Mick. He was her responsibility after all.

"Mick, your hand please," Isom reached toward him with his small slender hands.

Mick did as he was ordered. Isom made a chewing sound, and then spat a sickly green ball of what could only be described as slime into his little hands.

Mick closed his eyes as the little creature cupped his hands around Mick's and was rubbing vigorously. However instead of screaming like he thought he would do, Mick opened his eyes and saw his hand glowing bright green.

Isom withdrew his hands and smiled.

"There you go; you'll be fine now."

"Um; thanks," Mick managed to choke out through teary eyes.

"What's wrong Mick?" Lucerna asked growing concerned, yet Mick couldn't say anything.

There was a strange feeling working its way throughout his entire body.

"What in the hell did you do to him? You little green bastard!" Lucerna shrieked.

"My my; what a potty mouth you have little girl," Isom reprimanded her, clearly offended.

"He will be fine in a moment, give it time to work."

By this time Mick's head was spinning out of control and he felt faint. He tried to talk but couldn't, and when he tried to move, he simply fell backward with his eyes wide open.

"Give what time to work? Look at him!" Lucerna screamed, kneeling down beside him stoking his hair.

"The wolf must have been rabid Lucerna. The Virdis knows this and is going through his blood stream to purify him. Give it time to work or he will die," Isom said in a sober tone.

"If he dies you will too," Lucerna looked at Isom with a deadly glare.

Isom could tell she loved him and was only speaking that way because of it. Human feelings always amazed him. The way they were with one another would never be acceptable in his world. Well come to think of it; he'd never been accepted in his world, he thought sadly.

"We need to move him into the tent Lucerna and wrap him up to keep him warm while the Virdis works. Here, help me child," Isom told her grabbing Mick's legs.

Lucerna reached under his arms and lifted the best she could. God he was heavy she thought working him into position to get him into the tent.

"Ok, I got him; let's go," she said.

They finally got him inside the small comfortable tent and managed to cover him from his feet to his neck with blankets.

"Should I prop his head up Isom?"

"No he'll be fine," Isom said and touched the back of her hand with his cold green twig-like fingers.

"Lucerna, he'll be okay; trust me," the small green creature said sympathetically.

"It's just. It's just..." she couldn't say another word.

She could not bear to think of life without him. He was her everything since her mother died. If she lost him; she lost her world. She knew what she would do. She would finish his mission, which was so important it cost him his life. Then go back to Lawrence and ring the life out of Valkriss for ever sending him on this foolish quest to begin with. After that, she didn't know if she could go on.

"Mick, please fight for me. Please Mick, I need you," Lucerna whispered into his ear, gently stroking his cold cheeks which had lost all their color.

"What's wrong with him Isom? He's cold to my touch," Lucerna said as giant tears rolled down her flushed red cheeks.

"I told you; let the virdis work. He will be healed. You have to believe me," Isom told her, repeating his claim again.

Poor child Isom thought, so young and so full of burning passion. He would give one of his little green arms to feel a taste of what she was feeling right now.

Yet not in three hundred years had there been any such love for him to feel. Not since Yalla his wonderful companion who had been killed by those foul abominations, who would one day see their demise at his hands. Then he would look for another, once Yalla's death had been avenged.

He was growing colder; was he dying? Is this what death felt like? He was floating and moving somewhere. If he knew which god to pray to; he would now.

He was afraid; he never thought things would turn out like this. He had failed his mission; this was his first and would be his last. Feelings of sadness washed over him cascading down like a waterfall.

Lucerna would be alone; left alone to do what he could not, alone to go on without him. He knew she was strong. He had seen her inner strength when her mother died. More than anything, she would probably be mad at him for letting a common old wolf do him in. He could hear her now, telling him that she trained him better than that.

Wherever he was, it was so cold he felt like he had been thrown into a frozen lake. If I'm dead, I shouldn't feel anything anymore; maybe I'm dying and hadn't got there yet?

Where would his spirit go to? He hadn't had time to figure out this whole afterlife thing everyone talked about. Well, it was too late for that; blackness wrapped itself around him like a cocoon.

"Isom what is this Virdis you keep talking about? Is that the slime you put on his hand?" Lucerna asked, drying her tears.

"That 'slime' as you're so vulgarly calling it is what will save his life. And yes for your information, it is what we call Virdis. We have used it for centuries for the healing of all things," he told her sitting by Mick's feet.

"You have? Has it been used on humans?" Lucerna asked not taking her eyes off Mick's cold face, which had a greenish hue to it in the light the lumen wood torch.

"Well; we normally don't associate ourselves with humans. I do only because I'm on a mission to Sindara," Isom said crossing his arms.

Oh great; another man on a mission Lucerna thought angrily to herself; just what she needed.

"I asked if Virdis had ever been used on a human before, Isom."

"Like I told you, we don't go around humans very often. So to answer your question; no it hasn't as far as I know of."

He barely finished his sentence before Lucerna flew on top of him knocking him outside the tent, rolling around on the ground outside.

"You trite little bastard; you used something you wasn't sure would work! I'll beat you to a pulp," Lucerna roared furiously.

Thankfully Isom was able to wriggle loose and made a mad dash for a nearby pine tree, melting into it the second he hit it.

Lucerna was stunned by what she had just seen. The little green bastard ran right into a tree and disappeared from sight. She walked up to the large pine tree and touched it with her hand, wondering if what she saw had really happened or if she was going mad.

"I'm sorry Lucerna, if I've made you angry," the tree spoke in Isom's voice.

"So you want to play games with me; huh? I'll show you games," Lucerna said, picking up a burning log from the fire and walked back over to the tree.

"Come out of there right now, you little monster, or I'll burn you out!" she glowered.

"Lucerna I said I'm sorry. Now put the fire down and step away from the tree."

"I told you," she said and held the burning piece of firewood near the pine.

There was a swooshing sound which caused her to drop the log and before she knew it, she was hanging thirty feet upside down above the ground.

"I told you that I am sorry. Now, I will not say it again. Besides; hurt me and your friend dies," Isom's voice came through the pines limbs.

"Enough; put me down!" Lucerna demanded.

"Will you try to hurt me again, or burn me?" Isom asked.

"No," she replied.

"Swear it," Isom demanded.

Lucerna hesitated a second and the branch holding her quivered.

"Swear it, or I'll drop you on your head girl," Isom said shaking her a little, for good measure.

"Okay, I swear. Put me down, you're making me sick," Lucerna spouted.

Isom lowered her to the ground gently, and then appeared to walk right out of the tree.

"I would have not used Virdis if I thought it would harm Mick in anyway. The wolf was rabid otherwise they usually leave us alone. Mick would have never made it to the next town. Even there, no one would have been able to do anything for him. They would have killed him fearing he would spread rabies."

"I'm sorry Isom; I'm upset over Mick. He's more to me than just a friend. Don't tell him though; he may get a big head, if you know what I mean," Lucerna told him.

"Well I'm glad to see that you think he will get better," Isom said smiling.

"How long till we know?" she asked as she turned and look toward the tent.

A bright green glow was coming through the opening of the tent and was increasing in intensity.

"What's going on Isom?"

"It's almost over."

"What is?"

"The healing my dear."

There was a burst of the most beautiful emerald green light Lucerna had ever seen, and then it went dark.

"It's done," Isom said solemnly.

Lucerna crawled into the tent, holding the lumen torch in front of her and could see color had come back into Mick's face. It no longer had that sickly pale gray to it.

"Mick, are you okay? Can you hear me?" she asked leaning over him and gently shaking his shoulder.

There was a flickering of his eyes as they opened. He was silent at first.

"Mick; are you okay?" Lucerna asked again, still worried.

"I'm…" he started to say before she kissed him.

His lips were cool and soft. She was overcome with joy he was alive.

He was shocked and excited all at the same time. Her lips were so hot and wet, it sent shocks of electric down to his body.

"Oh Mick, I'm so happy you're alive!" Lucerna said and kissed him again.

If he had known all it would take to get a kiss was to get bitten by a wolf, he would have done it a long time ago.

"Thank you, Lucerna," Mick stumbled to find the words.

Oh great you just thanked her for kissing you, real smooth loverboy.

"What happened, Lucerna? I remember sitting by the campfire, and then I couldn't move. I was cold and felt like I was floating," he said dazed.

"The wolf had rabies and the medicine that Isom used on you healed it," Lucerna said smiling and tearing up again.

"What's wrong? You okay? Don't cry. I'm feeling better, I promise," Mick told her, attempting to rise up, but she reached out and pushed him back down gently.

"Just lay there; I'll get you some water. You must be thirsty. The sun is almost up. Don't you move Micknia! I'll be right back," Lucerna ordered with stern affection.

"Okay okay, I won't," Mick said in a defeated tone.

He knew when Lucerna meant business; you better not mess with her. He still felt cold, when he heard Isom speak.

"Glad to see you're well," he said smiling, sitting at Mick's feet.

"I still feel a little funny," Mick told him.

"It's natural; you're very lucky I did what I did, or you would have been dead for sure," Isom replied matter-of-factly.

"Thank you Isom," Mick said warmly.

"You are very welcome my friend. It was the least I could do," Isom said as Lucerna crawled into the tent, completely ignoring him.

"Here you go Mick; drink, but not too fast. I don't want you to get sick," Lucerna held the canteen up to his mouth.

He took a couple of drinks before she took it away.

"There that should do. How are you feeling?" she asked as if she was the doctor and he was her patient.

"Better; a little weak that's all," Mick said managing a half smile.

"Here, eat some of your favorite jerky. If you eat, you'll feel better," Lucerna handed him a piece.

Mick tried a bite and spat it out in disgust.

"Yuck," Mick spat.

"What's wrong Mick?" Lucerna asked worried.

"It tastes awful."

"It the same barbequed turkey jerky you had yesterday, Mick. Maybe you're not well after all. I'll get you to a doctor," Lucerna told him reassuringly and looked back at Isom glowering.

"It's just some side-affects, Lucerna; that's all," Isom said looking worried she was going to try to jump him again.

"And what side-affects are those, Isom?" she asked accusingly.

"Well since the Virdis is comprised of our essence and we're vegetarians, he may not have much of a taste for animal flesh for a while. He'll eat more salads; at least it will be healthier for him," Isom said, doing his best to lighten the mood inside the tent which was growing tense.

"I'm fine, Lucerna; I'm just not hungry right now," Mick spoke up.

"Oh now I know you're sick," Lucerna looked at him and laughed.

He was glad to see her happy.

"I just need to get some fresh air; that's all."

"Ok, but take your time. Here, let me get out of your way," she said heading out and opening the front flaps for him; Isom followed out after her.

The morning sky was clearing. It looked like it was going to be a beautiful autumn day. The outside air was rich and full. Mick could almost drink it like water from a cool spring. He never realized how wonderful nature could be. He would definitely have to get outdoors more often after his mission was over, he thought.

"Do you feel well enough to travel today Mick?" Lucerna asked when they got outside.

"I'm fine; don't worry about me."

She looked at him closer for a second when she noticed.

"Mick, your eyes; they're green. They've changed color. It must be the rabies trying to come back. We have to get you to a doctor now!" Lucerna demanded.

"Lucerna, rabies will not make your eyes change color," Isom stated matter-of-factly.

"Well then, what…" Lucerna stopped mid question.

"You, you did this to him with that damn Virdiious."

"Virdis," Isom corrected her.

"Whatever it is; look what it's done to his eyes. Will they change back? I liked his blue eyes," she said fuming.

"If you expect me to be honest with you, then don't get mad when I answer you," Isom told her.

"Okay okay, for crying out loud. Will they change back, Isom?"

"I'm not sure if they will or won't. Virdis has never been used on a human. We'll have to wait and see," he turned his attention to Mick.

"Now Mick I want to look. How many fingers am I holding up?" Isom asked, holding up two slender twig-like fingers.

"Two. Now will you two stop bickering, I'm the one who was hurt, remember" Mick told them, frustrated.

"We have things to do and a destination I would like to get to sometime this year."

"I'm sorry Mick; you're right," Lucerna said, feeling bad for over acting.

She didn't know why she acted the way she did when it came to him anymore.

"Shhh; someone's coming. They're on horses, at least twenty," Isom told them.

Mick's heart sank; he had survived a rabid wolf attack only to be killed by Mr. Riner. His nerves were going into overdrive.

"Oh great, now he wants to show me how much he loves me! He probably sent his guards; I bet he's not even with them. Just told them to go and find his wayward daughter," Lucerna was having a full blown tissy fit now.

"Aren't you going too hid or something, Isom?" Mick asked when he looked over and saw him still standing there.

"Never again," Isom said crossing his arms.

"It is time humans and our kind meet. Mankind and nature must learn to be as one and not war against each other as we have in the past. No more will we hide in the shadows and groves in the forest. We will stand in the light and be known. We will let your kind know they are not alone on this earth and they have to share it like the rest of us do."

Isom finished his grand speech as the sound of hoof beats grew louder. The only thing Mick was thinking was that Isom was going to be a witness to his execution at the hands of Lucerna's father. Maybe he could run for it, but he knew he wouldn't get far.

In the next minute a squadron of at least twenty guards in full armor rode up and stopped in front their small campsite.

He swallowed hard; Lucerna didn't have to worry. She was his daughter. He couldn't kill her; only ground her for the rest of her life. But him; he was a whole other story. He wasn't related in any way to Mr. Riner. He was just a young teenage boy, who he would blame for luring Lucerna out of Lawrence. Probably thinking they were going to elope and get married without his approval.

Mick did his best not to look too shaken by the sight in front of him. Although nearly every eye was on Isom instead of him, which made him feel a little better.

Mr. Riner dismounted from his large gray stallion; handed the reins to a guard, and walked up to Lucerna. The fierce angry look changed into a worried frown when he looked down at his daughter.

"Lucerna; what in the world are doing you out here?" his voice deep and warm with compassion.

Lucerna was shocked he was with the guards and didn't say anything at first.

"I… I left you a note. I didn't think you'd mind; you work so much," she said having no fight in her.

"Lucerna, you're my world, my only child. The reason I wake up every day and work like I do is for you. Everything I do is for you, darling. I know it's not been the same since your mother left us, but you can't go running off with any boy who will let you," he told her gently and glared at Mick when he spoke the last words.

"Dad! He never let me do anything! I found out where he was going and followed him. He never even told me he left. I found out on my own," she said now glaring at Mick too.

Oh great; now both of them are mad at him, Mick thought, still trying to figure it out whether he should make a break for it or not.

"Well, you're safe now; that's all that matters. We'll deal with this when we get back home," Mr. Riner said hugging her.

"Now you listen and listen good; I'm going with Mick to Sindara. He's been hired as a courier to deliver a message there, and I'm not going to let him go without me," Lucerna said defiantly.

"I will deal with Mick when I get you and him back to Lawrence, Lucerna. Now pack your things!" Lucerna's dad said losing his temper.

"Dad, I'm not one of your guards you can order around. I told you, I'm going with him! And you're not going to do anything to Mick. I told you it's not his fault I left," she said in a heated tone.

"Now little girl," he said, before Lucerna cut him off midsentence.

"What did you call me? I have you know, I'm the same age as mom when you two met and fell in love," Lucerna said steely, feeling her blood running hot through her veins.

"That's not fair, Lucerna."

"What's not fair is you can't stand the thought of losing your little girl as you called me or the fact that I am becoming a woman," she said crossing her arms.

There was an awkward moment of silence as neither one of them were willing to admit defeat.

"Tell you what I'll do, Lucerna. If you are going to accompany Mick here to Sindara, then we will go with you. You will not go alone," he told her, softening his tone.

"Oh Dad! Really? You do love me," she grabbed him and hugged him tightly.

Lovely, Mick thought; when Valkriss hears about this, he was going to be a dead duck. He'll probably have him clean the bathrooms with a toothbrush forever. Well, on the bright side there should be no trouble the rest of the way. He would get his mission completed, which should make the old goat a little bit happy.

On the negative side of things, he wouldn't have a chance to be alone with Lucerna. With Isom tagging along it would have been hard enough without Mr. Riner. Damn it, damn it, this wasn't working out like he thought it would.

How in the world had things got so complicated so fast, he'd never know?

"Hi sir," Mick said meekly to Mr. Riner.

"Did I say you could talk yet, son?" Mr. Riner boomed in his deep bass voice.

"Dad!" Lucerna smacked him on his chest.

"Kidding; just kidding, Mick. I'm glad to see you're both okay and unhurt," Mr. Riner looked at him with a deadly smile while trying to sound light-hearted.

"Captain Waldrop."

"Yes sir."

"Send Morris back to Lawrence, he can take charge until I return. I'll send couriers when we reach Cinnibar and Sindara. Send word if you need anything," Mr. Riner ordered.

"Yes sir; anything else sir?" Captain Waldrop asked.

"That's all Captain."

"Squadron dismount; rest and allow the horses to water and feed."

After Riner gave the order there was a rustling of metal and horses shuffling as they began carrying out his orders.

"Now that's taken care of, why don't you introduce me to your little friend here."

"Dad, this is Isom; he's a sapling. We saved him from a rabid wolf last night," Lucerna said proudly.

"A rabid wolf; see why I don't want you out here," Mr. Riner told her again.

"Now dad, don't start with that again. Besides, you're here now."

"Okay; well it's nice to meet you Isom," he said extending his right hand.

"Sorry dad, saplings don't shake hands with humans, germs you know," Lucerna told him.

"Oh, okay then," Mr. Riner said and raised his hand like he was waving.

"Dad, he gets the point. He's not stupid," she said quietly.

"Sorry, first time I've met one of your kind," Mr. Riner said, a little embarrassed.

"It's okay Mr. Riner. It's a pleasure to meet you sir. You have a strong and fiercely independent daughter," Isom said pleasantly.

"Oh, if you only knew the half of it," Mr. Riner laughed.

"Dad! You're embarrassing me," Lucerna said when she noticed some of the guards listening.

Lieutenant Trevilians walked up to Mr. Riner and reported, "Sir, our horses are done in for today, and the men need rest before going on."

"Fine, set up camp. We will stay here and leave at first light. We'll stop and re-supply in Bentree on our way to Cinnibar," Riner ordered.

"Yes sir," Lieutenant Trevilians replied and done an about face.

"I hope that will be ok with you; Mick?" Mr. Riner really wasn't asking.

"Oh yes sir, of course; no problem here sir," Mick spoke up trying his best to hide his growing resentment.

This was his mission and his alone. It was bad enough for Lucerna to come along. Now he had a full company of Lawrence's guards with him as well, not to mention a sapling; who for some unknown reason had taken a liking to humans.

He always tried to look on the bright side of things, but this was getting ridiculous. There was nothing he could do about it now. His mission was still the same, and he would see it through to the bitter end. Somewhere deep inside him, he got a feeling this was the beginning of grander things to come.

Chapter 15
Stormy Night

"Where's Isom?" Lucerna asked as she rode close to Mick.

"He likes keeping to the forest. I guess it will take him a while to get used to being around humans."

She was trying to pass the time which seemed to drag on forever since her father joined them. She was tired of the men's constant talking; tired of riding, tired of sleeping on the ground. Come to think of it she was just tired and couldn't wait until they were all safe and sound back in Lawrence. And whether Mick liked or not he was going to see a real doctor when they got back.

The only thing she was looking forward too now was being able to see Sindara. She had heard many stories of all the wonders it held. Like the Mage Quarter where you could shop for magical trinkets till your heart's desire or went broke.

Now that her father was with her she would be able to spend all her allowance on goodies instead of supplies. After passing through Cinnibar she was now the farthest from home, she had ever been. It was the last place they went as a family to see the Solstice Festival before her mom died. It seemed like it was a lifetime ago, Lucerna thought sadly.

Mick looked over at Lucerna, who had been riding quietly for the last few minutes. He could always tell whenever she was thinking about her mother. He rode in as close as he could.

"Want to have some fun tonight?" Mick asked.

She instantly brightened up and leaned toward him.

"What do you have in mind?" she asked.

"I managed to get some things at one of Cinnibar's markets. I think you'll like them," Mick said grinning.

"Oh," Lucerna said caught off guard thinking of something completely different.

"What do you mean, 'oh', you're always interested in new things."

"Never mind; what did you buy?" she asked, hoping Mick wouldn't pick up on the fact she had hoped for something else, like a kiss, other than showing her some trinket he bought. Men are so dimwitted.

"If you're not interested, it's alright," Mick said with slightly hurt feelings.

"Mick don't be mad, I'm just homesick that's all. What time do you want to meet?"

Mick knew she wasn't interested, but maybe he could cheer her up anyway.

"Wait until midnight when everyone's asleep. I'll tap on your tent with a stick, okay," Mick told her, and then saw Mr. Riner eyeing him.

He pulled away from riding so close to her. She gave him an understanding nod.

She rode the rest of the day lost in thought until they stopped to set up camp. At least men were good for something she thought sourly watching them working to set up the tents.

The best thing that happened on the whole trip was also the scariest, when she kissed Mick after the wolf attack. Maybe they would kiss

again tonight and she cheered up at the prospect
of being alone with him. It gave her butterflies
just thinking about it.

She wondered if he felt the same way. She
looked over at him working on his tent. There
was something different about him, an air of
confidence he never had before. He looked in her
direction and almost caught her staring before
she looked away quickly.

Time passed slowly for Lucerna, lying in
her tent waiting to meet Mick at midnight. She
had just dosed off when she heard three light taps
on the tent.

"You awake?" he asked whispering.

"I'm up," she answered in a hushed voice.

"Good, come on."

"Coming."

She crawled out of the tent quietly and
followed Mick into the woods, where he led them
to a small clearing.

"Mick, let's not get too far from the camp,
it's dangerous out here," Lucerna said tugging at
his tunic.

"This is as far as we're going. I didn't
want us to be seen," he informed her.

"What do you mean seen? We don't have any torches."

"Just watch," he said as he dug through his old leather pack and pulled out something round wrapped in dark cloth.

"What is it?"

"Ah, I got your attention now," Mick said beaming and slowly untied the string.

The instant the dark cloth slid away from the glass jar, a beautiful yellow light filled the clearing.

"No way! I can't believe you found any for sale. Mick, you went to the black market district; didn't you? Those can't be bought by the public. How many did you get?"

"Four."

"How much did they cost?"

"I got a good deal, only one gold for them," Mick said proudly.

"What are you going to do with Mulciber flies, Mick? You can't be seen with them, you'll get fined and I'll never hear the end of it from my father. He'll go on and on about what a bad influence you are one me."

"I'm going to turn them loose."

"Mick you can't, most Mulciber flies are raised by licensed growers and wouldn't be able to survive if you turned them loose. You better cover them back up before we're seen," Lucerna said looking around nervously.

"I didn't think about that."

"It's not your fault; you didn't know."

"It was a spur of the moment thing," Mick said frowning.

"Ah Mick I'm sorry. I didn't mean to make you feel bad. We can keep them.

I'll go to the library when we get back and find out how to take care of them," she said, making an attempt to cheer him up.

"I just hate seeing things in cages, that's all. They keep them there until they die and then discard them like trash."

Lucerna had never heard Mick talk like this. He must be getting sick again.

"Mick their just flies."

"Oh; so that gives people the right to cage 'em up and do whatever they want with them."

"I didn't mean it like that."

"Well then; how did you mean it?"

"Are you feeling okay; ever since the wolf attack, you've been acting strange?"

"I'm fine Lucerna; just drop it."

"I been watching you and you won't even eat meat anymore. I saw the guys making fun of you the other night when you wouldn't eat any of the venison they fixed. And you won't eat your favorite food anymore either. Also your eyes haven't changed back," she added.

Oh great Mick thought she's on another rant.

"Do you have any?" Mick asked.

"What?"

"Any turkey jerky."

"Yea; why?"

"Give me a piece and I'll prove to you I'm fine," Mick said putting the Mulciber flies away.

"Here," she said and tore off a small piece and reached it to him.

He popped into his mouth.

"Yum," Mick smiled, but as soon as he bit down on the meat something terrifying happened.

He could see a turkey about to be butchered and heard its last gobble before its head came flying off. He watched as it flopped on the ground bleeding to death, blood spurting everywhere.

He instantly grabbed his throat. Lucerna thought he was choking and ran behind him and proceeded to beat him on his back until the piece of jerky flew forcefully out of his mouth.

"Are you okay?" she asked after she saw it fly out, but thumped him a few more times for good measure.

"I won't be if you keep hitting me like that," Mick said and spat on the ground in front of him making sure all the remnants of the foul animal flesh was out of his mouth.

"I'm sorry I made you eat it," Lucerna said apologetically.

"It's okay my mouth was dry, that's all," he lied.

"You sure you're alright?" she asked again.

"I'm fine, now quit worrying about me. We better get out of here before your dad finds us; kills me and grounds you for life," Mick said attempting a smile.

"See you in the morning," she said and kissed him on his cheek and then left quietly back to the camp.

At least one thing hadn't changed was the way he felt about her as he watched her go.

"Okay Isom you can come out now. I know you're there," Mick said to the empty darkness.

Isom stroll out from behind a nearby tree.

"It's worse than I thought Mick," Isom said sounding way too serious.

"What's worse than you thought?" Mick asked.

"Something else has happened to you other than the side effects from the Virdis."

"What do you mean?"

"How did you know I was nearby?" Isom asked

Now that he thought about it, he wasn't sure.

"I just felt a small magical presence and then you came into my mind. Why?"

"I was inside a tree. There should have been no way you could have known I was near. I know the Virdis has made you more in tune with nature, but not like that," Isom said, starting to ponder to himself before Mick interrupted him.

"Which reminds me," Mick said and went on to explain what happened when he tried to eat the jerky.

"Mick I think the Virdis has imparted some of our sapling qualities to you. We eat only plants, no meat ever passes our lips. Yet I have never seen it glow like it did, when I used it on you. I thought it was because you were human, but there must be more to it."

"Why?" Mick asked, growing more interested.

"When you sensed me just now, you shouldn't have been able to. Although you were healed by our essence, only another sapling can detect our kind. To my knowledge no creature; man, or beast can sense our presence when we commune with nature. We can be caught off guard of course, by rabid wolves," Isom smiled, "but not if we are hidden, like I was just now," he finished.

"Oh," Mick said confused.

"What does it mean?" he asked Isom, who fell silent for a moment.

"I don't know, but we need to find out. You travel on to Sindara. I know you have an important task to finish. I'll meet you back in Lawrence, hopefully with some answers."

"Where you going?"

"To speak with someone who will have the answers we need."

"Who's that?"

"The Unimodus."

"The what; who?"

"Sorry; he's the eldest of our kind. Very wise and very knowledgeable about many things; he will know."

"Why is it so important?"

"You are very young and even I don't fully understand. If I'm right a new convergence could be happening."

"What's that?"

"When I was no bigger than a twig, The Unimodus told us of a time when man and nature would be as one again. We would live in harmony as we once did in times past."

"How does that happen?" Mick asked.

"I don't know, but to quote The Unimodus; 'The one saved by nature, becomes nature," Isom said before going silent a moment then spoke again.

"Go on to Sindara. I will meet you in Lawrence when you return."

"How will you get to the tavern without people seeing you?"

"Don't worry we have our ways; besides when did people scare me?" Isom said with a snort.

"Can I tell Lucerna?"

"Of course, she is true to you."

"What do you mean?"

"I forget how dimwitted humans are when it comes to love."

"You mean?"

"She loves you," Isom said pursing his lips together in an attempt to imitate people kissing and making full sound effects.

"Oh; OH!" Mick said dumbfounded by what he just heard; after another round of mock kissing Isom got serious again.

"It's nearly dawn, you need to get back before you're missed," Isom said standing up.

"Wait; what am I supposed to do about Lucerna?"

"Why are you asking me for advice? I don't know how humans relate to each other. All I know is love when I see it and you two love each other," Isom said.

"I do?"

"Mick if you don't know how you feel, I can't tell you. Now we wasted enough time, let's go. I'll see you in Lawrence," and with those words Isom disappeared into the thick forest.

It was a good thing Mick didn't sleep as much as he used to. He felt fine after only sleeping two hours before one of Riner's men woke him with a rude, "Get up boy," and then kicked him.

Mick knew Mr. Riner had told them to treat him rough. He didn't mind it too much. Maybe he could get in his good graces if he just went along with it. However if one of those idiot guards kicked him again, good graces or not he would have it out with him.

He hoped to talk to Lucerna when they stopped for lunch since Mr. Riner believed in getting an early start which barely gave him any time to dress and grab a bite to eat before heading out. In two days they would be in Sindara.

He wondered if he should use the aura candle to tell Valkriss what's happened, yet he told him to only use it in an emergency. This didn't exactly classify as one and he would find out as soon as they got back no doubt. Mick could only imagine the hell he was going to catch. What's done is done; he thought and saddled up.

The weather was turning sour along the coast; a fierce storm was rolling in off the Saline Sea. The sky grew darker by the minute. Mick didn't need to look at the sky. He knew the storm was coming, something about the way the air smelled, it was so fresh.

In his mind he could see the far away lightning imparting its life giving energy to the earth. The distant sea was raging amidst the flashes of brilliant light. Everything was clearer now than it ever had been. He was like a blind man seeing for the first time. The newness of life had awakened him from a long slumber.

It was midafternoon when the storm broke and they found shelter in an old barn not too far from the road. Riner sent one of the guards to the farmer's house to tell them they were going to wait out the storm in the relative safety of the old structure.

Mr. Riner was an good man and even paid the farmer for its use. He could have just as easily commandeered it, since he was an official of the kingdom. Mick was learning more about

Riner on this trip he thought as he unsaddled Jenny.

Unfortunately being constrained to the confines of the barn meant he would have to wait and talk to Lucerna until everyone went to sleep.

It was nice to be under a roof as the cold rain pounded against the old weather beaten barn which smelled of livestock and hay.

The afternoon slipped into evening as the storm grew in intensity. There were times the booming thunder shook the old barn to the point where Mick thought it was going to collapse on top of them. He could see the frightened look in the horses' eyes which reflected everyone's nervous mood.

Night time arrived with even more lightning ripping, tearing the sky apart. No one spoke much when they got ready to turn in for the night; rest was going to be doubtful unless the storm abated.

Lucerna must have been frightened, because she slept close to her father. Mick didn't blame her; it would be nice to have a parent in times like this. He drifted off into a deep sleep listening to the sound of the heavy rain, not long after he woke with a start.

Something wasn't right. He could feel evil lurking in the darkness, not far off and closing fast; more than one. They were moving in a tight pack directly at them, there wasn't much time. He threw off his blanket and rushed over to where Mr. Riner lay sleeping.

"Mr. Riner, wake up," Mick said in a low voice which was all it took to wake him.

"What is it boy?" Riner asked, eyeing him warily.

"Something's out there."

"What do you mean?"

"I can't explain it now, there's no time. I heard something out there in the distance. You better wake your men," Mick told him.

"Pray you're right Mick," Mr. Riner said grumpily as he got up and roused the men.

By then Lucerna woke up.

"What's wrong dad?" she asked half asleep.

"Mick had a bad dream or something; nothing to worry about. We're going to check things out just to make sure," he told her in a clam voice.

When she looked up at Mick she knew right away something was wrong. She grabbed

her sword lying next to her and pulled her boots
on.

"Lucerna don't worry," Riner tried to
reassure her, but it was no good she knew Mick
well enough to know he wasn't joking.

By that time the rest of the guards were
stirring about and getting torches lit. Riner
looked out into the darkness and heard something
he couldn't identify off in the distance.

"Baxis, Keyes," Riner called the two men
over.

"If things get out of hand, take Lucerna
and Mick and ride for Sindara, we'll follow
behind," he ordered.

"Yes sir."

"Lucerna; Mick you understand."

"Yes sir," Mick automatically responded.

"But dad," Lucerna started to argue.

"You heard me; now saddle your horses,"
Riner said as he looked out once more.

"Lucerna don't worry we won't go far and
we'll turn around and come back for him," Mick
whispered to her.

"We better," Lucerna told him menacingly.

Mr. Riner looked back at his daughter.

"Don't worry dear it's just for your own safety. Everything will be okay; it's always good to be prepared. Mick probably had a bad dream that's all," he finished with a reassuring look and looked at Mick who was standing beside Lucerna.

"It's alright," Mick spoke up, and then he felt their presence again; now they were in a rage.

He had never felt such a blood thirsty savagery before in his life. It sent chills down both arms and caused his hair to stand on end.

"Well Mick," Riner said.

"Yes sir?"

"Where's your monsters?"

Before Mick could answer, Mr. Riner turned and looked out from the old barn again.

"On guard men!" Riner shouted. Suddenly pairs of red eyes where circling the barn sending the horses nearly bolting in fear.

Damn it, of all things to encounter when he had his daughter with him Riner thought angrily. He had only faced the deadly Scarious twice in the past. They were cunning; fast, and a powerful foe in any number. He counted at least a dozen sets of eyes.

"Everyone stay tight. Baxis, Keyes as soon as you get the chance get Lucerna and Mick out of here!" Riner ordered.

"Yes sir!" they answered in unison.

Before Mick or Lucerna could protest four beasts came crashing through the side of the wall sending broken boards flying in all directions and three horses bolting.

Two more charged Riner sending him flailing backwards trying to regain his footing. He was doing his best to keep them at bay. Lucerna ran straight at them.

"Get off him; you monsters!" she screamed hitting one with her sword barely cutting it.

It was enough to cause it to turn around and swing its muscular arm hitting her in her midsection sending her flying backwards.

"Oh no you don't, you bastard!" Mick yelled and jumped in between them swinging his sword side to side.

By that time Riner killed the one he was fighting and turned and struck the one in front of Mick from behind causing it to throw its arms up howling in pain. Mick took the opportunity to stab as hard as he could through its chest, killing it. Riner looked at him with a nod of approval, before they were on the defensive again.

Everything seemed to be a blur to Mick. The foul beasts had surrounded the barn and now there was no way out. Baxis and Keyes had been killed. The rest of them formed a tight group in the middle of the barn facing an uncertain outcome.

Within seconds another wave was on them managing to break them apart. The guards were fighting for their lives. Mick stayed close to Lucerna and Riner.

They fought with every ounce of strength they had, but it wasn't going well. Riner was hurt; Lucerna was doing her best to fend off their attacks. Mick was knocked to the side. He regained his footing and charged back to her side, fighting desperately.

Out of nowhere a man jumped right into the middle of the fray. He moved with cat-like grace killing everything that got in front of him.

The remaining black devils sensing defeat was fled as fast as they came.

"You all alright; I was riding by when I heard the fighting," the stranger asked.

Riner was the first to speak.

"We owe you our lives, stranger," He said breathing hard.

"Glad I could help," he replied in a raspy tone.

"Dad you're hurt," Lucerna's voice cracking.

"It's nothing; I'll be okay, just a scratch," Riner said trying to breathe easier in a vain attempt to restore her confidence.

Yet she could see he was bleeding profusely from his right side.

"Sit down and let me take a look at that," she ordered.

"Here let me take a look at it," the stranger said as he stepped a little closer.

"Name is Jules Brannigan by the way. Now let's have a look at that wound," Jules told Riner pointing at it.

"Mick help the guards round up the horses; will you?" Riner said breathing hard.

"Yes sir," Mick said.

He wanted to thank Jules, but he was busily tending to Riner with Lucerna looking more worried by the second. He took one last look at Jules before he turned to help the guards.

Getting a closer look at him now he was much older than Mick realized, with a graying beard and hair to match. He carried a long silver sword and wore a large silver ring with a blue stone, inset with a silver sword like the one he was carrying.

A ring that looked a lot like the one Valkriss wore. With no time to ponder anything further, Mick turned to go help the others.

By the time he finished and got back to Lucerna and Riner, the stranger had already left.

"Lucerna I'm fine," Riner told her batting her hands away as he got to his feet swaying a little.

"Dad you're not fine, you're injured. Now sit down before you fall down," Lucerna told him pointly.

"I have to see to things."

There was no stopping Mr. Riner, it didn't matter who you were.

"Alright then let me help you at least," Lucerna said impatiently as she put her arm around him trying to steady him the best she could.

"Mick quit standing there gawking, and help me," she said straining under her dad's increasing weight.

"Oh sorry," Mick said unsure of what to do.

"Here, get on the other side and help me support him," Lucerna directed.

"I'm fine," Riner said as Mick put his arm around him, but he didn't pull away and slumped putting more weight on them.

Damn he was heavy Mick thought and wondered if he was going to be able to hold him up, if he got any weaker.

"I got you sir," Mick grunted.

Lucerna was struggling as well, trying to hold him up.

"Dad; please sit down, we can't hold you up much longer," Lucerna with a strained voice of someone carrying an oversized load about to drop it.

"Okay, help me to that bale of hay over there," Riner agreed.

They managed to get him the few steps to it and sat him down. Both were breathing hard from the exertion.

"Where's everyone? How many have we lost? I need answers. Where's Captain Waldrop?" Riner asked.

"Sir, Baxis; Keyes and Makeil are dead, two others are hurt, but will be okay," Captain Waldrop reported running up to them.

"You're hurt Captain," Riner said.

"No sir, it's those foul bastards' blood. Pardon my language Miss," Captain Waldrop apologized seeing Lucerna was there by his side.

"It's nothing, I've heard worse," Lucerna said dismissingly.

"Can everyone travel tonight?" Riner asked.

"Yes sir; but…" the Captain said before being cut off by Riner.

"But what Captain?"

"You don't look to be in any shape to travel."

Nonsense, I'll be fine in a few minutes; just need to get myself together that's all."

"Listen to Captain Waldrop dad," Lucerna urged.

"Hey you all alright?" a man's voice out of nowhere asked, causing everyone to jump and grab their swords and turn around quickly to see who it was.

"Whoa! I'm Millis the owner of the farm. A man stopped by the house and said you folks had a bad run-in with the Scarious," he said holding his lantern higher, showing he was still wearing his sleeping cap.

"I didn't mean to alarm you," Millis quipped.

"Quite alright," Captain Waldrop said. Riner began to say something and then fell backwards.

"Dad!" Lucerna screamed; everyone looked back and saw he was unconscious.

"Let's get him up to my house. Here put him in the cart over there, easier than carrying him all the way," the old farmer said, pointing to a two wheeled wooden cart used to haul hay.

Lucerna and Mick each grabbed an arm while Captain Waldrop grabbed his legs and laid him gently in the cart.

"Get a blanket," Lucerna told Mick, absentmindedly wiping her father's forehead with her handkerchief; whispering, "It'll be okay," to him.

Captain Waldrop and another guard pulled the old creaking cart up to the front door of the nondescript farmhouse.

They carried Riner into one on the large downstairs bedrooms and placed him on the bed. The house was spacious yet sparsely furnished with the basic of necessities and had a smell of disuse; mothballs, Mick thought.

"Now young Miss I can take a look at him, if you wish. I'm quite skilled at doctoring my livestock, people ain't much different," Millis told Lucerna.

"He's my father, not an animal!" Lucerna said with a tear stained face.

"No offense Miss, was just saying that's all."

"Is there any doctor's close?" Lucerna asked.

"Afraid the nearest one's in Sindara. At least a day's ride," Millis said plainly.

"Lieutenant Trevilians ride to Sindara. Find a doctor and alert the authorities that there have been a Scarious attack."

This time it was Lucerna giving orders. She was so embolden by seeing her father laying there injured it never occurred to her she had no authority to command anyone.

However Trevilians knowing it needed to be done offered no objections and with a, "yes mam" was out the door after having a word with Waldrop.

"Now Miss if you don't mind," Millis said moving slowly to Riner's injured side.

Lucerna looked like a fierce mother lion protecting her cub.

"Don't worry," Millis told her softly.

He removed the makeshift bandage and saw three long deep slash wounds on his right side.

"They need stiches and the wounds need to be sterilized before infection sets in. Here hold these bandages tight while I go get supplies," Millis told Lucerna.

"Can't we wait for the doctor?" she asked, choking back more tears.

"He won't make it dear," Millis said matter-of-factly.

"Alright, then go ahead. If you make it worse, you'll deal with me," she said coldly.

"Yes Miss," was all Millis said as he headed for the kitchen to get the things he needed. Captain Waldrop followed him.

"Will he make it?" he asked.

"He will, if I can close the wounds without infection setting in," Millis told the captain gathering his supplies.

"Now if you don't mind captain, I'd like to get on with it," Millis said impatiently.

"Sorry," Waldrop said stepping aside.

He knew the old farmer would be the best hope they had to save Riner.

When Millis returned Mick slipped out of the room unnoticed and went back to the barn. He knew what he had to do like it or not. He lit the aura candle and spoke Valkriss' name into it just like he had been shown.

He waited a second and spoke his name again, "Valkriss are you there?" Mick asked in a hushed voice.

Finally a small image of a man's face appeared in the flame.

"Hello Micknia," it said. Yet he didn't recognize the face or its voice and immediately blew out the candle.

Damn he thought; what could he do now? He had to think. He knew there was only one thing to do. He would have to continue on without anyone. Once his mission was over he could get back and check on Lucerna.

After all he wasn't any good to them standing around worrying. He knew better than to go back to the farmhouse and tell Lucerna. She already had enough to deal with; besides she would try to talk him out of going. He would leave a note on her saddle, so she would know he went on to Sindara.

He had Jenny saddled and in no time was on the road. Jenny seemed to sense his urgency and ran at a gallop. Hours passed and finally dawn broke before she let up to a trot.

The storm had passed, by the time the morning sun rose. Mick wasn't tired and Jenny was holding up well, so he rode on, arriving in Sindara at midday.

He went straight to the Auckley Council of Mages building. It wasn't hard to find being the tallest and most colorful cobalt blue with blazing silver trim.

After being asked to wait a few minutes in an enormous atrium decorated with lavish furnishings. He was called back to the inner chamber to meet the man Valkriss had told him to give the scroll to. Mick was stunned to see it was the same man who had appeared in the aura candle.

"How did you know it was me," Mick asked remembering that he called him by name.

"Now Micknia, I would not be the head of the council if I didn't know things, now would I?" he answered.

"Besides I was using one last night when you tried to contact Valkriss," he smiled.

"Oh," Mick said confused.

All this was beyond him. He had enough on his mind without trying to figure out how magic worked.

"Here you go sir," Mick said handing him the scroll.

"Thank you young man; you are a brave and hearty soul to come so far from home."

"I'm sorry, I have little time sir. I have to get back," Mick replied, trying not to say too much.

"Ah yes; I believe some unfortunate events have befallen your companions."

Mick automatically tensed.

"Do not worry young man, as I said; I know many things. Besides, are we not on the same side?"

"Sorry sir."

"No need to be; I have already dispatched aid to your friends. You are welcome to rest before your journey back if you like. However my guess is you don't know need much rest do you?" the old man smiled and raised an eyebrow.

Mick didn't like the way he asked rhetorical questions and got the feeling he knew way too much.

"I'm sixteen, I don't need much rest," Mick retorted.

"Of course; is there anything we can get you for your journey back?"

"No thanks sir," Mick answered.

"Safe journeys and eagles speed," the old mage blessed Mick and he turned and left without another word.

The ride back seemed to fly by. He would ride until Jenny got tired and let her rest, then ride on again. She was an amazing animal. When he got back to Lawrence he was going to buy her from Valkriss. The thought of buying any animal repulsed him. He knew it would be the only way he could keep her.

"Would you like that girl?" Mick asked and Jenny nodded in approval.

She and Mick had bonded and he would not be separated from her.

When he arrived back at the farm he saw it had been transformed into a mini hub of activity. Not only had the Ackley Council sent mages, but Sindara had dispatched a full battalion of soldiers to canvas the countryside for remaining Scarious.

Mick dismounted and tied Jenny outside and went into the farmhouse. As soon as Lucerna saw him, she came running grabbed him and kissed him nearly knocking him off his feet.

"You're safe, and dad's going to be fine. The old farmer knew more than I gave him credit for. Even the healing mage that came from the Auckley Council was impressed by his skill," Lucerna told him.

Mick was still stunned by the kiss to say anything other than, "that's good."

"Did you get the scroll delivered? I got the note you left me."

"Yeah, I got it done."

"Good; they say dad will be able to travel in another day or two and we can get home."

"Sounds great," Mick said, still thinking about the kiss.

"Come on, dad wanted to see you as soon as you got back."

"Is he mad at me?"

"No silly," she told him as she led him down the hallway holding his hand.

He could hear the old farmer complaining of how the attack had brought such a rapid response when he couldn't get help when one of his prized goats was killed by a wolf.

They entered the bedroom where they found Mr. Riner sitting in an armchair beside the bed.

"What are you doing up? You're supposed to be in bed," Lucerna scolded him like an old mothering hen.

"I was getting stiff from all the bed rest and Millis told me it would be good to move around a little," he told her frowning.

"I guess it's okay," she said as she walked over and placed a blanket over his legs.

"Darling I'm fine; quit worrying," he told her gently batting away her hands.

"You're just like your mother, always a worry wart. Now if you don't mind I'd like to have a word alone with Mick," Riner said and looked around the room at the captain and the others.

"You too Lucerna," he added when she wasn't going with the others.

"I'll go to the kitchen and make some more chicken soup," she said brightly.

"Sounds great," Riner said as Lucerna kissed him on his cheek and followed the others out closing the door.

Mick's stomach began to get tied in knots. Riner's face became stone cold. Here it comes he told himself, bracing for what was to come.

"You were brave in the barn Mick. I see why Lucerna is so fond of you," he paused before going on.

"Out of respect and love for her I have not asked you why you're on this mission of yours," Mr. Riner said pointly, waiting for Mick to answer.

"I'm asking now," he said when Mick remained silent.

"My job was to deliver a message to Sindara," Mick replied flatly.

"Who sent you?"

"Sorry sir, I can't tell you."

"Can't; or won't?"

"I'm sorry, I can't."

"Mick until the attack, I was simply entertaining my daughter and saw the trip as a good way to spend some much needed time with her that I haven't been able to do since… her mother passed away," he said as if he was fondly recalling a memory.

"Sir this much I can tell you. I was hired to take a scroll from Lawrence to Sindara."

"So, Valkriss didn't send you?"

"No; he allowed me to go. Said it would be good for me to see the sights, as he put it," Mick said determined to hide as many facts as possible.

Riner stood up from the armchair. He was an imposing man when standing full height.

"I must say, you're a talented liar."

Mick swallowed hard and stood his ground.

"What do you mean sir?"

"Don't play games with me. Why did one of my men see you in the barn trying to contact Valkriss using an aura candle?"

Damn it, Mick thought.

"Sir, I hope you can respect the fact I was asked to tell anyone about my mission."

"Except my daughter?" Riner's anger now rising.

"After she found me; I told her. I trust her with my life."

"You do; do you?"

"Yes sir."

"Micknia understand one thing. The details of your mission can remain secret unless they affect Lucerna. Then no more; do I make myself understood?"

"Yes sir."

With that Riner sat back down in the chair. For the first time Mick could see the toll the stress of losing his wife had taken. Now the fear of something happening to his daughter was gnawing at him like an endless hunger.

"One last thing Mick."

"Yes sir?"

"You can trust me."

"Of course."

"Now if you'll excuse me. I'm sure Lucerna is waiting outside the door with more of that infernal chicken soup," Riner said grimacing.

Soon they were back in boring old Lawrence with nothing to do but listen to Valkriss bitch; harp, and moan about how he nearly blew everything because of a damned ol' girl. He wouldn't even let Mick explain what the circumstances were or anything. He was so unfair.

However he didn't punish Mick as bad as he thought he would. His punishment came in the form of tongue lashings, which he received at least two times a day for three weeks. He even resorted to hiding in the guest rooms as often as he could.

With Holly gone, the old man had fewer people to vent on. He also managed to sneak off and secretly meet Lucerna a few times a week through the long winter which made life bearable.

Mr. Riner had grounded her hard for worrying him like she done. He brought her up to speed on everything Isom told him and how he was supposed to meet Mick back in Lawrence and didn't. He was going to look for him. However he had no clue where to begin; besides Lucerna threatened to beat him if he did.

They formed various theories as to the ring the stranger wore that looked like Valkriss'. Lucerna filled him in on how Millis, the old farmer wore a ring like the one he described. They came up with everything from secret societies to cults, but in the end they had no concrete proof.

Chapter 16
Wizzys

"Don't worry dear if he bites you, I have some extra Silverberry Licor left you can have," Holly said clearly amused.

"Har har, everyone's going to think it's funny until I lose a limb," Michael said grumpily, making Holly laugh even more.

"Okay Ravis needs his rest and I think we can use a good lunch. How's that sound?" Holly asked.

"Sounds great, I'm starving," Michael said.

"You're always hungry. It's not fair if I ate the way you did, I swear I'd be three hundred pounds," Holly jealously pointed out.

"You are getting a little thick around the middle," Michael said jokily.

"What did you just say mister?" Holly said with a growl in her voice.

"What...who me... nothing why?" Michael said smiling, looking up in the air.

"Careful dear, I know where you sleep. Accidents happen," Holly said with an evil grin.

"Now; get in here and help with lunch before I make you starve," she ordered gruffly and smirked at Michael.

"Yes ma'am," Michael said and walked into the kitchen with his head down, pretending like he was a little boy in trouble.

He watched Holly for a moment when Livies caught his attention in the living room making a racket in her bag.

A short white candle sitting on the windowsill over the sink suddenly lit, and caused Holly to jump back with a little yelp. Michael was watching Livies play in her pouch when Holly jumped.

"What's wrong?" Michael asked, thinking she saw a spider or something. He looked over at her and saw her pointing at the candle in the window.

"Garian surprised me that's all," Holly told him.

"Oh I'm sorry dear; I didn't mean to scare you like that," the image of Garian's face in the flame of the candle spoke.

"I wanted to apologize to you and Michael about my unexpected departure and let you know I'll be returning tomorrow."

Apparently the voice had gotten Livies attention as well, and she came into the kitchen to see what all the commotion was about. As soon as she looked up and saw the face in the candle she started yelling.

"Help, big on's, help Livies; wizzy, wizzy, he'll get us," Livies squeaked in panic, hiding behind Michael's legs shaking.

"It ok Livies, he is Garian, a friend to us. This is his house we're staying in," Michael said patting Livies on her head.

In that second, Ravis let out an ear-splitting howl and came half-limping, half-running as fast as he could into the kitchen, so large in size he almost didn't fit through the door. He almost gave Michael a heart attack. He thought for sure Ravis was going to tear his backside off.

"LIVIES CALL RAVIS DOWN!" Holly yelled.

"It's okay boy. Wizzy scared Livies; that's all, it's okay, boy; settle down now; you're going to hurt yourself again," Livies told him stroking the fur under his chin.

Then a strange thing happened, Ravis went back down to his regular size.

"Oh my, it seems I have new houseguests. Please pardon me if I startled you and your wolf, little one," Garian's gentle voice carried through the candle flame.

"Who you calling 'little one', you big ol' meanie wizzy. I'm tall where I come from, thank you very much," Livies said bravely, still not moving away from Ravis or Michael.

"You have no need to fear me; Livies is it? My name is Garian; I was just talking to Holly and Michael," Garian said.

"Kruckles don't trust wizzys; they hurt wolves and snatch us up if they can," Livies said still shaking.

"My dear, you have nothing to fear from me or anyone else while you stay in my home," Garian said trying to reassure her, which seemed to help a little. Michael felt her quit shaking as much.

"And if you'll excuse me, I shall see everyone tomorrow. My sincere apologies for the fright," Garian said and the Aura candle went out, not even leaving a smoke trail.

"You didn't scare Livies, you mean ol' wizzy," she said much braver now that the face in the flame was gone.

Holly crossed the room quickly to check on Ravis, who was still at Livies' side.

"You okay, boy?" she asked gently, running her hand down his injured flank which caused him to flinch.

"You get back in there and lie down and be good a boy."

Ravis wouldn't move.

"Livies, would you tell him to go lay down? He needs rest."

Livies never said a word out loud, but Ravis went back into the living room and lay down on the round rug in front of the glowing fireplace.

"Livies, how did Ravis grow like that?" Holly asked, ever curious. Michael turned to hear the answer too.

"It's their reaction when they get ready to attack," Livies said.

Oh great that didn't make Michael feel any better.

"How interesting?" Holly said deep in thought.

It was hard imagine how powerful the Lunaris Cult had to be to control these wolves against their will.

"He wasn't going for me; was he Livies?" Michael asked.

"Livies don't know; his mind was cloudy because he's hurt. He just knew Livies thought she was in danger from a wizzy," she chirped like it was nothing.

"You mean a wizard Livies?" Holly asked.

"That's what we call them mean ol' culties," Livies replied.

"Ah, okay I got you dear," Holly said understandingly.

"Well that was quite rousing to say the least. Now what do you say we get back to having some lunch?" Holly said, getting her things together on the table.

She picked up some smoked ham, bread, and a little something for Michael as well.

"Ah you shouldn't have. How'd you know it was my favorite?" Michael asked Holly smiling.

"Valkriss told me." She beamed, seeing how happy he was.

He grabbed the small keg of Rockbite and carried it over to the counter to open it. After all that he could use a good drink. He couldn't find anything to pull the cork out. He couldn't risk hitting it, the mead would spill everywhere. He tried to pull it out with his fingertips with no luck. Then with his teeth and had no luck either.

"Damn it," he cursed quietly to himself, so Livies wouldn't overhear him.

"Oh dear," he looked at Holly exasperated and pointed at the cork.

"Would you? I can't find anything to open it," Michael asked sweetly.

"Sure; Flecto Cortex," Holly said lightly with a whirl of her right index finger.

That caused Livies to run and hide behind the door leading into the kitchen.

"Holly, are you a wizzy too?" she asked in surprise.

"Livies not all wizzys are bad ones. There are many, many good ones; I helped Ravis, didn't I?" Holly said.

"Yeah, but you used herbs for that; I saw you," Livies countered.

"You're right, however good wizzys use good magic to help, just like I used good herbs to help Ravis. Some people call using herbs magic," Holly said as she prepared lunch for them.

"Herbs not magic, its nature. All Kruckles use herbs and many other plants. We don't call it magic," Livies said inching her way back into the kitchen and closer to one of the chairs.

"You won't use bad magic on Livies or Ravis will you?"

"I promise Livies; I will never use bad magic on you or Ravis," Holly said, raising her right hand in the air as if making an oath.

That satisfied her and she climbed up the chair to the table where she placed her little bag and sat down beside it.

"Livies, how do you know Michael isn't a wizzy?" Holly asked.

"Mitchel packs a sword. Sword-swingers are too dumb to use magic," Livies said matter-of-factly.

Holly busted out laughing. Michael couldn't help but grin. He knew Livies never meant anything by it. It was just her way of putting things.

"No offense Mitchel; you know Livies likes you. You're not like those dumb sword-swingers. You a smart sword-swinger, you are," Livies proclaimed after hearing their reaction; like she was making him special.

"Why thank you Livies; I think," Michael told her.

"Livies, do you like human food?" Holly asked as her and Michael sat down to eat.

"Depends; what you got?" Livies asked raising an eyebrow.

"We have smoked ham; bread, mustard, pickles, hmm," Holly said trying to remember what else they had in stock.

Sadly due to the lateness of the season, fruits and vegetables were hard to find, good ones anyway.

"Livies likes pickles dipped in mustard," she squeaked, smiling showing her pretty little white teeth.

It was hard not to love the little tike, Michael thought, even though she was a bit funny looking.

"I'll fix it right up for you," Holly told her getting a small saucer and placing two medium sized dill pickles on it with some mustard.

"Now Michael would you like the same as Livies, dear?" Holly asked with a smile.

"Um, no thanks," Michael said and snarled his nose.

"Next time you say I'm getting fat, that's all you're getting to eat," Holly laughed while she sliced the ham and bread.

"Never another word," Michael said solemnly.

"Better; now get over here and eat," Holly ordered.

They sat at the table enjoying their lunch, hardly talking while they ate.

Afterwards they went to the living room to sit and relax each with their stomach full. Livies jumped right in between Holly and Michael on the couch. She plopped her little pouch in her lap and seemed content humming softly to herself which was hypnotic.

"Livies, would you mind if I asked you a few things?" Holly asked.

"Livies don't mind, big on'. What ya want to know?" Livies loved to talk and seemed to be opening up to Holly and Michael quite well.

"Tell me about Goshen," Holly asked.

"You would like it there. There are giant mushrooms, very good eatin'. Though we don't get enough black truffles because they are dangerous to hunt. They grow close to them mean ol' culties," Livies said in her little girlish tone.

"Do you mean the Lunaris Cult, Livies?" Holly asked.

Livies looked concerned.

"You know them?" she asked in a hushed whisper.

"Garian told us about them, we have never been to Kemlah," Holly said.

Livies relaxed a little and continued talking.

"We even trade with the big on's in the port of Kilar. It's not far from Goshen. Most of Kemlah is pretty safe, except where the wizzys are, and parts of the Samaramoon Forest are kinda bad. But Livies tell you something, if you keep secret. Will you?" Livies asked all serious.

"Cross your hearts and hope to die?" she added.

"We do," Michael and Holly said in unison.

"Us Kruckles got special powers," Livies said proudly.

"You do?" Michael asked with a smile which Livies took as disbelief.

"Oh Mitchel don't believe Livies. Would Mitchel like to see?" Livies asked sweetly.

"I'm sorry, Livies, I didn't mean to doubt you or anything. It's okay; you don't have to show me," Michael said.

"Are you scared Livies would hurt you bad?" she asked in an excited squeal.

"Yeah Mitchel, you're not afraid are you?" Holly teased.

"Of course not," Michael rebutted.

"We can't do it in here. We have to go outside," Livies said jumping off the couch.

"Ladies first," Michael said and followed them out the front door.

"Mitchel, you stand here beside the house," Livies ordered.

"Don't do any permanent damage, Livies,
I kinda like him," Holly said amused.

"No worries, Livies knows what she's
doing," she said and walked about fifty feet
away. She called out something that Michael
couldn't hear.

He saw something small flying through the
air right before it hit him and exploded into a
cloud of orange colored dust. He instantly started
sneezing and couldn't stop. Holly laughed as
Livies came running to them.

"See, Livies told you she had power. You
okay, Mitchel? Livies didn't want to hurt you
bad. Just teach you a lesson," she giggled.

"I think he'll be fine," Holly said still
laughing.

"Now let's get you back inside Livies,
before someone sees you out here," Holly told
her. Livies went in first followed by Holly and
Michael still sneezing.

"How long... will... this last?" Michael
finally got out in between two sneezes.

"Not long, Livies used her weak sneezing
spore powder on Mitchel. Livies likes Mitchel
and didn't want to hurt him much," Livies said.

Once they were back inside, the door opened again and Garian came in.

"Hello Garian," Michael said and stifled another sneeze.

"We thought you weren't coming back until tomorrow?" he asked.

"Change of plans," Garian smiled.

"You're not getting a cold, are you Michael?" Garian asked.

"Just allergies, it's nothing," Michael replied.

"Now where are my new guests?" Garian asked curiously.

"Are you a good wizzy, old on'?" Livies asked peeking out from behind Michael's leg. She had to make sure herself, not believing anyone else.

"Why yes, I try to be. My name is Garian, and yours?" he asked politely.

"Livies and my wolf Ravis is behind me; so don't think about doing anything suspicious, or there'll be trouble," Livies said in her most courageous voice.

"I would never dream of it; I Promise. There; is that good enough?" Garian said smiling warmly.

"Mitchel and Holly trust you, so Livies will trust you too," she squeaked, bounding over to him and stuck out her tiny little hand out for Garian to shake.

"You know Livies, you are the first Kruckle that has ever been in my house and that's saying a lot," Garian said looking down at her.

"Mitchel told Livies you all are going to her homeland come spring. Is that true old on'?" Livies asked.

"You may call me Garian. It sounds better than, 'old on'. And to answer you, yes, if everything works as planned, we will be going to Kemlah this spring," Garian told her, which made her break out into her little happy dance.

"Yay Livies happy; thanks Gerian."

"But right now, we have a lot of planning to do. We will have more visitors coming soon to stay with us, and we must make ready," Garian looked up from Livies to Holly and Michael.

"No problem, just let us know what you need, we'll do everything we can to help," Michael told him.

"Same here," Holly spoke up.

"Livies and Ravis too, we can help too."

"Thank you all for your willingness," Garian said sincerely.

"I'm sorry to be hasty, when I have just returned, but if the reports are true, we do not have much time to work. Our first order of business will be to expand my house and get it into shape to accommodate what's going to be needed soon. But for the minute, I have brought back with me some excellent food stocks from my travels. Would any of you care for some?"

"I believe our little friend here will appreciate this," Garian said as he reached into his pocket and pulled out a black truffle as big as his hand.

"Ooo is that for Livies?" she said already dancing in place.

"I thought I should bring you a little apology gift for startling you the other day," he said and reached the large truffle to her waiting hands.

The black truffle mushroom was as big as both of Livies hands were. As soon as she got it she went over to the fireplace and sat down eyeing it. She smelled it and then took a small nibble.

"Oh, oh! Yum, yum; solid grade number one!" she said.

"So many kind thanks Gerian. Livies hasn't had a number one grade in ten years."

"You are very welcome Livies," he told her smiling.

"Now how about you two? Interested in something to eat?" Garian asked heading for the kitchen.

"Sure, I'm always hungry," Michael perked up at the sound of food.

"How could I have guessed?" Holly said with a playful sneer as they followed him into the kitchen.

They sat at the table while Garian filled them in on the plans he had to change the house and what to expect come spring.

"You can't be serious Garian, there's no way we can defend against, let alone defeat a force the size of what you're describing," said Holly worried.

"You're right, we and the Stonebrook soldiers can't; however with the help that is coming, we stand a chance."

Holly knew she had to get word to Valkriss. She would just have to use an aura candle of Garian's. As far as she knew they had no recall memory of anyone who used them.

"That's all we can hope for; regardless whether we have a thousand men or ten thousand. Soladar will still come when the snow melts and the northern passes are free," Garian continued

They spent the entire winter going over battle plans and renovating the house. Michael found out just how useful magic really was when you need to get things done and didn't have a lot of men or time to do it.

He didn't know whether it was the thought of the impending spring attack or simply staying busy from sunup to sundown.
However time was on a fast track, barreling toward the spring destruction.

He had hardly noticed how fast until looking out the kitchen window one day and saw beautiful yellow lilies had sprung up outside.

Soon they were joined by Caleb and Ember, who Garian introduced as friends of his who had come to help. To Michael, both were quiet and content to keep to themselves in the newly built basement, which suited him, just fine.

Chapter 17
Wisterium

The Solum Lands were left as nature intended; forgotten by time, left in their pristine state, untouched my man. Its true name long lost through the eons of time. Few ever ventured here, afraid of the many legends that told of unfathomable creatures able to devour a person whole.

Of course little is to be believed when it comes to bibble babble nonsense, Ember thought. One must assume with a logical mind the tales of terror were told to scare off would be poachers who would exploit the natural riches of such a place.

He didn't care; the more people who believed the stories, meant less competition for him. He would have all the goodies to himself. He deserved it after all; it was him who found it.

After years and years of research, it was him and him alone who found it. Not some foolhardy, sword-swinging swashbuckler. Hmm I like that, I'll have to write that down in my journal later, but for now there's just too much to do, he thought.

He had waited patiently until winter ended and the weather had faired enough to make the journey.

Yes indeed, he had too much to explore in this new found land. He was sure it held untold riches. Yet there was one thing in particular he wanted; no needed more than anything else. The reason he began his search for the Solum Lands in the first place.

Wisterium; the one herb which had always eluded him in the past. All those fruitless searches, traveling to the farthest reaches of the known world. He hoped this miraculous herb wasn't just another useless legend meant to drive reasonable men like himself insane.

The sad part was most people spent their entire lives in search of treasure: gold, silver, and all manner of precious gems.

However Ember spent his life acquiring herbs, potions, and artifacts of the ancient world. Why most would toil in vain, trying to get their greedy little paws on non-living metals and stone was beyond him.

Unless of course they could be used in an artifact or brewing a concoction of some sort. He had heard stories of alchemists using various metals in their attempt to discover the legendary philosopher's stone; however none had succeeded to his knowledge. But even if it had been discovered, who in their right mind would openly admit to it, for fear of provoking thieves and would-be fame seekers. People who would do anything for a chance at immortality.

Was he any different? He wanted fame and glory, but for a different reason. He wanted to help others, and this herb was the key to making that happen.

Its properties were astounding to say the least, able to extend the life of potions indefinitely. When added to healing elixirs, they would cure any ailment.

Wisterium exhibited an ability he called adaptogen, because of its varied ways of interacting with other substances as well as the body.

He had one special reason his search had taken on a new sense of urgency. Garian had informed him Soladar was moving south as soon as winter ended. With the help of the newly recruited Vorlocks and their necromantic magic, no one would be able to withstand their disease based magical attacks.

The hideous dark curses, would cause the flesh to rot and fall off of a man in a day and could only be cured with help of Wisterium-aided healing potions.

Ember didn't think of himself as a healer by any means, just someone who liked to help others, and if doing so he gained, then so much the better.

At any rate, anything he could do to get in the way of Soladar would be better than standing around twiddling his thumbs waiting to be his next victim.

If he found out, his life would be forfeited. Little cold shivers ran down his spine at the idea of facing Soladar's fury. He could keep the herb a secret as well as its uses. He would surely keep its location hidden, but he knew he couldn't keep its abilities concealed from those who would surely need it.

Besides it was worth way too much fame and glory. If he perished at Soladar's hands because of it, it would just add to his legacy. People would celebrate him for years to come.

Maybe they'll make a holiday in his honor; Ember James Lyndhurst Day, oh that did have a nice ring to it. Maybe even change his name to Ember the Great. That brought a wide smile to his face. Was he crazy, he wondered? Not really, he just desired to be famous.

Ember grew up being a nobody from nowhere who received help from no one. And he knew a great many just like him, who society had swept away and forgotten about.

Thank the high heavens, something sparked inside him at an early age that ignited an all-consuming passion to learn about everything he could. It didn't really matter what the subject was, he would read about it until his curiosity was satisfied.

Before long he would pit his wit against Soladar's power. Would that be enough, he wondered, or should he just keep hoarding all the spoils to himself, as he had done since he was young?

Though he was only twenty-five years old, he had managed to accumulate a treasure trove of goodies, all squirreled away safely in his secret lair, as he like to call it.

His 'lair' was nothing more than a remodeled cave he found near the shore of the Saline Sea, half way between Cinnibar and Sindara. It was a perfect location, close enough to the port of Calumet in Cinnibar yet with Sindara close by as well.

With both cities close, he could sell his finds; at least the ones he could part with. The ones he prized, he stored in his cave. He used magic to camouflage the entrance and excavate it deeper with storage rooms off to each side.

The thing he was most proud of was the permanent teleport circle he made in the center of the cave. Anytime he was out, all he needed to do was simply draw a temporary teleport circle on the ground and teleport directly into the cave from anywhere without any trace left behind.

The only drawback was he still couldn't figure out how to teleport himself holding large items. Note to self, work on that when I get back, making a mental note to remember.

He found the cave when he was sixteen and been hoarding ever since. At first they were small things, little trinkets he picked up here and there. Then bigger and better things as he got older and wiser on what valuables to collect.

Okay, get yourself back to work he told himself. Let's find this herb before sundown and he set out cautiously exploring this strange and exciting land. It would be dark soon; about two hours, he noticed, as he held up his hand to the horizon to see how many hand-widths were between it and the setting sun.

He had read several descriptions of Wisterium, but how reliable they were; who knew? The best reference book, *Pardus Magiorium* described it as three to three and a half feet tall with round purple shoots at the tips. The body of the plant was red with spade shaped leaves of the same color. It was supposed to grow in shady, well drained valleys.

At least that would make for a good campsite if he wasn't successful finding it today he thought as he walked toward a forested hilly

area which would be perfect habitat for
Wisterium.

This would definitely be better than
discovering Flame Powder from the Boiling
Sands near the Neither Region. He accidently
found when he was searching for this place. He
tried to name it after himself, yet some damn
mage from the Auckley Council in Sindara
claimed to have discovered it two years prior.

They were probably just jealous. Besides
'Ember Powder' sounded much better than some
generic ass name like, Flame Powder. Just goes
to show you how lacking in imagination those
snobby high and mighty mages really were.

The powder was truly wonderful stuff to
experiment with, if you were careful how you
handled it. He learned that the hard way after
dropping just a few grains on his pants and
setting them ablaze burning his inner thighs
before he could put it out. He was just glad it
wasn't any higher up on his leg, he thought with
a snicker. That would have been far worse.

From then on he was extra careful
whenever he handled the powder. It was light
grey in color and cool to the touch, with a gritty

feel. It would ignite any combustible material wet or dry on contact.

Thankfully he had a fire-proof pouch that enabled him to carry plenty back to his cave for storage where he put it in metal containers for later use and experiments.

The pouch was invaluable carrying some with him as well. It proved extremely useful starting campfires when conditions were wet. He wasn't very skilled with fire based magic, or the use of flint and steel. His best abilities lay in mental based magic; teleports, illusions, and invisibly.

Invisibly was his favorite by far and so handy when trying to sneak a peek at ladies in taverns. He always felt a little perverted when he tried, which explained the fact he hadn't been very successful at it.

The last time he tried, he got so nervous he lost his concentration and caused the invisibly to wear off. He got a good slap across the face and thrown out of the tavern to boot.

He tried to play the whole thing off like he dropped something on the floor. However when you suddenly appear out of thin air on all fours near a ladies dress, it doesn't look good.

If she just hadn't screamed like a wild banshee, he thought grimacing. He would have made it out, without getting ruffed up so bad. After all, he was just looking and there wasn't any harm in looking, all guys did it.

They were jealous he had the skill to do it and they didn't. Still though, he hadn't tried it again. He was going to do it the old fashioned way from now on, winning them over with his wit and charm.

He was working on some great lines. He had already used one, when he was in a tavern in Lawrence: "Hi, my name's Ember. Can I light your fire?" Although the last fiery barmaid slapped him.

He was sure any woman with half a brain would immediately see what a fine catch he was. He had so much more to offer than those, dim witted muscle bound freaks with swords. Hmm that's another good phase I'll have to write down in my journal later too.

He didn't have anything against them. He had never met any intelligent ones before. One day the world would marvel at his knowledge and praise him wherever he went. He would show them all. They would never laugh at him again or whisper mean things about him, behind his back.

"Damn it's dusk," Ember cursed out loud.

He found the best place he could and made camp for the night. The night passed without incident and he woke up early. He was most certainly going to have to come back here. There were so many strange and wonderful things here; it would take years to explore fully.

He wished he could draw a permanent teleport circle here like the one in his cave, but he had to use a teleport spell on a scroll he had traded for.

He had bought a copy of the *Advance Teleportation Codex* book in Calumet and read some of it. He had the basics down, but finding time to practice was a chore. It was more fun finding things than working your butt off practicing magical enchantments over and over.

He sat and ate some of his dry rations and washed it down with some spring water he collected near his camp. He packed up his belongings and continued his search. It had be here, just had to be, he kept telling himself over and over as the day drew on and the sun rose ever higher.

He couldn't believe his eyes; wait check it first.

"Yes, Yes I found it; Wisterium!" he burst out loudly, before he was able to contain himself.

Of course he would; he put the work into it. He knew all along he would find it eventually, he thought confidently with the biggest smile he ever had in his life.

He pulled out his worn copy of *Pardus Magiorium* and opened it to the bookmarked page on Wisterium.

It said to collect the purple buds at the tip for use in potions; leaves were used in salves; and the roots should be dried and ground up into a fine powder for use in magical spells.

Oh sweet, Vehementer; he had hit the mother lode! There were at least ten Wisterium plants he could see within a twenty yard circle of him.

He went to work collecting the precious plant as if he were a surgeon collecting organs, separating each plant part into different pouches he brought just for the task.

He filled every pouch he had with him and wished he could take more. He had to make a map, he thought quickly. That way he would be able to get back without trouble.

He drew the best one he could – he was never much of an artist – yet the crude map would be good enough to guide him back. To any other it wouldn't make any sense and now for a teleport circle back to his lair. He carefully drew out the symbol on the ground with his powder and chanted.

"Portus Vecto," nothing happened.

"Portus Vecto," he said again this time louder; still nothing.

"Ah hell," he cursed out loud, should have known this would happen.

They were stories of magic not working right in the Solum Lands. At least some of the damn legends were true, he thought bitterly.

Walking took time, he had to get out by dark he thought. If he could get to the border he could use a temporary teleport circle; otherwise it's going to be another overnight stay.

He certainly didn't want to be in this wild land with who knows what kind of creatures roaming around. He was lucky enough to make it so far without any unfortunate encounters. He knew his luck would not hold out long, it had never been a friend to him.

Finally he reached a point where he thought a teleport circle would work. This time it worked and he was safely ensconced back in his lair. All his other treasures were mere trinkets compared to what he had now. And now that he knew the location of where to get more, he had it made.

He managed to buy a nice gentle mare and set out with his supplies in tow. Riding was not a skill he was very good at. If he was honest with himself, he was afraid of horses. So when he bought this one, he made sure to get one that was old and very forgiving of people.

At least Stonebrook was only a day's ride, even pulling the small cart from his cave. He would look just like another trader traveling to peddle his wares now that the warm spring weather was upon the region again.

Chapter 18
Earth Magic

The wind blew softly through the forest gently rustling the tender green canopy of budding leaves overhead.

Nightfall still came early this time of year; yet each day grew a little longer as spring approached. Coldness emanated from the earth forming a frosty layer of fog floating just above the ground, lending a dreamlike look to his surroundings. No matter how many times he'd been in the woods, it always amazed him, having something different to be seen in every place.

There was always a sense of excitement, yet today he had an overwhelming feeling of foreboding. The forest was too quiet.

He knew all too well what that meant, someone or something was out there. He slowed his pace to hear better; finally stopping.

Not even a bird chirping. He went into an extremely sensitive state of mind, a trance-like state. He became keenly aware of the faintest sound. The stirring of air caught his ears; they were coming up behind him.

Those foul malicious beasts he had been trying so hard to escape from. They had lent him no reprieve since Keswick, pursuing him now into the sixth day. They couldn't be more than a mile behind him and would be on him before long.

He was getting too tired and angry to run any longer. If he just had a horse, might as well pick a place to fight that's at least his choosing, Caleb thought. He found a small clearing with a short hill that had been cut in half by a shallow creek eroding it in times of hard rains. It formed a natural U-shape, perfect for channeling his best earth spells.

He had a slender one handed sword, yet his greatest skill lay in magic, trained from a child in the use of earth magic. It came so naturally to him that by the time he was twelve, he was better than those twice his age.

This fight would surely test his abilities to their fullest. He drew lay lines on the ground in front of him, which would aid him in the battle to come. Lay lines were lines an earth mage could draw in the ground and would act as channels.

One thing he learned early was how to channel the earth's natural energy and focus it with his spells. Once he had accidentally moved his house when he was only ten years old. He mislaid the lines and got a good scolding from his mother, when she got back from the market and found the house was fifty feet from the cobble stone path. He still smiled whenever he thought of it, in spite of himself.

Finally he finished his preparations and could hear them closing the distance. Those foul wretched beasts; anger consumed any lingering fear.

He began to focus on seeing and feeling all the energy around him. All living things had energy, even though it was diminished a little due to the season. He knew to draw down deeper.

Focus, he told himself harshly, see the energy in the air; earth, water, everything even the trees though dormant still stored it, he concentrated harder.

Little red and blue lines began to appear in front of his eyes which gleamed with power.

Now the first waves of Scarious were in sight. Caleb's hands went up from his side, palms up as he spoke in a booming voice.

"Shield me!" suddenly in the place where he drew the first set of lay lines, an invisible wall shot up from the ground in a split second.

The black devils in the lead smacked hard into it. Stunned at first, they wasted no time searching for a way around. Others beat furiously on it, throwing huge stones, beating on it with limbs ripped from nearby trees, and even trying to tear through the barrier with their steel-like claws. Once they were on the hunt they would not be denied their prey.

It wasn't long before they breached the first defense, but Caleb was just getting started. He was going to use every element to aid him in his fight.

The beasts soon closed the gap to the second set of lay lines. They sprung like a trap, the instant they were triggered. The earth became thick muck and swallowed the beasts to their knees. The natural concave shape of the bank behind him would act to intensify his channeling that would soon begin in earnest, now that they were in range.

"Earth, aid me. Air, hear thy call. Fire, come to me. Water, thy friend, defend me." Now all four elements were activated, he was ready. They rushed him and he focused on his best fire spell.

The black devils who been trapped by the second set of lines were close to being free while more were coming up from the rear when he cast an incendiary cloud, catching four in the middle, their screams were drowned out by the exploding spheres. Although his fire spells were weaker than his earth, they were still deadly.

He chanted, "Ignis Orbis," an arc of fire shot out in front of him, sending beasts running with their hides on fire. More closed in and now he was surrounded, just like he planned.

He dropped face first to the ground with his arms outstretched, the second they encircled him. The instant his fingers hit the dirt, they immediately sank into it along with the rest of him; melting right into the ground.

It was one of the trickiest spells he'd learned and always proved useful. It allowed him to disappear in one spot only to reappear in another. The only drawback was it was a short range spell and he had to reappear in a place within sight. However this was exactly his plan. The beasts would be right in the middle of the U-shaped earthen bank that would become their tomb.

He popped up a hundred feet behind them, chanting while his arms were still half buried in the ground, "Earth close upon my enemies."

The U-shaped bank came alive and closed together like two giant hands around the remaining devils sealing their fate forever.

He was weaker than usual after the fight. He hadn't had anything to eat of substance in two days. At times, he dreaded fall and winter months, not just because his magic diminished, but as he grew older, it was getting harder and harder to cope with the cold.

If he had his way, he would move to the Dwarf Islands south of Cinnibar, named after the dwarves who colonized them.

They left long ago preferring the safety of their ancestors' mountain homes to the annual storms, which could rage for weeks in the summer months. He frowned at the thought of giant waves and tropical storms, yet in recent years the weather had improved with no major storms to be heard of.

About his luck, as soon as he got settled in to a nice island home, he would get wiped out by a storm. Was there any place that didn't have its drawbacks, he wondered?

All that would have to wait, though. For now Soladar would have to be dealt with; exactly how, he didn't know. All he knew was him or anyone else would never be safe again as long as he drew breath.

He did have one hope in an old priest he heard about who lived in Stonebrook. A man named Garian; who if the tales were true, wielded immense power and would surely to help him.

It was widely known he was at odds with the Soladar. Caleb didn't know why; all he knew was an enemy of Soladar's was a friend of his.

Caleb saw first-hand the destruction Soladar caused. Flashbacks of the ruins of Tallan were still fresh in his mind. Intense fires raged for thirty days and nights before finally burning out, having nothing left for fuel.

The blackened ruins were an eerie sight in the pale moonlight. Wisps of smoke drifted through the air mixed with the smell of charred wood and death.

Destruction of this scale could only be caused by someone like Soladar. Only his incredible power could have caused such complete and utter devastation. It was one thing to read about such things in books or listen to a sad bard's tale, yet to see it firsthand was surreal, numbing the senses

After seeing the destruction of Tallan, he knew which side he was on. Now that his beloved mother was gone, he didn't have to worry about anyone missing him.

At least from what he knew, which was little since his mother never spoke of his father only saying he died shortly after his birth. As the years passed his questions were met with silence, so over time he stopped asking.

He had to make it to Stonebrook. That would be Soladar's next logical target after sacking Tallan. Sindara was his home city, it was too far south for now. Stonebrook was north of Cinnibar and would have to fall when Soladar moved south.

Caleb rested a little before setting off again. He knew he wasn't more than a day's travel at most if he traveled through the night to reach it. He used a favorite spell to draw energy from the earth and give him the strength he needed to overcome the fatigue.

Soon dawn was embracing the land once again with the warm rays of the springtime sun, thawing the land from the winter's grip.

He was at Garian's by midday, tired and ready for rest, but first there were things he needed to know.

Chapter 19
Vorlocks

Damn them to the fires of Hell itself! I will see their blood run freely. I will spill it upon this earth. Not one shall escape my wrath, in my anger they will perish! My heart consumed with fury; rage, and indignation. My soul locked in eternal battle between good and evil.

Screams of my torment cause the heavens to tremble; tears of lament flood the earth beneath.

In ancient times, it was foretold one would come and the earth would tremble with every step he took. He would become one of the scared ones, taking within him the power of chaos, dealing death and destruction to all who oppose him.

None shall stand against him; any who do, their strength shall waste away like a delicate flower in the desert sun.

Yet his power shall not be whole until the completion of the Parca Staff, and then his power will be absolute.

"Go; find more slaves to do my bidding," Soladar commanded, his voice dripping with distain.

"Raid and plunder as you like, yet bring any captives alive; NOW GO!" Soladar finished in his deep booming voice.

"Yes master," grunted the Scarious leader and slowly turned to go.

"One last thing," Soladar spoke again. The enormous black devil turned back to face his dreadful master.

"Kill any who resist, but leave Stonebrook alone. I have special plans for it. Seems Adrelia and Michael have sought the aid of Garian, who will pay for his betrayal. I will deal with him personally," Soladar finished.

"Anything else master?" the foul creature asked before leaving.

"That is all," Soladar said, dismissing the beast with a wave of his hand.

Now that spring had come, his forces were ready to march south. They went forth in astounding fury, all were struck with awe. Village after village fell; most without a fight, many were already empty. People fled in terror as news of the invading forces of Soladar were on the move south.

Word finally reached Stonebrook and they sent calls for help to Cinnibar; Helcon and every village in between.

Soldiers finished reinforcements to the outer defenses as fast as they could, figuring they had two to three days before they faced the full wrath of Soladar.

Little did they know they would be dealing with a new terror in Soladar's arsenal; Vorlocks. They are born of evil and raised on the hatred of all that is good; lovers of filth, consuming anything warm-blooded. These were the foulest creatures known to walk the earth, if that's what they did.

They preferred the blackness of night to spread their terror upon the land. If one was even rumored to be in an area, that place was avoided by everyone. Even the hardiest adventurer would not dare tread into that territory.

The Vorlocks were descended from an ancient warlock cult that worshipped the god Vor. A dreadful; malicious monster of a god, who demanded all manner of sacrifices, even human. To show their true devotion to their god, they transformed themselves into the creatures now known as Vorlocks.

Not only could they perform magic, but had incredible strength and flew using leathery wings. They have no neck, their head being part of their upper body. They have two pair of short arms which extend from their wings, and razor sharp claws protruding from their fingers.

They can move in and out of shadows at will, having black leather-like skin, making it nearly impossible for them to be seen at night. They're even mistaken as shadows in the daylight.

The Vorlocks most fearsome weapon is their magical prowess, which has been maintained through the centuries. Their warlock spells still effective as ever and anyone who ever faced one and lived to tell the tale knows full well why they are to be feared.

The warlock cult that formed the Vorlocks was made up of the most devilish wizards and mages. They delved into the deepest, foulest necromantic arts.

Their downfall however, was at the hands of Glollas himself, who died after killing Kavanaugh their high leader.

Decimated; their remnants scattered to the four winds and now were reunited under Soladar. He promised them a return to their original glory and power. Soladar knew there would be no counting on brute force alone to win the battle to come in Stonebrook and defeating the one he loathed to think of; Garian. He would take care of him just like he had Delwen.

Oh what fun he was going to have. The Vorlocks were going to have another souvenir. And if they were lucky, they would have the son of Delwen right beside his father. They should be very pleased to finally have an end to the bloodline of Glollas and revenge the killing of Kavanaugh.

He didn't care whether they were happy or not, as long as they did his bidding. If they didn't, they would join their dearly departed leader in eternal slumber.

He had to make sure no one killed Garian except for him. It was his doing and his alone which set the chain of events in motion to begin with. Soladar thought angrily to as he stood surveying his massive army which was preparing to camp for the night.

The Vorlocks were the leading edge and would travel on through the night taking up forward positions and would signal an alert in the event of an early counteroffensive. They also went first because they simply preferred nighttime, which suited Soladar just fine. Besides, they were making the rest of his forces nervous.

Soladar had a three prong attack laid out for Stonebrook. First the Demergos would come up from their home out of the Alleghany Swamp and attack the Cinnibar forces.

Then, with the Stonebrook forces helping them, he would attack with his Vorlocks on Lawrence's army which was coming in from the west and drive them into Stonebrook.

Finally he would use the bulk of his Scarious army to come in from the north and close in on the city like a vise. He would hold the remaining units in reserve until needed and use them to deliver the final death blow.

Soladar knew speed would prove to be the winning move in this chess match. He would have his revenge on Garian, take Adrelia and be long gone.

Had it not been for Garian, his fate would have been completely different. He would not be the raving lunatic he was now. Although at times and in some sadistic way he was glad he was the way he was now, having access to power beyond imagination.

Soon he would be able to do what he was unable to do so many years ago, destroy the Orb of Chaos. With the three parts of the Parca Staff finally reunited, he would control Time and Fate and be counted as one of the gods.

He would be the one who wielded unprecedented power, able to restore what once was; order and no more freewill. He could even turn back time and capture the love of Ezmora, the mother of his beautiful Adrelia.

With his contacts in Lawrence, he had been able to locate Adrelia and would have had her had it not been for that continued thorn in his side; Michael.

The air around Soladar crackled with energy as rage welled up inside him again.

"Oh yes Michael, I know your secrets. I know them well," Soladar whispered into the wind, as if he was talking to it.

Now with the Solaris staff, all he had to do was acquire Tellus the Earth Staff, and Noctila the Moon Staff. Once he was finished with Stonebrook, he would be off to Kemlah for the moon staff.

The earth staff would be a little trickier; though he knew it was at Castle Lake. Its exact location there or even how to retrieve it was unknown.

According to the reports he had, the dwarves hid a scroll deep within their earthen caverns. It contained one word which when spoken near the staff would cause it to rise to the surface.

His plan was to combine the sun and moon staffs together and with its power defeat the dwarves, for they were a formidable foe indeed.

What Soladar did not know was Garian had already found the earth staff and he would meet the full force of its power, head on in the battle of Stonebrook.

A seething boiling rage overtook Soladar whenever he thought of what Garian had cost him. The air crackled again with an electrifying terror, causing nearby devils to panic and run away.

In another day's travel, he would be in position to launch his attack. He would have to divide some of his forces, sending units south and join the Demergos to intercept Cinnibar's army, which would answer Stonebrook's call to arms.

Any soldiers coming west from Lawrence he would outflank, getting behind them, and drive them into Stonebrook. There he would fall on them like a sledge hammer, crushing them all together with his main force.

Chapter 20
Sir Lawrence

Lawrence's forward units met fierce resistance and were making little headway. At least they kept some of Soladar's forces occupied and kept them from joining the fight south of Stonebrook.

Little did anyone know that the famous general himself would be leading his entire army eastward to join the fray, leaving behind only enough to protect the city.

Sir Lawrence had heard about Soladar's destruction and now was the time to act. It was time for him to join with Cinnibar and Stonebrook. He hoped the combined might of the armies would be enough to prevail.

A dream worth dying for, he imagined as he sat staring at the flickering flames of the campfire. The sound of footsteps and rustling of armor brought him out of his thoughts.

"Sir, I have reports from the forward scouts near Stonebrook," Captain Azurus spoke while standing at attention.

"At ease captain and deliver your report," Lawrence spoke crisply, having no time for pleasantries.

"Sir; Cinnibar's forces have broken through Soladar's southern lines and have reached Stonebrook. Our forward Calvary units have met stiff resistance ten miles east of here. They're holding now, but not much longer," the captain spoke in a shaky tone.

"Steady yourself solider," Lawrence said in a firm reassuring voice.

"Sir, our scouts also report Soladar is mustering his main forces to the north of the city. The ones we're encountering are splinters off his main army, meant to keep us from reaching the city in time," Captain Azurus finished.

"Is that what you fear, captain?" Lawrence questioned.

"No sir; Soladar has unleashed a new terror, which attacked our scouts on their return. Two were killed only four returned," the captain added quickly.

"I want to see the surviving scouts; now," Lawrence spoke a little more harshly than he had meant to.

"Sir, they're being treated for their wounds. Shall I get them from the medic tent?" Captain Azurus asked.

"No, I will go to them," Lawrence said getting up.

"Captain Azurus sound the ready alarm. We make for Stonebrook tonight," Lawrence commanded.

"But sir; you wish to travel at night?"

"Did I stutter Captain? Get ready to march; you have two hours," Lawrence finished, turned and left without another word.

The time for talk was over and now action must follow. Lawrence walked through the camp to the sound of the ready alarm setting soldiers scrambling in a rush of activity.

He knew his troops better than anyone, and he knew they would follow his lead without question.

He finally made his way over to the medics area located in the center of the encampment so the wounded could be protected from all sides.

As Lawrence approached, his chief army surgeon was coming out of the main hospital field tent. When he saw Lawrence, him and two of his assistants stopped and saluted.

"Evening sir," Chief Surgeon Darias spoke in a young sounding voice, betraying his age.

"Are the scouts well enough to speak?"

"One of them may be in a while," Darias answered.

"Three have succumbed to their injuries," he went on.

"Most grievous indeed," he finished nearly muttering to himself.

"Might I have a word with you in private, sir?" Darias asked as he waved for his assistants to leave them alone.

"What is it chief; and why so private?" Lawrence asked curtly.

"Sir, the scouts' injuries were not; were not normal," the chief said with his brow furrowed deeply.

"Out with it, man; we don't have all night," Lawrence spoke, his patience wearing thin.

"Sir their injuries were not from sword or arrow, but by magic; a most foul magic of which I have never seen before. It caused their flesh to rot and fall off, even to the bone. That's what killed three of the scouts. The fourth one lived because I was able to amputate his left arm and stop the spread of the deadly rot. No medicine I have; ointment or otherwise worked," Darias continued.

"The surviving scout keeps talking about being attacked by a bat-like human. I gave him something for the pain as well as his nerves," Darias finished.

"Is he able to talk at all?" Lawrence asked.

"I doubt it, sir," Darias replied.

"He may be in better shape in the morning; I'll have one of my assistants do hourly checks and will send word to you as soon as he is well enough to talk," he finished.

"That will do Chief; we'll leave a small detachment here with you to operate as our rear base of support. Make sure the dead scouts are buried quickly, so no disease spreads," Lawrence ordered.

"Yes Sir."

Lawrence's mind was racing. He had heard Soladar had a deadly new weapon, and soon they would find out just what that was. Lawrence didn't put anything past Soladar. He knew the stories well enough to know he would use anything or anyone to get what he wanted, Lawrence thought returning to his tent, which was already being packed for the move.

Captain Azurus stood waiting.

"How long till were ready to move, Captain?" Lawrence asked.

"Thirty minutes sir, and we'll be ready. We're getting extra enchanted lanterns ready now so we'll have sufficient light for the horses and men. Where should we station the mages sir?"

"At the rear captain; that will be our little surprise for Soladar," Lawrence said smiling.

Fortunately Lawrence forged an unlikely alliance with the Auckley Council of Mages in Sindara. He still was unsure why they had sent a diplomat to him over the winter with promises of new cooperation. He was very happy they did now that he was going up against Soladar and his minions.

They had sent one hundred twenty of their best mages in answer to his call, which was a hundred twenty more than he thought they would send. He learned growing up, talk was cheap and action spoke louder than words.

This would place him deeply in their debt and they knew that. Because of that; it was an unwelcomed addition to his ranks, although a much needed one now with this new horror filling Soladar's masses.

"I'll take the lead captain, when we're ready. Call up my knights, they'll ride with me," Lawrence ordered.

"Yes, sir," Captain Azurus responded and turned to carry out the orders.

Lawrence knew he could trust his battle hardened knights to deliver a punishing blow and hopefully act as a spearhead to break up Soladar's forces into smaller groups then encircle them.

So far it seemed Soladar had underestimated the strength and size of his army. Lawrence had called in his reserve units, and with the help of King Galanar, mobilized the local legionnaires. His forces now numbered five thousand strong, with one thousand knights in full battle armor.

One problem though; what was this new threat Soladar had, Lawrence wondered? He had little understanding of magic if that's what it was that had killed the five scouts. He preferred to place his trust in the cold hard steel of his sword. The sounds of horses approaching brought him out of his thoughts again.

He turned around and before him one thousand knights in full battle armor surrounded by light bearers on all sides stood ready.

Captain Azurus walked up with the reins of Lawrence's horse in his hand.

"Here you go sir," the captain said handing the reins to Lawrence.

"Thank you captain," Lawrence said as he mounted his massive pale grey warhorse.

"Captain," Lawrence said.

"Yes sir?"

"One last order for you; find Tiberious and get him to me in Stonebrook as fast as you can."

"But sir, he's not been heard from in four years," Azurus said stunned.

"Well then, you better hurry and find him. Now, Captain," Sir Lawrence said stiffly.

"YES SIR!" Captain Azurus said, evidently frustrated at not being able to join in the battle of and rode off in a full gallop.

"On my mark! Forward march!" Lawrence shouted as he took the lead.

He wondered if this would be his last battle, as they rode toward Stonebrook.

There was an eerie silence in the forest, an unnatural calm settled in the ranks of the troops. The only sounds to be heard were of jangling armor and horses. This would be the largest fight Lawrence had been in since the Great War and would cement his position to take over the throne.

King Galanar had no heirs, and all eyes were on him. He would show them he was worthy.

"Ride hard men, our troops need us!" Lawrence yelled. "Let us ride to victory. May the Gods be with us!"

With that they quickened their pace.

Before long they were joining the fight head on with a vengeance.

"Knights to me! Stay tight! Charge!" Lawrence gave the command with ferocity born of pure determination. Steel clashed like thunder tearing through the sky.

"Leave none alive! Fight on to Stonebrook! Break their ranks!"

Sir Lawrence rode up to his field commander of his Calvary.

"You got here just in time, sir," the seasoned soldier told him.

"Round up all the men you have left and make a push for Stonebrook. We'll handle things here commander," Lawrence ordered.

"Yes sir," the commander replied and turned to round up his remaining men. Lawrence could hear him off in the distance.

"First Calvary, on my mark, Second Calvary close in behind. Close ranks; onward march!"

"Sir we have something coming in from the north hitting our left flank. The men can't see them sir," Grahn his major general of the fifth battalion reported out of breath, his armor showing signs of the raging battle.

"Bring the mages in from the rear. Get every light bearer we have up there NOW!"

"YES SIR!" Grahn snapped a salute and rode off at full speed.

"Knights to my side!" Lawrence shouted the order for them to reform.

The knights immediately formed up behind him in an arrow-like formation.

"On my mark! Left flank; forward march! Do not break formation!" Lawrence moved with them to fight this new terror of Soladar's.

Whatever it was, it would die just like the others.

The sky in front of them lit up as the light-bearers concentrated their efforts ahead of them. Red; white, blue, and yellow streaks screamed overhead from the incredible barrage of magic missiles being launched at shadowy figures.

"What are they sir?" Fultz, one of his most loyal knights asked as they closed in.

"Don't know, but we're getting ready to find out. Make sure the mages have plenty of cover," Lawrence ordered.

"Yes sir," Fultz said and rode to the rear of the battalion to relay Lawrence's order before riding back up to join his place beside him.

"Knights close ranks! Shields up!" Was the last order Lawrence was able to get out before they were being swarmed by shadowy winged creatures.

"Light-bearers to the front; NOW!" Lawrence yelled as loud as he could.

"We've got to see what we're fighting or we are all going to die!"

Every time he swung his sword, it struck nothing but thin air.

"Damn it, show yourselves cowards!" Lawrence screamed angrily.

Finally the light-bearers got close enough so they could see what they were up against. At first sight, Lawrence's stomach was sick. He had fallen right into Soladar's trap. They were being attacked by Vorlocks and would all die if he didn't do something fast.

"Tell the mages to use their best fire power, NOW!" he ordered Grahn.

"Yes sir."

They were being swarmed on every side. Most soldiers were simply fighting thin air not even seeing their enemy until it was too late.

"Get all our units out of here. Reform half in front leading our way to Stonebrook and the rest guard our rear flanks. Gather all troops and move out as fast as possible," he gave the order, hoping it wasn't too late.

Something flew at him from the shadows knocking him off his horse.

"Finally bastard, show me what you're made of; let's see if you bleed?" Lawrence seethed with rage as the accursed vorlock came at him.

He spun left bringing his sword down hard catching the spineless half-breed human in its midsection, nearly cutting it in half.

"Guess you can die, you ugly son-of-a-bitch," he said smiling, right before he was knocked to the ground by another one.

"Oh yeah, now it's getting fun. Fight like a man, coward," Lawrence spat at the leathery black figure.

The most intense pain he had ever felt seared its way into his right shoulder.

"You're not trying to bite me are you; you skimpy no good for nothing devil," Lawrence said through clenched teeth, god it was great to feel so alive.

Every muscle in him was surging with power, energy he hadn't felt in years.

Now back on his feet, the vorlock in front of him was doing something with its hands like working a spell. It wasn't fast enough and within a blink of an eye Lawrence had sliced it down the middle.

His trusted horse never left his side during the whole fight. Once he got back into his saddle, he looked around and saw everyone was moving together toward Stonebrook.

"Sir, you okay?" it was Grahn asking as he rode up beside him.

"Just a scratch, nothing to worry about. Is everyone moving out?"

"Yes sir, we've suffered hard losses. If not been for the mages, we would have lost even more," Major General Grahn reported.

"Let's try to get to Stonebrook; they can't be faring well even with the aid of Garian. Dispatch a man to warn them against what's coming if they don't know already.

"Also send one to General Holt let him know we're coming in hard from the west, so there's no confusion when we arrive," Lawrence ordered and then rode fast to catch up to the others.

Chapter 21
Battle of Stonebrook

"Mother Earth, hear thy call; aid us in our time of need!" Garian's voice boomed over the intense battle.

A great rumbling sound grew to a deafening roar as the earth rose up in answer to Garian's call, reinforcing the crumbling walls of the city being torn apart by Soladar's fury. Thankfully Cinnibar's army had managed to fight their way through the southern enemy lines and reach Stonebrook just in time as the main assault was taking place.

Now Sir Lawrence's army came in fighting from the west. Lawrence rode straight into the heat of the raging battle followed by his knights.

"Fight hard!"

You could hear him call out as he reared up on his stallion, crushing a bullyworg underneath. He rode through the main front gates, which were thrown wide open to allow

Cinnibar's army in to fight Soladar's attacking forces from the north.

"Have you seen Garian?" Lawrence asked a nearby soldier.

"Up ahead, he's reinforcing the walls."

Once he was closer, it wasn't hard to spot Garian. He was standing near the rear entrance, staff in hand, working powerful spells to keep Soladar's minions at bay.

"Looks like you can use some help, old friend," Lawrence said.

"Glad to have you," Garian said his spirit being raised having added help.

"We have a big problem. We were attacked by Vorlocks directly west of here, and they're fast on our heels. The Sindara mages were the only reason we could make a break for it," Lawrence said grimly.

"I had suspicions, yet I didn't think he would go that far. I see now he will stop at nothing to get what he wants. Get fifty knights and take them to my house just southeast of the main gate. I'll be right there; the earth shield will hold a while yet," Garian told Lawrence.

"Okay old friend; I'm going to trust you on this one," Lawrence said and rode off to find Grahn.

General Holt had set up a field headquarters near Garian's house.

"Good to see you General Holt. It's been a while," Lawrence said dismounting from his horse.

"Has anyone seen Major General Grahn?" Lawrence asked.

"Right here sir," he spoke up from behind him.

"Damn it man, you gave me a shock," Lawrence fumed.

"Sorry sir,"

"No need. Round up fifty of my best knights and bring them here to me as fast as you can," Lawrence ordered.

"Yes sir," Grahn said, already mounting back up on his horse.

"General Holt; did my message get to you?" Lawrence asked quickly.

"Yes, coming from anyone else and I would have thought they had lost their mind. Vorlocks of that number haven't been heard of since the times of Glollas," Holt said.

"If I hadn't been there general, I'd thought it a tall tale myself," Lawrence said as Garian walked up.

"Hello gentlemen; my apologies there's no time for pleasantries. Now if we can meet inside my house for a moment," Garian said.

They followed him inside and saw that he had made his house into a mini headquarters of sorts. The living room had been cleared of all furniture and a large table sat squarely in the middle with papers piled high. There were people running to and from every direction in the house. It was much larger inside than it appeared it could be from the outside.

A tall lanky red-haired young man was working furiously in the kitchen measuring and placing some kind of powder into small bags.

Garian's front door opened, in came Michael with Livies riding on his back her head barely out of a pouch followed by Holly and Ravis. Every one of them looked as if they had been in the thick of the battle.

"You called for us Garian?" Michael asked.

"Yes; this is Sir Lawrence and General Holt. They've come to help. However I'm afraid we have something that's going to be difficult to content with on its way as I speak. Vorlocks attacked Lawrence's troops as they were coming in. I suspected Soladar was up to something and now we know. However fate has brought us help; Ember would you care to join us a minute?" Garian asked.

The tall slim red haired man who was in the kitchen walked into the living room.

"This is Ember; he is preparing small pouches of Flame Powder which will be our best weapon against the Vorlocks. Our supply is limited, and we must use it carefully. Lawrence, we will give foil pouches to those fifty knights I asked you to round up. They are to use it only against vorlocks, nothing else. It will burn anything that is combustible and they will not be able to put it out thanks to a little additive of mine," Garian instructed and noticed Lawrence sway a little.

"You alright Lawrence?" Garian asked.

"It's nothing, just a scratch from one of those bastard vorlocks, managed to get me on the shoulder; that's all," Lawrence said sweating profusely.

"Let me see," Garian told him.

"Ember get the healing salve with Wisterium mixed in it. No time like the present to see if it works. Lawrence we haven't had time to try this out yet, so you'll be first," Garian said.

"Oh great just my luck," he grimaced.

"The vorlock's diseased touch can kill a man in less than twenty-four hours, and there's no known cure. Or there wasn't until now. Take that piece of shoulder plate off," Garian directed.

The wound on his shoulder was now solid black and spreading down his chest.

"Here, let me see your hand," Garian said pouring a small amount in it.

"Now rub it in well."

As soon as Lawrence did, he felt a tingling sensation and color returning to the affected area.

"Ember, looks like you saved my hide. I will not forget it. Garian, how much more do you have?" Lawrence asked moving his shoulder, amazed it was already healed.

"Just glad I could help," Ember said humbly.

"It was Ember here who brought us the Flame Powder and Wisterium. He has proved extremely useful," Garian said proudly before returning to the battle plans.

"Now, once the earth barrier breaks, Soladar will come at me first. We have an old score to settle. He will use his forces to overrun the city and provide him the distraction he needs," Garian spoke quickly.

"A distraction for what?" this time it was Holly who spoke up.

"Why to kill me and kidnap you of course," Garian said with a sickenly light tone.

"Like to see him try," Michael said gritting his teeth and feeling his old friend rage beginning to boil again, his grip tightening on his sword.

"There'll be time for that Michael. Holly, I know there's no use to try to talk you into staying inside my house is there?" Garian asked one last time.

"Not a chance in hell; I got some payback to dish out myself. Besides I can't let you men have all the fun; can I?" Holly said smiling.

"I'll stay close to Michael," she said gripping his arm, reassuring him.

"I like a woman like you Holly. We need some in our ranks. If you know any, send them our way," Lawrence said beaming.

"Sure thing," Holly said a little bashful about the praise Lawrence lavished on her.

"Okay, now Lawrence we need those fifty knights and the Auckley Mages to fight the Vorlocks. Keep them at bay at all costs. We cannot have them entering the city. Caleb's a very talented young man, he will direct the mages.

"Anyone who gets hit by a Vorlock, bring them to my place. We have set up a small infirmary in the second room on your left. Ember and his assistants will treat them with the Wisterium. All the other injured, take them to the main hospital set up inside the Stonebrook gates.

"Lawrence you and the rest of your knights can be the forward assault force when the barrier breaks.

"General Holt, we need to protect the rear and send one battalion on each side of the city's walls and hit Soladar's army from both sides at once. It will drive them straight into us," Garian paused.

"What if he overruns us?" Holt asked.

"Have your battalions fall back to the rear and come into the city using the front gate and help us with Soladar's main assault," Garian answered.

"Do we have any more help on the way?" Lawrence asked.

"Sindara's forces have been hindered by Soladar and he has managed to cut off the Helconian Warriors as well. We have what we have, I'm afraid," Garian said gravely.

"Then it will be enough!" Lawrence declared, looking around the room seeing faces full of resolve, though one troubled him.

Michael was a spitting image of his father at that age. If he only knew it was him who had given the order which resulted in Delwen's death. He wondered how Michael would feel about him then.

If he lived through the battle to come, he hoped Tiberious would provide the answers to why Delwen and now Michael were connected in all this.

"The earth barricade is ready to fail; any questions?" Garian waited a second.

"May the gods bless us with victory," he told them as they filed out of his house, where the knights stood ready.

"Ember get those pouches and show them how to use them," Garian told him before heading off into the city again.

"All right men; listen and do whatever Ember tells you to do. To disobey him is to disobey me; understand?" Lawrence ordered, to the sounds of men yelling.

"YES SIR!"

Then he mounted up on his stallion and rode off to round up his troops. A few of the Vorlocks had already broken through and were making their way towards Garian's.

Oh hell here they come Ember thought. He told the knights what to do as quickly as he could and then ran back into the safety of Garian's house. He was there to help. This wasn't his war to fight. He'd be damned if he was going to get himself killed, especially now that he had his new fame.

Livies rode in a little pouch on Michael's back, which he made for her since she would be safer there than riding on Ravis, who was right beside Holly. Michael swore that damn wolf spent more time with her than he did.

Ravis was already enraged and stood well past Michael's chest. Any human or beast with half a brain that saw him immediately ran away, and any who didn't Ravis made extremely fast work of them.

There was a deafening boom and the earth barrier gave way. Soladar was immense and looked like he was two stories tall riding on nothing more than the air itself. Fire streamed from the staff in his hand, as bright as the summer sun burning everything it touched.

Garian struck the ground with the earth staff and dirt flew up covering the buildings that had been set ablaze.

Scarious now came in droves, wave after endless wave. Holly was doing her best, using her most powerful spells. Lawrence and his knights charged right into the heart of them, cutting them down like mowing wheat.

Lightening came striking down at Soladar when he moved toward Holly, who had gotten separated during the chaos of the invading horde.

"Honos, grant me the strength I need!" Michael shouted, killing everything in front of him.

Livies was quite useful throwing her bags of mushroom spores, blinding some, causing other to gag, and even managed to set a couple on fire. Yet Michael could not get to Holly before Soladar did.

"No! Holly!" Michael yelled.

"I have you now, my dear," Soladar was smiling insanely.

"Really! We'll see!" Holly screamed and ran straight at him.

He looked at her with the welcoming smile of a parent.

"Ilire Illum Exploria," she screamed, pointing her wand directly at him.

Intense searing yellow fire erupted from her wand and flew directly at Soladar, who simply batted it away with a wave of his staff. In another second, he had her enclosed in a giant invisible hand which held her in midair.

Michael redoubled his efforts trying to reach her, yet he was knocked to the ground sending Livies scrambling out of her pouch.

"Run, Livies! Get Ravis and get back to Garian's!" Michael yelled over the noise of the ensuing battle.

"Livies never leave Mitchel!"

Michael couldn't get another word out before they were overwhelmed again fighting for their lives. Ravis was absolutely ferocious, tearing devils apart left and right with Livies now riding on his back, throwing spore bags as fast as her little arms could.

Everything seemed to stop for a second. The sky opened up and massive lightening came down striking around Soladar preventing him from moving. Then an equally bright flash of fire broke through it. The ground shook so violently it seemed as if every building was going to crumble.

"Ahh Garian you have it!" Soladar's voice boomed as sunfire shot out toward Garian who made a huge wall of earth come up to protect him. The heat of the fire was so intense that it turned the earth into molten lava.

"Water, thy friend, aid thee!" Caleb spoke and water gushed forth from nearby wells and turned the lava into black glass.

"Looks like you could use a little help Garian," Caleb said running up to his side.

"The vorlocks weren't enough for you?" Garian said before they were on the defensive again.

All the while Michael was desperately trying to get to Holly when he finally managed to get underneath the invisible force holding her. He went swinging wildly at it, yet to no avail. If he couldn't harm it, he knew one he could. He charged at Soladar with every ounce of fury in him.

Soladar saw him coming and pointed the Solaris staff at him and engulfed him in fire, which never fazed him. Now Soladar knew he was right. In the next second, he hit Michael with a force spell which sent him flying backwards over a hundred feet, knocking him unconscious.

It's truly a shame when you little piss ants think can take me on. I will slay every one of you. Get the staff, Soladar, you must have it; forget Adrelia; forget everything. All will be yours once the Orb is destroyed. Time will be at your mercy.

A turn of fate will make it as though none of these worms ever lived. You will be the supreme god, Soladar's was mind racing.

Soladar directed all his reserve forces into the fray overwhelming their opponents just long enough for him to get at Garian forgetting about everyone else. They fought as told in epic tales of old, yet in the end, it was Soladar who managed to overcome Garian using the one thing he knew Garian valued more than he did, human life, which was just a means to an end for Soladar.

Unfortunately the bastard's little helper mage had wrangled Adrelia from his grasp while he was busy with Garian. Nothing mattered now he had Trellis.

Now there was only one piece of the puzzle left to get: Noctila. And with that, he would do what he could not years before.

Once he had the staff, he withdrew his forces which had been on the losing end of the battle. He would increase his ranks and make sure to attack Lawrence, Cinnibar, and Sindara while he headed for Kemlah. With their destruction, there would be no interference when he returned to destroy the Orb of Chaos.

"Their retreating!"

Word spread quickly to all the others, who were overjoyed with their victory. However it had been a costly one, which left many dead and wounded. The hospital was flooded with injured, and there were a steady stream of vorlock victims going in and out of Garian's.

"Mitchel, Mitchel; Oh Mitchel. What's Lives going to do without her Mitchel!" she wailed over Michael's chest, not realizing he had only been knocked out from the force of the blast.

"Livies let me check him!" Holly told her frantically trying to see if he was breathing.

"Oh Mitchel! What's Livies going to do without you?" she whimpered with tearful eyes.

"Livies tried to help Mitchel, but wasn't fast enough. Now Mitchel has left Livies all alone. I know; I know I got more Gamuca, that will help him, won't it Holly? Holly a good wizzy; help bring him back to Livies, please. Please bring him back. You're such a good wizzy," Livies was in hysterics.

"Livies, he's breathing, Michael's going to be okay," Holly said with tears in her eyes as well.

"Yay, Yay! Livies knew Holly the good wizzy could do it. You brought Livies' Mitchel back to her. Livies never forget Holly for bringing Livies' Mitchel back to her," Livies said, dancing around in circles.

"What's all the fuss about?" Michael said opening his eyes and tried to rise up, only to be tackled by Livies hugging his neck.

"Okay, okay, Livies. I'm fine. Where's everyone?" Michael asked still dazed.

"Right here," Holly said smiling. Michael heart soared when he saw her.

"What's going on? Where's everybody else?" he asked looking around.

"Soladar's forces are retreating; we've won for now at least," Holly told him.

"What do you mean for now?" he asked trying to unwrap Livies from around his neck.

"Soladar got Garian's staff and then vanished," Holly said.

"Bastard's a coward. Wouldn't fight me like a man, had to hide behind his magic."

"Boy you weren't kidding when you said magic didn't work against you. I saw you run right through Soladar's sunfire."

"He's damn lucky I didn't get within swinging distance of him," Michael said grimly.

"Let's go check on the damage and help the injured, but first, Livies honey, you're going to have to get off me so I can get up."

"Only if you let Livies ride in my pouch on your back. And you must promise Livies you will not get hurt no more. You scared the daylights of Livies, Mitchel. No more, okay?" Livies told him wagging her tiny little finger in his face.

"I promise Livies," Michael said and hugged her, then allowed her to climb back into the large brown leather pouch on his back, which Livies preferred instead of her wolf now.

Soon they found Garian along with Caleb at his side directing others where to take the wounded. Sir Lawrence was busy having his troops clear the battlefield of the injured and dead.

He sent word to have all his units who had stayed behind to double-time it to Stonebrook to provide as much assistance as they could.

General Holt had been killed by Demergos that had regrouped and sprung a surprise attack on the rear flanks. Still it was Lawrence's army which had suffered the most casualties.

He had lost Major General Grahn and a fourth of his best knights, yet he was steadfast in his resolve, never showing any sign of weakness.

"Well Garian, it looks like we live to fight another day," Lawrence looked over at Garian who was taking a second to look up at the sun rising over the horizon.

"Indeed Lawrence, alive we are. Let us live for the day when bloodshed is no longer needed to ensure freedom," Garian spoke like the true sage he was.

The early spring dawn broke across the sky. It would be a beautiful day as there was not a wisp of a cloud anywhere to be seen.

How ironic Michael thought, amid all the devastation there was beauty to be seen, if only one looked. He knew there would be more terrible times to come, but for now he had Holly and a new little friend, feeling Livies wiggle inside her pouch.

I hope you enjoyed,
My sincerest thanks,
Greg Carter

Author's Bio:

Greg Carter grew up in rural Eastern Kentucky without many modern conveniences. His fondest memory is the bookmobile stopping by his house every two weeks in the summer; allowing him to check out books. Reading has always been a treasured source of endless entertainment; naturally leading him to write.